Relentless Pursuit

by

Kathy Ivan

D1520715

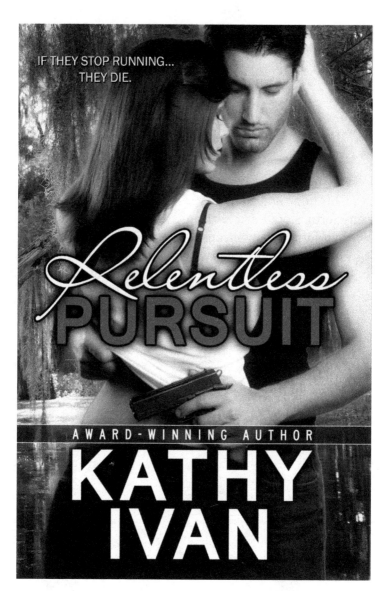

IF THEY STOP RUNNING...
THEY DIE.

Relentless
PURSUIT

AWARD-WINNING AUTHOR
KATHY
IVAN

Chapter One

With a sigh of relief, Jinx's naked toes met the cool porcelain tile of the kitchen floor. She stooped and picked up the three-inch heels she'd slid off the moment she stepped through the kitchen door of her pride and joy. The cracker-box of a house she'd scrimped and saved for, finally making that all-important down payment a year and a half ago. Looking around with a sense of pride and accomplishment, she grinned. *This is mine. Nobody can take it away from me. Except the bank, and just let 'em try. That damn sure ain't gonna happen.*

It was a huge change from the way she'd grown up. Moving from town to town, never staying in one place long enough to put down roots or develop any kind of lasting friendships. She'd finally struck out on her own and moved away from the family she loved, who drove her stark-raving bananas, and fulfilled the nesting urge that sizzled beneath the surface for as long as she could remember.

The kitchen was a cheerful mix of blues and yellows, bright and airy and filled with sunshine. The scent of fresh herbs from her little window box garden perfumed the space, a tacit reminder she'd missed lunch. Maybe there was time for a quick shower before her brother, Carlo, showed up. He'd called earlier to say he'd finished his job sooner than expected and dropped his load off early. He had gotten a nice bonus check, so dinner was his treat. Dress nice he'd teased, because they were celebrating.

"About darn time he pays for a change." She winced at the tinge of bitterness underlying her words. She loved her brother, actually adored him. Growing up her older brother had been the one constant in her life, the person she could count on to always have her back. Three years older, he'd been the one to celebrate her victories and a shoulder to cry on. The one who held her during the nights she cried herself to sleep when Mami and Papi said they'd have to move again. Always sneaking away in the dead of night, elusive, trying to stay one step ahead of their latest mark. Although she loved her family, the life they lived, the excitement they craved from one more grift, pulling one more con, wasn't for her. She despised everything about it.

Laying her purse on the kitchen counter she stretched her arms overhead while she worked the kinks out from sitting behind a desk all day long. Working at a bank may not be a life of excitement, but she'd had enough of living an alternate kind of lifestyle and craved the stability the assistant manager's position offered. She'd worked damned hard for her stable, settled life. So what if it was monotonous and boring and—different from how she'd grown up. She'd found her place and was happy. Yep, happy.

Muffled voices from the living room stopped her in mid-stretch and she froze. *Voices?* Ah, Carlo must have gotten home before she did. *Wonder who's with him?*

Listening for a few seconds, she cringed when she recognized the other voice. *Vladimir Dubshenko.* Crap. What the hell was he doing in her house? Carlo's friend and sometimes employer, he was an attractive enough guy. He stood a little under six feet tall with blond hair styled in an expensive, professional cut. His icy blue eyes always gave her the creeps, though she couldn't put her finger on an exact reason. All she knew was he made her skin crawl every time she saw him. *Which was getting more and more frequent all the time.*

He'd started calling her about six weeks ago, asking her out. What was up with that? He had to be at least twenty years older than her, and while it wasn't a huge problem there wasn't a hint of chemistry between them. *Nada, zilch.* At least on her part anyway.

With the less-than-open floor plan of her older house there was a solid wall separating the kitchen from the living room, with an opening that led to a short hallway. When you rounded the corner and took two steps you were in the living room. That big, thick wall was the reason the voices were muffled. In her bare feet she tiptoed around the butcher-block island, crossed to stand just on the other side of the dividing wall and tried to catch a few words of their conversation.

She really hoped Dubshenko didn't have another job for her brother. Rumors ran rampant he was into things that skirted the wrong side of the law, although he'd never been convicted. Terms like *Russian mob* and *smuggling* were but a few of the illegal activities bandied about in connection with Dubshenko's organization.

"Carlo, where is my package?" Dubshenko's cultured accent was easy to hear now that Jinx had moved closer. She remained just out of their line of sight. Gut instinct kept her on the opposite side of the wall. *Wait*, it said. *Find out what's going on.*

"Mr. Dubshenko, it's like I told you when I called. The contact in Houston never gave me any package. Ivor swore you knew about it." Carlo's pleading voice caused a frisson of alarm to course through her body, chill bumps popped up along her skin. The stark terror in his words sent shivers racing along her spine. Her big, brash older brother wasn't afraid of anybody, or anything. Yet here he stood whimpering like a beaten pup before a reputed mob kingpin—who dominated *her* living room like he owned the place!

"Carlo, Carlo. We both know that's not true, *da*? The package was delivered on schedule. To you."

"No, Mr. Dubshenko! I swear I never got any package. I did everything exactly like you said. I waited, but..."

"Did you? Yet here you stand almost a half a day earlier than you were scheduled to arrive. If you had waited in Houston for my package...how are you home so early, my friend?" Dubshenko's voice, so level and calm, sent another round of chills coursing through Jinx, and she rubbed her arms trying to ward off the impending feeling of doom.

What had her brother gotten himself into this time? He'd been trying to keep his nose clean, and she'd given him the benefit of the doubt over and over again because she loved him. But if he'd slid back into shady criminal dealings this was the last straw; she'd have to kick him to the curb. As much as she adored him she wasn't getting pulled back into that life—ever again.

"I swear, sir, I waited. The pickup never showed and

Ivor told me he'd handle things and I should finish my route." Carlo's pleading voice appeared to have no impact on Dubshenko, though the whiny tone wasn't something she was used to hearing—not from her big brother. He never bowed or scraped to anybody, yet here he was sniveling and groveling like a misbehaving two-year-old.

Jinx knew her brother well enough to know he told the truth. Well, mostly. There was something he was definitely hiding, but what?

"Is Ivor Gregorski your employer, Carlo?" Dubshenko's smooth voice bit like glass, sharp and with a distinct edge.

"No, sir, Mr. Dubshenko."

"Who is, Carlo?"

"You are, sir."

"*Da*, that is right, I am. I gave you one small job to do. Make a short detour with your truck, pick up a package and deliver it to me. But do I have my package? *Nyet*."

A thump sounded, distinctive and familiar—the sound of a fist meeting flesh—followed by a muffled grunt.

Had he hit Carlo?

Jinx took a step forward intent on confronting Dubshenko. Regardless of his questionable affiliations he was in her house—her *home*—and if he'd hit her brother there would be holy hell to pay.

"It seems we have a bigger problem here than a missed delivery, Carlo, do we not? Ivor assured me he delivered my special package to the designated rendezvous area."

"I...I...okay, I made the pickup. Only, she got lost."

Carlo blurted out the words followed by the sound of another punch.

She? Wait—what? Jinx was totally confused. They'd been talking about a missing package and now it's a she? Crap on a cracker, what had her brother gotten himself mixed up in?

"Mr. Dubshenko, I swear it wasn't my fault. She jumped from the truck while it was moving. By the time I pulled over she had disappeared. I hunted everywhere, but she'd just vanished." There it was again, that pleading tone in Carlo's voice. Jinx winced at the sound, plus thinking about the horror she felt at a girl obviously so terrified she'd jump from a moving semi-truck.

"Why was she not sedated and in the back of your truck as you were instructed? Can you not follow the simplest instructions, Carlo?"

"I thought she was asleep, sir. Plus, there wasn't anywhere to put her in the back of the truck. It was filled up with the goods to be delivered to your warehouse. And there's no air conditioning back there; she'd have suffocated in this heat."

"That was not your decision to make. I really have no use for someone who cannot follow orders."

Everyone stopped talking and an eerie silence filled the house. Should she step out, announce she was home, maybe diffuse the situation before things escalated further out of control?

Jinx took another tentative step forward into the little hallway, giving her a perfect view of the main living room and the three men currently occupying it. Her brother Carlo, Vladimir Dubshenko and a behemoth of a man with black hair and dark brown eyes. Across his forehead a jagged scar bisected it from the middle of his scalp across one eyebrow, ending at the outer corner of his eye. It puckered at the edge and pulled the lid in an upward direction, making him look like he had a perpetual grimace marring his expression.

Nobody noticed her, their attention focused solely on her brother. She froze at the sight of the gun held in Dubshenko's grip, pointed straight at her brother's head.

What the hell is going on? Why does he have a gun?

"Carlo, I am very disappointed. You have failed me. The reason I am so successful in all my business endeavors is I do not tolerate failure." Carlo's eyes widened, circles of white in a pale face. He shook his head vehemently, though no words left his mouth.

"Don't worry, though, I'll take good care of your sister. I have very special plans for my dear Jennifer."

"No!" At Dubshenko's words Carlo rushed forward, straight at Dubshenko. "Don't you touch Jinx. You leave her alone!" Before he'd taken more than two steps Jinx rushed forward into the living room.

"Get away from my brother, you son of a bitch!"

Everyone froze. Dubshenko took a single step back from Carlo before turning toward Jinx. With a jerk of his head, his bodyguard grasped Carlo's arm keeping him from rushing toward his sister.

"What the hell is going on?" Jinx's voice rose with each word until her sentence ended on a screech. She inhaled deeply, trying to see a way out of this decidedly screwed up situation. Dubshenko held the gun in his hand, once again pointed at Carlo's head, a sadistic smile twisting his thin lips. He barked out a laugh at Jinx's entrance.

"Ah, my dear, we weren't expecting you quite so soon. I'm afraid you've interrupted your brother and I finishing up some rather unpleasant—business." Dubshenko's precise English held barely a hint of an accident. "I am happy to see you though. You've been avoiding my calls."

"I don't understand. Why are you holding a gun on my brother?"

"Jinx, stay out of this. Leave right now." Carlo jerked his head toward the door, his eyes so wide the whites showed, a pleading look was on his face.

"No, I don't think so. I'd much rather Jennifer stay. She is a part of this, after all."

"She doesn't have anything to do with this. Damn you, leave her alone." Carlo struggled against the dark-haired goon's hold. Both his arms were pulled back nearly far enough to dislocate his shoulders, but he still fought to break free. Jinx knew she needed to defuse the situation and fast, or somebody was going to get hurt.

"Mr. Dubshenko…"

"Jennifer, my dear, how many times must I tell you to call me Vladimir?" Jinx winced at Dubshenko's use of her name. Growing up she'd always been called Jinx by her family, a term of affection. People at work of course called her Jennifer or Ms. Marucci, but to hear her name said in Dubshenko's oily voice, well…eww.

"I'm sorry. Vladimir, I don't know what's going on, but can't we talk about this rationally? Whatever Carlo has or hasn't done I'll make sure he makes it right." Jinx figured offering to play peacemaker might get Dubshenko to lower the gun he still held pointed straight at her brother's head.

"I'm afraid your brother has something of mine he has yet to deliver. Actually, you have two things don't you, Carlo?"

Carlo flinched which was all Jinx needed to know Dubshenko was telling the truth. Carlo had something important that belonged to the deadly Russian, and was terrified to hand it over.

Dubshenko laughed, deep bellied and full of enjoyment. "Carlo, Carlo. Did you think I wouldn't find out what you did, you stupid fool? I know everything. Every move you make I have someone watching, reporting back to me."

He strode forward until he stood within inches of Carlo. Jinx held her breath as Dubshenko rubbed the barrel of the gun against her brother's cheek. Sweat trickled down the side of her face, yet she remained frozen in place, afraid to move, afraid to breathe. Any sudden movement could set off Dubshenko and he would pull the trigger.

"What?" Carlo's voice cracked, as the cold metal of the gun pressed against his forehead so hard, Jinx saw the skin dent inward.

"Where is it? I won't ask again. I'll just—kill your sister."

Dubshenko whirled around, the gun now pointed straight at her. Okay, things had gone from what-the-hell-is-going-on straight to this-son-of-a-bitch-is-pointing-a-gun-at-me!

"Carlo, I don't know what the hell you've done, but if you've got something that belongs to Vladimir," Jinx glanced at Dubshenko and watched him preen at her use of his given name, "give it to him now."

"Listen to your sister," Dubshenko glanced over at the goon still holding tight to Carlo. "Get his phone."

Tall, dark and loathsome grabbed Carlo by the arm and began patting down his pockets, quickly finding and pulling out his cell phone, which he promptly handed to Dubshenko. Jinx studied Carlo's face intently, watching her brother for clues. He quirked a brow as Dubshenko scrolled through his phone, focused on finding whatever he thought her brother had. Knowing Carlo, whatever Dubshenko was looking for wasn't on his phone. *Well, not that phone anyway.*

With a muffled curse, Dubshenko tossed the cell phone on the floor. He stomped on it with the heel of his expensive, shiny black shoes crushing the plastic case into dozens of pieces.

"I am not a stupid man, Carlo. There are numerous hackers in my employ who will find where you have hidden it, and when they do your life is forfeit. It's only a matter of time." Dubshenko walked over to Jinx, and cupped her cheek in his hand. She tried wrenching her face away, but his grip tightened to the point of pain. At the barely disguised lust in his eyes, Jinx stilled. He wanted her to fight, struggle against his hold. She could tell from the way his breathing sped up he liked inflicting pain.

"In the meantime, maybe I'll spend a bit of quality time getting to know your sister a little better. More…intimately."

"Don't touch her you son of a bitch!" In an unexpected move Carlo broke free from the bodyguard's hold and raced across the living room toward Dubshenko. He grabbed the hand Dubshenko held the gun in, and both men grappled for control of the weapon.

A bark of the gunfire erupted, and time seemed to freeze. Everything reduced to herky-jerky movements that flickered and sputtered like an old-time kaleidoscope. It was a moment out of time, surreal to watch. Her brother's body jerked with the impact of the bullet hitting him in the center of his chest. A circle of bright red—such a small amount at first—bloomed outward from the darkening hole. Carlo's knees buckled, and his body sagged to the ground.

Jinx didn't realize she'd screamed until she saw Dubshenko and his bodyguard turn toward her. Dubshenko shook his head, a moue of distaste puckering his lips.

"Get her." He motioned with the gun and the scarred, black-haired giant advanced toward her. Adrenalin zinged through her like a bolt of electricity and she spun, sprinting toward the kitchen. *Gotta get away. Gotta run. He's gonna kill me.*

A hand latched onto her arm and Jinx yanked, feeling the stitching in her sleeve tear loose with her jerking movement, but at least she was free. *For the moment.* She snatched the wire bowl of lemons sitting on the butcher block island, tossed the entire thing toward her assailant. It bounced off his chest and he batted it away, still advancing on her. She looked around for something else to use for a weapon. The block of knives was too far away and he'd be on her in an instant, well before she could get one pulled free. *The sink.* Grabbing the bottle of dishwashing liquid she aimed and squeezed, the stream of pink liquid hit him square in the face. He stopped advancing, wiped at his eyes and bellowed a curse in a heavy Russian accent. Yep, he definitely worked for Dubshenko.

While he smeared the soap across his face trying to clear his vision, Jinx aimed the creamy, slick liquid onto the floor at his feet. Hopefully, he hadn't seen that since his eyes had tears running from them. Maybe spreading out the dish soap bought her a few extra seconds. Squirting the remainder of the bottle onto the tile, she prayed the newly slick surface might slow him down.

She chucked the now-empty plastic bottle at his head and sprinted toward the back door, snagging her purse on the way out. Her one thought—my cell phone's in my purse. I've got to call the police, get an ambulance for Carlo. *Oh, Carlo, please don't be dead.*

The doorknob slipped beneath her soap-slicked fingers when she twisted it, and she lost her grip. An angry outburst peppered the air behind her. Dubshenko had entered the kitchen behind his cohort and Jinx's fingers scrambled against the lock. *Did I turn the dead bolt when I got home? Why won't the damn door open?* No, the lock was still in the unlocked position. It was just her stupid clumsiness that kept it from opening.

The knob twisted—finally—and she tugged the door inward and raced out into the humid evening air. Sweat immediately pooled between her breasts and plastered her shirt against her back. Droplets beaded along her forehead. Ignoring the discomfort, she ran.

Get to the car, call the police. Get to the car, call the police. The refrain played over and over in her head keeping a relentless beat that matched the rhythm of her bare feet skimming across the grass and dirt of the backyard. The brittleness of the dry, brown grass stabbed at her naked soles, but the pain never penetrated. She kept running.

"Jennifer, my dear, come back inside. We can talk about what happened."

"Go to hell, you son of a bitch!" She didn't even bother turning around, knew too much time had already passed. Was Carlo still alive? Tears flowed down her cheeks with the realization—he was dead. The gunshot wound, all the blood. His unconscious body slumped to the floor. There was no way he'd survived a point blank shot at such close range. Her brother was dead. Now she was running for her life from the very man who had killed him.

She had to get away. Knew if they caught her she'd die. Legs pumping, breathing became more and more difficult as she raced full out. Her bare toes caught on a rock and she stumbled on the uneven terrain, barely staying erect when she traversed the side yard where it changed from grass to the concrete and broken pavement and spiky weed of the city sidewalk in front of her house.

She stopped short, her feet stomping on the hard concrete at the sight of a huge black limousine parked just feet in front of her, its engine idling. There wasn't a doubt in her mind it belonged to Vladimir Dubshenko. The big black behemoth blocked her car in, effectively trapping her.

Changing course, she darted toward the right, through the small line of perfectly manicured bushes dividing her yard from the house next door. Thanks to her fastidious neighbor, Mr. Swanson, the neatly trimmed hedge rose to about waist high. Hunkered down low, she ran in an awkward loping gait. She did her best to stay hidden from view. If she could make it past her next door neighbor's backyard, there was an open alley, and then green space with lots of trees and dense foliage behind their houses. She could hide. Jinx was good at hiding—she'd been doing it nearly her whole life. Louisiana was abundant with greenery, wild and lush, though the last couple of years with the drought things weren't as verdant as they'd been. There was still enough overgrowth and dense vegetation to mask her from ruthless thugs bent on ending her. She'd use every advantage she had to stay out of Dubshenko's clutches.

Behind her, running footsteps and heavy breathing sounded closer and closer. Grabbing her side, she winced at the stitch of pain. She held her hand pressed against it as she ran. She might be a curvy girl, bigger than society dictates considered beautiful, but she was in great shape physically. She could outrun this clown.

Not much farther, just across the alley. She could make it. Before she'd taken two steps, a body slammed into her, knocking her to the ground. All the air in her lungs whooshed out at the impact. Momentarily stunned, rough hands grabbed her and flipped her, slamming her back against the hard-packed earth.

"Stupid bitch." Dubshenko's goon grabbed her arms, and Jinx thrashed wildly. She couldn't give up. If he took her back to Dubshenko...

With an upward swing, the heel of her palm slammed into his nose pushing upward. Blood gushed out and he yelped in pain, turning her loose to grab at his face. Raising both feet and bending her knees, Jinx rocked backward onto her shoulders, and kicked forward with both feet, catching him in the chest and toppling him backward. Scrambling backward in a crablike crawl she finally regained her feet, grabbed up her purse from where it had fallen when she'd been tackled and took off running. But not before she saw Dubshenko rounding the corner from her yard and striding toward them.

"Jennifer, stop right now. Do not make me hurt you. Come with me and I will explain everything." His quiet voice had Jinx running even harder away from both of the men. *Explain. Yeah right. He gets his hands on me,*

I am one dead chickie. I saw him commit murder. He knows I'll testify against him. No way he'll let me live.

By now, her feet were a torn mass of open cuts and she was sure they were embedded with heaven only knows what, but she'd worry about that later. Fortunately, since buying her little cottage she'd taken many nature walks through these woods and she was familiar with them, knew where the best ins and outs and hidey-holes were. A few more yards and she'd be home free. Dubshenko wouldn't dare shoot at her out in public where any of her neighbors might hear it and come and investigate, or better yet call the police. But then again, he'd already killed Carlo, maybe he wouldn't think twice about killing anybody else who got in his way.

Riding high on an adrenalin-induced burst of speed, she raced across the open alleyway and into the relative darkness of the trees. She didn't dare stop to look behind her, still running. Think, Jinx, where's the best hiding place close by? Get out of sight. About fifty yards in, there was a fallen over tree lying in a small dried up creek bed. She could hide behind it, wait for it to get full dark and then outwait them.

She heard Dubshenko at the edge of the alley calling her name. The fear-laced rush of adrenalin was wearing off, and the reality of the evening's events started sinking in.

Her brother was dead. Murdered by one of the biggest Russian mafia leaders in the state. He ruled New Orleans seedy underbelly from everything she'd heard. He wouldn't stop looking for her. There really wasn't much choice. She'd have to go to the cops. Trusting the police—not the best option—but she'd tell them everything she knew so they could at least start an investigation. After that, she'd do the one thing she was good at. The one thing she'd been doing her entire life.

Disappear.

Chapter Two

Nothing in the world compared to the feeling Remy got every time he walked through the doors of the station; the smell of burnt coffee, sweaty bodies and stale, musty sex perfumed the air. Uniformed cops led handcuffed perps toward the holding cells, paperwork in hand. Even the buzz and pop from the overhead fluorescent lights felt homey and comforting.

Damn, I love my job.

Sauntering through the front door, he managed to make it farther into the bull pen, took a sharp right and meandered all the way to the back wall where a beat-up, scratched to hell and back, tan and chrome metal desk sat. It had definitely seen better days, but occupied a place of pride, the narrow space by the window. The nighttime lights from downtown New Orleans shown through the panes of scratched glass as revelers paraded by on their way to a night of parties and debauchery in the Big Easy. It was still early enough in the evening that people lined the streets, heading for Bourbon Street and the French Quarter and all the touristy-type fun New Orleans was famous for.

Plopping down in his equally beat-up office chair with the padded armrests wrapped in duct tape with stuffing sticking out, he opened his desk drawer and pulled out the file for his current case. The one Cap called his obsession. He began his daily review of the ever-growing file of the scumbag POS who still roamed the streets of his town, Vladimir Dubshenko.

Remy hadn't been able to find a way to nail Dubshenko's ass to the wall yet, but it wasn't for lack of trying. The District Attorney never felt there was enough evidence to make a case stick. Remy planned to change that fact pretty damned quick. Vladimir Dubshenko was a walking, talking menace to every single person in this town. There wasn't a law he hadn't broken—drugs, prostitution, gun running. You name it, Dubshenko had his sticky fingers all over it. Unfortunately, every time Remy rounded up enough evidence and injured parties to arrest the scumbag, the witnesses tended to disappear before an indictment could be handed down.

Remy lounged back in his chair, his Nike-shod feet rode the corner of the desk as he perused the photos again. The same way he did every night when he checked in at the beginning of his shift. He was well aware if he didn't get results soon Captain Hilliard would pull him off Dubshenko's case and assign it to somebody else.

No way in hell was Remy letting that happen. Too many of his friends had been hurt by Dubshenko, but with his Russian mafia connections and a fortune in illegal funds, he was untouchable. As it was, Remy skirted around all the national alphabet guys trying to get a solid lead. Truth was, at this point he wasn't particular who nailed the son of a bitch, just as long as he was taken off the streets.

Slapping the file down on his desk, Remy grabbed another folder out of the drawer. He'd been riding this damn desk for way too long now. Since being shot weeks ago helping his cousin, Connor, apprehend a whacked-out serial killer who'd kidnapped Connor's wife, Captain Hilliard had turned him into a desk jockey. He knew the imposed paperwork detail had more to do with his being off duty and in Baton Rouge at the time the whole FUBAR situation went south than for his actually being shot. Hell, it was barely a scratch. He should have been back out in the field long ago instead of riding a chair. Yet here he sat trying to solve cases sitting on his derriere.

He needed to be on the streets mingling with the crowds of people. His brother, Max, called him a chameleon, able to blend in with the crowds and his surroundings better than anybody else he knew. Maybe tonight Hilliard would give him a break and put him back on the streets.

Coffee. I need coffee.

A quick stroll to the front break area, and a cup of hot black tar soon filled his hand. Taking a sip, Remy sighed. Ahh. Thick, bitter and several hours old, it still tasted like home. A tingle ran down his spine and he frowned. His instinct was on high alert and he shot a quick glance toward the front door of the precinct and froze, the cup halfway to his lips for that second swallow.

She was tall, long-legged and breathtakingly gorgeous. Golden blonde hair flowed down past her shoulders, half-falling out of the upswept style which he was sure started out the day neat as a pin and perfectly coifed. The wavy length cascaded around her, and resembled a halo surrounding a beautiful but ashen face. His eyes skimmed down the royal blue blouse. Which was torn and streaked with dirt and twigs. Plus, there were mascara smudges beneath her startling sapphire eyes as though she'd been crying and wiping at them.

She was pale. Too pale. Her eyes darted around, moving from one side of the room to the other, and Remy noted the death grip she held on the purse— gripped so tight her knuckles appeared white. He watched her posture straighten as she took a deep breath, pushing those gorgeous breasts up and out. *Dayam*. Watched her as she braced herself and started forward toward the staff sergeant's desk. She limped and favored her right side. A quick glance downward and he noted the scratches and dirt marring her legs and bare feet. *Bare feet?* What the hell happened to this angel?

That same gut instinct that made him look up when she'd walked in told him he needed to talk to her. Needed to be the one to help her. Maybe it was that he couldn't stand to see a woman hurting. Maybe it was seeing the sheen of unshed tears visible even from several feet away. Maybe it was the fact she reminded him of, Theresa, his brother's wife and his dearest friend on the planet. It might have been any or all of those things, but regardless of the reason it had Remy striding forward, intercepting her before she reached the front desk.

"Sweetheart, can I help you?" Remy kept his voice soft, instilling concern, gentling her like a frightened kitten. One wrong move and he knew those claws would flick out, scratching and drawing blood. His intent gaze never left her face, reading the panic evident behind those big blue eyes.

"I...I need to report a crime." Her fingers fiddled with the clutch in her hands, worrying at the broken clasp, another thing he noted in his earlier perusal. His trained, observant gaze took in her chipped nail polish. Several of her nails were jagged and broken. Along with the unevenly buttoned and torn blouse—scratched and bloody bare feet—she looked like she'd been drug through a bush backwards.

"I'm Detective Remy Lamoreaux. Let's go back to my desk and you can tell me what's happened, okay?" Motioning toward his desk at the back of the room he ushered her forward, his hand light against the small of her back, easing her onto the straight-backed, wooden chair next to his desk. It wasn't comfortable, but then again most of the people who occupied the chair weren't stunning blondes. Moving around her, he plopped into his own chair and gave her a reassuring smile.

"Let's start with something easy. Can you tell me your name, sweetheart?"

"Yes, of course. I'm Jennifer—um—Smith." She took a deep breath, and Remy's eye strayed once again to her breasts beneath the silky, blue material. Hell, he was a red-blooded guy, which meant he loved breasts. Plus, he wasn't blind, the woman was stacked.

He loved women. All women. Shape, size didn't matter. The fairer sex should be treasured, cherished. Besides, he'd have to be dead not to notice she had a great rack. And watching her ass when she'd walked toward his desk? *Oh, hell yeah.*

Remy reclined back in his chair maintaining his comforting smile despite her obvious lie. *Hmm, definitely a fake name. Won't meet my gaze. Ms. Smith is hiding something.*

"Okay, Jennifer. Is it alright if I call you Jennifer?" At her barely perceptible nod he continued, "You said you wanted to report a crime. What happened?"

"Somebody killed my brother." Her words broke off as a sob escaped, and her eyes filled with tears. Remy immediately straightened.

Killed her brother? Was she reporting a murder?

He didn't work homicide anymore, hadn't for several years. He'd transferred over to vice when the death and carnage became too much. Drugs, prostitution, illegal gambling, those he could deal with. The nightmares that came from seeing man's depravity and disregard for human life, after a while, had gotten too much. So he'd done the only thing he could to stay sane and on the right side of the badge. He was much happier working with New Orleans' seedy underbelly.

"Killed? What happened?" Keeping his tone soft and calm he encouraged Jennifer to give him more facts. If this turned out to be legit, he'd call in somebody from homicide and turn the case over to them ASAP.

"My brother sometimes crashes at my house when he's in town. He's a long-distance truck driver, coast-to-coast, so staying with me makes more sense than keeping his own place. Plus, he kicks in a couple bucks to help with the mortgage and expenses." She rubbed her fist against her right eye, smearing more black mascara beneath it. "He called this afternoon, said he'd be in today instead of tomorrow—that he'd made good time and dropped off his haul early. Don't make dinner plans, he said, he wanted to take me out. He wanted to splurge and go to the French Quarter and make a night of it."

Remy passed over a box of tissues, and she pulled

one out, blotting at the tears soaking her cheeks.

"I left work and went home to get changed. I don't know why, but I went in through the kitchen door instead of the front door, which I'd normally do. I heard loud voices coming from the living room. They were arguing."

"How many voices did you hear?"

"I heard Carlo, he's my brother, and one other voice, although there were two other people with him."

"Did you recognize the other voice, Jennifer?" She nodded, her head bowed. Remy couldn't read her face with the fall of blonde hair obscuring her features.

"Whose voice did you recognize?"

"It was…" She jumped, startled at the sudden ring of the cell phone inside the purse she held clutched in her lap, before letting out a chagrined laugh. "Sorry." Remy watched all the color drain from her already pale face as she read the caller ID. Snatching the phone from her trembling fingers, he scanned the phone, biting back a curse at the name displayed. *Dubshenko*.

"You know Vladimir Dubshenko?"

"I've met him. I don't really know him."

Remy ran a hand across his face, trying to think while the cell phone kept ringing. "Okay, go ahead and answer it—put it on speaker. Don't tell him where you are."

"Alright." Sliding her finger across the incoming call icon, she answered in a shaky voice, "Hello."

"Jennifer, my dear, where are you? I've been so worried. You left so abruptly. Carlo and I were expecting you for dinner." Her eyes widened at her brother's name, and Remy watched her teeth tug at her lower lip before answering. Her eyes met his and she mouthed the words, "That's a lie."

"Mr. Dubshenko, you know why I'm not there. What the heck is your problem?" Remy couldn't help but grin at her very visible shudder while talking to Dubshenko. She was just too cute even in the midst of all this drama.

"Jennifer, what is this Mr. Dubshenko nonsense? I've told you to call me Vladimir, my dear. So you will be home soon, yes?" Remy shook his head vehemently no.

"What is wrong with you? I'm not going home, especially if you're still there, you bastard. You shot Carlo—you killed him!"

Remy stiffened at her words. Dubshenko was the shooter? Jerking free a piece of paper off his desk, half-listening to the conversation, he scrawled out a message on the blank sheet. In large block letters he wrote: **GET CAPTAIN HILLIARD OVER HERE NOW!** Lifting the page up, he waved at the rookie standing in the doorway. He held the note steady, pointing at it with his right hand. "Now," he mouthed. The rookie took off at a run, and Remy turned back to Jennifer.

Snatching up another piece of paper, he scrawled across it before turning it toward Jennifer. *Did you see Dubshenko actually shoot your brother?* Jennifer read the note, and a tear trickled down her cheek. She mouthed, "Yes."

There was a long pause with dead air on the phone before Dubshenko finally spoke. "Jennifer, where are you? I hear voices in the background. It almost sounds like—are you at the police station?"

"Yes, I am, you son of a bitch! I was there. I saw what you did, and I'm going to make sure you rot in jail for the rest of your miserable life, you murdering bastard!"

"That is too bad, my dear. You have made a very big

mistake. Perhaps you should change your mind. There's somebody here I think you'd like to talk to." Muffled voices and scuffling sounds reverberated through the phone's speaker before finally a soft, weak voice came over the line.

"Jinx—don't tell the police anything. Come home."

"Carlo?" The phone slid from Jennifer's fingers and Remy lunged for it, catching it before it hit the floor. Dubshenko already knew she was at the police station, so he had nothing to lose.

"Hey, Dubshenko."

"Well, well, is that you, Detective Lamoreaux?" Remy could practically hear the smirk through the phone's connection.

Remy glanced up and saw Captain Hilliard stalking toward him, his imposing presence a comfort and a curse. The man was a great captain, an excellent leader, but he was old school and did things by the book. Most of the time that was great, and Remy had no problem following orders. But with the captain standing beside him, he wasn't free to tell Dubshenko what he really thought of the bastard.

"Yep, Vlad, it's me. Surprised?"

"I'm only surprised Jennifer ran to the police for such a small…misunderstanding. As you heard, her brother is very much alive and well."

"I heard the alive part, but as far as well, that hasn't been established yet. How about I come over there and see for myself exactly how Carlo is?"

"And will you bring his delightful sister with you, Detective? I do so wish to clear up this unfortunate incident."

Remy looked at Captain Hilliard, trying to gauge his

take on Dubshenko's motives. Cap didn't have all the details, but he was good at reading situations and acting on them. Hilliard motioned for him to keep talking.

"Unfortunate incident? Jennifer states she witnessed her brother being shot in the chest with your gun and your finger on the trigger. I think that's more than an 'oops my gun slipped out of my pocket, accidentally fired and hit him in the chest, don't you?"

Dubshenko laughed, "Detective, you have it all wrong. There has not been a shooting. Ms. Smith couldn't possibly have seen me with a gun. You and I both know I don't carry any weapons—don't we, Detective Lamoreaux?" Remy gritted his teeth at the reminder of one of his overzealous failures against Dubshenko. Another chink in the wall surrounding Dubshenko, but again he'd managed to slither right through the district attorney's hands on a technicality. Of course, it only gave Dubshenko another opportunity to needle him—which he took advantage of every chance he got.

"Well, Vlad, her story's easy enough to verify. Tell me where you and Carlo are, and me and a couple of the guys will be happy to come by and certify you're telling the truth, reassure our lovely witness her brother is safe and sound. A win-win for everyone."

Remy glanced up and saw the rookie he'd shown the note to earlier waving at him and pointing to the phone. *Really, dude?* He mouthed, "Take a message."

"Of course, Detective. I'm sure everything can be cleared up in a matter of minutes. Carlo, my friend, tell the good detective you are okay."

Remy waited one beat, then another, before the faint voice from earlier came over the phone. "Um, detective,

I'm fine, really. Everything's cool. I just need Jinx to come home and things will be good. Tell her to come back home." The male on the other end of the phone didn't sound okay to Remy, not by a long shot. Hilliard shook his head as though he, too, heard the pain underscoring the words.

"Carlo?" Jennifer stood next to Remy, staring down at the phone on the desk top. "I saw him shoot you."

"I'm fine, baby sis. Come home and everything will be good. I promise." A pained hiss followed by interminable silence filled the now-crowded corner of the police station before Dubshenko's voice came back on.

"My dear Jennifer, as you heard, your brother is very much alive. He wants to see you. Why don't you and the good detective meet with us and we'll clear everything up, and things will go back to normal, *da*?" Dubshenko's accent got heavier the longer he talked, and Remy, who'd dealt with him enough times to be aware of every nuance of Dubshenko's speech, knew what happened when the Russian got stressed. The body count started to rise.

Definitely more to the situation than he's letting on. He's panicked.

The rookie sprinted down the long pathway between the desks, and handed Remy the phone message. Dammit, he didn't have time for this, but his instinct, a cop's never-to-be-ignored hunches, had him glance at the name. *Theresa.* His sister-in-law and best friend, who also happened to be a very strong and powerful psychic. If there was one thing Remy learned after knowing Theresa for over a decade it was to never ignore any message from her. If she called him at work, it was pretty damned important.

The note read *bad pizza.* That was the whole

message? Bad pizza? Screw it, he didn't have time for cryptic puzzles right now. He'd have to call her back, or figure it out after he finished dealing with Dubshenko.

"Are you at Jennifer's house, Vladimir? I'd love to drop by and talk to you and Carlo up close and personal."

Dubshenko's laughter echoed through the speaker. "Detective Lamoreaux, you always entertain me. *Nyet,* we are not at the lovely Jennifer's house. Carlo and I are on our way to The Pearl, awaiting her company for dinner."

"Looks like you'll have a long wait. She's going to be tied up for quite a while—with me. I'm sure I'll find everything she has to say fascinating"

Dubshenko chuckled again, and the tiny hairs along the back of Remy's neck stood at attention. Something didn't feel right. Dubshenko wouldn't stay on the phone like this, not even for the opportunity to gloat over rubbing Remy's face in another failure to incriminate him. He was more the type to shoot you in the face and walk away, not stand around and chat for the sake of chatting. No, he was waiting for something.

"Please, Vladimir, promise me my brother is alright. I'll come meet you anywhere you want, I swear." Jennifer snagged the phone right off of Remy's desk before he realized her intent. He hated the desperate, pleading tone in her voice, the edge of barely suppressed hurt coloring her words.

Captain Hilliard shook his head. Remy knew without evidence proving her brother had been shot they basically had zilch. They didn't have any grounds to hold her. What could they charge her with, other than filing a false crime? He hadn't even started any paperwork yet, so they were between a rock and a hard place.

Remy believed her, though. Dubshenko or one of his goons shot her brother. As usual, luck was on Dubshenko's side, and Carlos still lived—for now.

"My dear, you heard him with your own ears. Your brother is fine. Why don't you come back? I'll send my driver to pick you up. I promise you a night you'll never forget." While Jennifer might not know Dubshenko well enough to read between the lines, Remy certainly did, and the threat was very real and very deadly.

In the distance the front door to the precinct slapped opened and a pimply-faced delivery boy in tattered jeans and a blue-and-white t-shirt walked in with one of those red vinyl containers used to carry hot pizza boxes. He looked around before heading toward the front sergeant's desk. A uniformed officer stopped him, spoke for a moment and looked around before he pointed back toward Remy's desk. With a grin, the kid strolled between the desks headed toward the cluster of cops milling around his desk.

Bad pizza. Theresa's message flashed into his brain and klaxon alarms blared in his head. The *Red Alert* signal from Star Trek screamed loud and clear. Nobody had ordered pizza. One of the cops would've asked him if he wanted to chip in. That was the way they always did things. Plus, it wouldn't be delivered straight back to the desks. Deliveries were left at the front where the delivery guy could get paid. Something stank to high heaven.

Son of a bitch! This was why Dubshenko was stalling, holding on the line. He'd been waiting for...

"Everybody down!" Remy shouted the words, throwing himself atop Jennifer and knocking her to the ground before shielding her with his body. He drew his gun from his shoulder harness. Bodies hit the ground all around him, officers responding with their own weapons drawn, and pointed at the pizza delivery kid.

"Whoa, dudes."

"Hands in the air." The uniformed rookie, Peterson, grabbed the pizza container when the hapless delivery man started raising both hands, and placed the red vinyl carrier onto a nearby desk.

"Chill out, guys. It's just pizza."

"Who ordered it?" Remy barked out the question, still covering Jennifer's body. He could feel every soft inch of her sweetly curved body beneath his. Her alluring curves fit him in a way he didn't have time to contemplate, but knew he'd remember later. Cops climbed to their feet, including Captain Hilliard, who eyed the red vinyl Peterson now held with suspicion.

"It's on the house, man. Gnarly dude outside gave me a hundred bucks to deliver pizzas for the fine cops at the New Orleans Police Department. Special delivery— said to ask for Remy Lamoreaux."

Bad pizza. The words whirled round and round in Remy's head. Something wasn't adding up. Theresa was rarely wrong about all that woo-woo crap. If she saw bad pizza coming into the precinct, it meant something.

"What gnarly dude?" Captain Hilliard's voice rang out.

"Tall, white-haired guy, talked kinda funny, like maybe he was from another country." The pizza guy cocked his head while he spoke. "Gave me the carrier and the hundred bucks, and sent me right in."

Remy started to rise off Jennifer's prone body when the uniformed cop who'd taken the pizza box from the delivery kid began peeling back the flap, the ripping sound of the hook-and-loop fastener coming apart.

"No, don't open…"

Remy's words were cut short as a deafening roar filled the air. The explosion rocked the building, plunging them into blinding darkness.

Chapter Three

All Jinx noticed when she peeled her eyes open was darkness. A wall of nearly impenetrable blackness, though her eyes slowly adjusted and images formed. Well, that plus the fact her head was killing her. Flat on her back a heavy weight pinned her to the ground. A warm, solid, breathing weight. Muffled sounds began penetrating the fog of smoke, and the smell of…was that sulfur…as her brain kicked into gear and she remembered the explosion, and the gorgeous dark-haired cop throwing himself on top her, protecting her from the blast.

"Are you okay, sweetheart?" The words whispered beside her ear rumbled in a hoarse voice laced with concern. Gentle fingertips brushed the tousled hair away from her face, tucking it behind her ear. A bright light shown downward, and she instinctively raised her hand blocking out the glaring intrusion. Flashlight, she realized, squinting against the beam.

"I'm okay. What happened?"

"Bomb. Probably a homemade pipe bomb from the look of things. Lots of bang, though not as much damage as C4. The pizza delivery guy carried it into the station." The cop's weight slowly eased off her, and Jinx immediately missed the security of his body pressed tightly against her. Odd, she usually couldn't wait to get out from beneath a man's heavy bulk. This felt different. Comforting, protected. *Safe.*

"Here, let me help you up."

"Thanks." She placed her hands into his outstretched ones. He gently tugged, steadying her when she wobbled on her cut heel.

Damn, why'd I take off my brand new shoes? Oh, yeah, right. Crazy Russians in my house.

A controlled kind of chaos surrounded them as a tall black man with salt-and-pepper hair, she thought she remembered him being called Hilliard, directed people, plainclothes and uniformed. Another uniformed cop lay on the ground as several people tried to stem the blood pouring from his mangled right hand. The beams from multiple flashlights streaked down the walkway between desks, and the warm humid night air poured through the gaping hole in the side of the building where the windows had blown outward. Outside, the shouts of officers trying to control the unruly crowd of ghoulish spectators, and the murmurs of the growing crowd hoping for a glimpse of the controlled chaos, could be heard.

"Ambulances are on the way, cap."

"How many injured?" The captain's deep baritone oozed confidence and calm, a rumble that echoed over the babble of voices. Jinx rubbed her hands along her upper arms, felt the trembling wash through her in the aftermath of the earlier adrenaline spike. *Hold it together. Gotta get out, check on Carlo.*

"Are you hurt? Bleeding anywhere, sweetheart?" The detective, the one who'd been protecting her, what was his name again—Remy—was asking her questions. *Concentrate, Jinx. Tell him everything's great so you can get to Carlo.*

"I'm fine, just had the wind knocked out of me. Look, things are crazy right now. You need to help your friends. I'll head out and you can…"

"Lamoreaux, she doesn't leave," Hilliard's voice interrupted. His sharp brown gaze seemed to see straight into her, plumb her every secret.

"You don't need me to stay. Obviously I made a huge mistake. I'll head home and straighten everything out and…"

"Sorry, sugar, but you're not going anywhere," Remy's voice interrupted. His hand latched onto her elbow, cementing her in place. She tugged, trying to wrench herself free, without any luck since his grip was solid, forceful and oddly comforting.

Remy glanced once toward his captain, nodded and turned back to her. "You heard the captain, you're here for a bit longer. Let's get out of the way and let the emergency crews do their stuff." Turning to the captain, he added, "Cap, I'm taking her down to interview two. Keep me posted."

Hilliard gave a brief wave of dismissal. Remy's hand slid against the small of her back as he guided Jennifer through the rubble and debris as they carefully made their way past the blast zone, and into the open area of the entrance to the station. The front doors were splayed wide, the warmth of the night air permeating the foyer. Temperatures had soared during the afternoon, and the atmosphere felt muggy, making it hard to breathe. Dust particles danced in the flashlight beams, yet Remy trudged forward continuing to the other side of the building. Guiding her down another hall, the darkness was illuminated by cops rushing forward, more flashlights and even a couple of lit flares penetrated the bleak gloom. Pausing in front of the second door they came across, Remy glanced at her. She knew he checked for signs of injury, his eyes raking her from the tips of her toes to the top of her head. His scorching look pooled heat deep in her belly and a spark of attraction arced.

Merde, now was not the time to be thinking about how attractive the cop was. How his eyes had crinkled at the corners when he'd smiled earlier, or the slight upward tilt of his mouth when he'd called her sweetheart. Think about your brother. Dubshenko denied shooting him, but Jinx knew what she'd seen. The argument she'd heard. The loud pop of the gun firing.

"Have a seat, Jennifer. Make yourself comfortable," Remy chuckled then added, "at least as comfortable as you can get under the circumstances." He laid the flashlight on its side so the light shone across the table top and onto the brick wall.

"I believe you. About Dubshenko shooting your brother. The good news—Carlo is still alive. The bad news—Dubshenko has him." He stood and walked over to a file cabinet in the corner of the small interrogation room, yanked open the second drawer and fumbled around inside.

Jinx waited with her arms wrapped around her body, not saying a word. She was afraid to say anything at this point. He was right. Dubshenko had Carlo, and if she gave the cops any information he wouldn't hesitate to kill him and dump his body in the swamps, never to be found.

"Ah, ha! Here we go." An old fashioned cassette tape recorder landed on the table. The light from the flashlight gleamed against its black and chrome plastic surface. The sheen was dull and worn from age and heavy use. Next, a couple of cassette tapes were plunked down on the table.

"Normally, we'd videotape our interview for both documentation and for your protection. Since the electricity is off, we're gonna do this the old-fashioned way." Grabbing up one of the cassettes Remy fed it into the recorder, and pressed play. The scratchy sound of the tape feeding was audible in the quiet of the room.

"Great. Hopefully this baby has halfway decent batteries, and doesn't conk out on us partway through." He smiled, and Jinx felt that little zing she'd noticed earlier.

Grabbing his chair he flipped it around, straddling it so he faced her. He pressed the play and record buttons simultaneously with an emphatic stab of his fingers.

"This is Detective Remy Lamoureaux of the New Orleans Police Department interviewing Ms. Jennifer Smith at 9:15 p.m., July fifteenth. This is a witness statement being recorded strictly on audio as there has been a bomb explosion at the station and power is currently off, so no video recording is possible. Ms. Smith, in your own words, I need you to repeat what we discussed earlier this evening regarding the shooting of your brother, Carlo."

Taking a deep breath, Jinx stated, "I have nothing to say."

"Ms. Smith, you came in and said you wanted to report a crime, that your brother had been killed. Is that correct?"

"Yes, but you know I was mistaken. You heard Carlo on the phone, he's not dead."

"No, he's not dead. But he sounded like he was in a lot of pain. You stated that you witnessed an assailant, whom you identified as Vladimir Dubshenko, fire a gun that hit your brother in the chest. That is what you reported, isn't it?"

"I don't have anything to say. This has all been a mistake. Can I go home now, detective?" Jinx crossed her arms over her chest, and rocked in the chair before she caught the nervous movement and abruptly stopped, freezing in place. No, she needed to leave, get Carlo away from Dubshenko and they'd disappear. Seeing what Dubshenko was capable of, bold enough to deliver a bomb directly into the heart of the police station, they weren't safe anywhere in New Orleans. Maybe not even in the state. Even if they ran she knew they'd never be safe. He'd hunt her and Carlo to the ends of the earth if it meant keeping himself out of prison.

Remy reached across and clicked off the recorder. "Jennifer, you can't go home. It's not safe. I want to protect you and your brother, but I can't do that, can't do my job, unless you work with me. Dubshenko is a monster. I've been trying to put him away for a long time, and like the rat he is he always scurries away through the cracks. With your eyewitness testimony and your brother's help we can arrest him, have him stand trial for attempted murder. That will get him off the streets for a very long time."

"You don't get it, do you?" She shot back. "You're right, he's a monster. I barely know the man, yet even I sensed that. After he shot Carlo tonight, when he realized I was going to be a problem—that I'd seen everything, he chased me. I took off and he hunted me." Jinx tugged at her torn and dirty shirt. "See this? I crawled through bushes and mud getting away from them. Ran through alleyways and into the woods hiding for what seemed like hours. I have never been so scared in my life. If he'd caught me I'd be dead right now." Jinx shuddered, remembering the acid in her stomach, the terror while she hid, knowing if Dubshenko or his bodyguard found her they wouldn't hesitate to execute her on the spot.

"You didn't see the look in his eyes. The soulless, icy depths with no sane person at home."

"That's why I have to put him away. You and Carlo are my best shot at that."

Jinx shook her head. He was a cop, he didn't get it. They never did. "Detective, my brother was working for Dubshenko. I didn't know it beforehand, but I heard them. People won't believe him. He'd be considered a bad guy, too. He's got a record. How much credibility do you think a jury is going to give to his story? I'll tell you—none. Most of the time the cops won't even listen to him."

"I'll listen to him." Remy's quiet confidence washed over Jinx in a calming wave, and she wished with all her heart she could give in, trust him, but she knew better. Cops were no friends of the Marucci family.

"Detective, I've got nothing to say, on or off the record. This interview is over unless I'm under arrest. In which case I want a lawyer."

Remy stared at her long and hard, and Jinx fought not to wriggle in her seat. He had the bad cop stare down perfect. Trouble was, after only a couple of minutes, she knew he wasn't the bad cop. He cared—something most police officers lost after being on the job for any length of time.

With a rough sigh, he turned the recorder back on. "Ms. Smith, you have declined to provide any further information, is that correct?"

"That's right."

"In lieu of Ms. Smith's refusal to answer questions this interview is concluded at 9:20 p.m., July fifteenth." With a flick of the buttons, he turned the recorder off, then leaned his crossed arms on the table.

"I wish I could convince you we can help."

A hard knock pounded on the door, and Captain Hilliard stepped through. "Interview can't possibly be finished already."

"Ms. Smith refuses to comply with the request for an interview."

Hilliard stared at her, and Jinx knew he was trying to figure out the best way to convince her to cooperative. Play the victim card? Threaten her with arrest? Didn't matter—nothing was going to make her say anything that might implicate her brother.

"You do realize Dubshenko is a violent man?"

Jinx rolled her eyes. Why else would she be here? The bastard had shot her brother right in front of her.

"I'm not going to sugar coat things, Ms. Smith—or whoever you really are. If your brother isn't already dead Dubshenko won't hesitate to kill him once he has what he wants. We," he motioned between him and Remy, "want to keep your brother alive. You need to tell us exactly what Dubshenko wanted from your brother."

"How many times do I have to tell you, I don't know!" Jinx stood, slamming her hands down onto the table. "He said Carlo lost his package, whatever that was, and that he had something else that Dubshenko wanted."

"Did he ever say what it was?" Remy asked, joining in the conversation.

"No, but it seemed really important. Dubshenko seemed to think Carlo gave it to me."

"Did he?" Hilliard again.

"No. Carlo didn't give me anything. He was excited when he called earlier about dinner, but that's it."

Hilliard leaned against the cement wall meeting Remy's gaze, and Jinx wanted to smack them. That damned male-to-male communication without saying anything drove her nuts. Her father and brothers did it too, and she wanted to pop them when they did it.

"Dubshenko's going to come after you—especially if he thinks you have something that is so vitally important he was willing to kill for it. Plus, if something has happened to your brother you're the only witness who can tie Dubshenko to his murder."

"Don't say that!" Jinx pulled in a deep breath, hands shaking so much she wrapped her arms around herself to still them. "He was still alive—you heard him."

"Think about it, Ms. Smith. He sounded weak and breathless, and most definitely in pain. A gunshot wound to the chest, unless immediately treated, often proves fatal."

Jinx bit back the sob threatening to escape. Did they think she was stupid? Of course she knew that. But crossing Dubshenko meant certain death, if not now then it was only a matter of time. She wasn't willing to risk herself or her brother to the honesty of cops.

"I need you alive and breathing until we can establish

enough of a case against Dubshenko to put him away. Your witnessing this attempted murder goes a long way toward that, but only if you're around to testify."

"Hold it." Jinx interrupted. "I didn't agree to be a witness to anything."

Hilliard nodded toward the table where Jinx saw the wheels spinning on the tape recorder. Damn it, lousy cops. They'd tricked her into talking, spouting off about Carlo's shooting and Dubshenko's involvement."

"That's not admissible. I didn't agree to anything."

"Not, you're right, Ms. Smith. It's not admissible in court. Dubshenko is an evil man. You've been here for a long time. Do you really think he's going to believe you didn't tell us everything?"

Jinx froze. Dammit, he was right. Dubshenko would never believe she hadn't willingly spilled her guts, told them everything. She'd voluntarily come in to report Carlo's shooting. Her shoulders slumped in defeat.

"What do you want me to do?"

Hilliard looked over at Remy. "Detective Lamoreaux is a cop I'd trust with my life, so I'm going to trust him with yours. Normally, we'd put you in one of our safe houses, but Dubshenko's too sharp. He'd find it in a second. There's always a paper trail with these things, and when there's a paper trail it's easy to find out just about anything. A safe house no matter how much we'd like to think it's secure…well, let's just say if the bribe is big enough no information is secure. Instead, we're going to put you both on the road, keep moving."

Hilliard pulled up a chair and motioned for everyone to sit.

"Okay, here's the plan."

Chapter Four

Carlo knew his chances of ditching Dubshenko and his goon, who Carlo had jokingly nicknamed Bubba, were slim to none. The gun shot earlier hurt like a son of a bitch, but hadn't done any real damage, though he'd be bruised to hell and back before the night was through. It would all be good, though, as long as Dubshenko didn't discover he wore Kevlar and sported a blood pack he'd popped seconds after the bullet struck.

Good thing he hadn't trusted Ivor Gregorski, that dirty lousy snitch, one inch. When he'd picked up *the package* for Dubshenko. plans to take things slow and continue investigating Dubshenko from the inside of his organization flew right out the window. He'd contacted his superior at the Drug Enforcement Administration and they'd kick-started the timeline up a hell of a lot quicker than planned. Hence, the bullet-proof vest firmly in place before he met with Dubshenko.

Things had gone off the rails when he'd shown up at Jinx's house earlier than scheduled. He'd planned to meet Dubshenko tomorrow morning, giving himself enough time to get Jinx out of town before all hell broke loose.

Instead, the Russian mob boss showed up without warning. He hadn't even had time to meet his contact, have him smuggle his baby sister out of the state. Yeah, she'd need to be that far away to be out of reach of Dubshenko's tentacles. Right now, nobody had a friggin' clue what was going on, or where to find the missing girl that Dubshenko kept referring to as *the package*. Like speaking in code would keep people from realizing the package was a person, not a thing.

Dubshenko thought the package Carlo was to deliver was his golden ticket. He had no idea Carlo had an even bigger package to deliver to the DEA. Carlo's new package was *the key* to shutting down Dubshenko once and for all.

"Carlo, your lovely sister has caused me a great deal of trouble. Unfortunate, indeed. I had an interested party lined up and willing to invest a hefty fee for such quality merchandise." Dubshenko laughed, and it took every ounce of willpower Carlo had not to reach across the limo's seat, wrap his hands around his throat and squeeze the life out of the evil bastard. Watch the bitterness and demonic gleam fade from Dubshenko's eyes as death swept this spawn of Satan straight into the pits of hell, from which he'd emerged. Instead, he balled his hands into fists and held his fury contained—biding his time, waiting for the opportunity to strike.

"It sounds like Detective Lamoreaux might keep her out of your hands, Vladimir." Carlo infused his voice with enough scorn and derision that Dubshenko couldn't misunderstand. He leaned back, checking out every inch of the luxurious limo. Maybe he'd find a weapon or an escape route, whichever came first. While he'd prefer to kill Dubshenko outright, it was more important to make sure Jinx was protected, and get his newly acquired information to his superiors. After this SNAFU, his cover was pretty well blown sky high. One big problem though—she didn't know what it was or where to find it.

"You've never met Detective Lamoreaux have you, Carlo?" Dubshenko chuckled before continuing. "The man is a clueless idiot. I will never understand how he earned his detective badge, unless he greased the wheels. Of course, he is such a—what is it you Americans' call it—a boy scout—he would never do something like that. The man has tried repeatedly to arrest me, but do you see me in his jail? No, and you will not."

Carlo doubted that. He'd heard things about Lamoreaux not only on the back streets of New Orleans, but from his bosses. Cops didn't come any cleaner than Remy Lamoreaux. The word they'd used to describe him–incorruptible. Guess he'd be putting his baby sister's life in Lamoreaux's hands. He damned well better be smart enough and fast enough to protect her.

Dubshenko glanced down at the cell phone in his hand as though willing it to ring. *Who was he expecting to call him? More importantly, what was he waiting to hear?*

He'd been pretty disoriented after the gunshot to the chest, his head bouncing on the hardwood floor of Jinx's living room when he'd fallen. Hearing her indrawn gasp, and Bubba chasing after her, his plan to fake his death flew out the window. Jinx's safety was his primary concern, and he'd crawled on his hands and knees toward the kitchen until his head cleared enough to chase after the two mobsters trying to kill his sister.

Luck had been on her side, and she'd escaped without injury. Unfortunately, he hadn't been so lucky. Bubba caught him and tossed him into the back of the idling limo and moments later Dubshenko climbed in, beads of sweat decorating his forehead, his suave appearance disappearing under the unexpected exertion of the chase.

"Expecting a call?" Carlo couldn't hold back the taunt.

Dubshenko's lips curved into a mockery of a smile, one that didn't reach his icy blue stare. His fingers slid across the screen of the smart phone like the caress of a lover.

"I sent a special delivery, a gesture of good will for my good friend, Detective Lamoreaux." He laughed and Carlo felt a chill crawl down his spine at the madness contained in Dubshenko's laughter. "I know it was delivered. I'm just waiting to hear how it was received. Hopefully, your sister shared in…"

The ringing cell phone cut off his words and he answered in Russian. Carlo's knowledge of the language was next to useless. He understood a word or two, but not enough to understand even a portion of what Dubshenko spouted. However, it was clear whatever was said on the other end did not make him happy. In fact, just the opposite seemed true.

Dubshenko's finger hit the end call button, and with a curse he flung the phone across the limo. Its case slammed against the darkened panel that separated the passengers from the driver's section.

"Bad news?" Carlo couldn't resist taunting him. He leaned back against the seat crossing his arms. Agony shot through him and he bit back an expletive as the muscles pulled, straining against his already bruising chest.

Who knew getting shot would hurt so damned much?

Dubshenko's gaze focused on him like a laser, and with a few muttered words to Bubba and a flick of his wrist in Carlo's direction, he leaned back against his seat. Carlo never saw Bubba's fist coming from beside him, although he felt the crack against his right cheek. His head snapped forward with the forceful blow.

"Dammit, that hurt."

"You forget yourself, Carlo. Speak to me with respect, or do not speak at all." Bubba grunted his agreement with Dubshenko's words.

"Yeah, right. Respect. You're gonna kill me, so why should I be respectful? So, what, if I bow down and kiss your Ferragamo's you're gonna let me live?"

Dubshenko tugged at the cuff of his shirt, before brushing off a speck of invisible lint from his jacket sleeve. Impeccably dressed, even in the sweltering heat appearance was everything to a man like him. "You might be interested to know, Carlo, there was an incident at the police station a little while ago." Carlo's heartbeat raced, the machine-gun's rapid beating forced a rush of adrenaline through his body. *What the hell has this bastard done?*

"Apparently, somebody smuggled a bomb into the police station. It went off right after your sister talked with Detective Lamoreaux. "

"What?"

"Yes. It seems a pizza delivery person walked in with a homemade pipe bomb concealed in a food carrier, and delivered it to the good detective. Things are chaotic, but several people have been injured and there are reported...fatalities."

No!

"Damn you, Dubshenko."

Boiling rage spilled through Carlo, nearly blinding him with the urge to end the son of a bitch who'd dared to hurt his sister, and he lunged toward Dubshenko intent on wiping the despicable smirk off his smug face. Before he'd cleared half the distance, Bubba slammed into him, taking him to the floor, his enormous bulk landing atop him with a resounding thud. A whoosh of air left his chest at the impact of all Bubba's massive weight pressing him against the floor boards.

Carlo couldn't catch his breath. His lungs burned with a silent plea for oxygen.

Can't breathe!

"Don't be a fool. My associate will snap your neck like a chicken bone before you lay a finger on me." Dubshenko uncrossed his feet and the last thing Carlo saw was his shiny black Ferragamo-encased foot, right before it made contact with the side of his head.

Chapter Five

The purr of the motorcycle's engine always soothed Remy. On a quiet night when the sweltering heat and humidity made the air nearly unbreathable and sweat coated his skin, hopping on his bike and letting her rip cooled him off, both physically and psychologically. His mind ran free as he sped down the highway. The vibration and smooth acceleration flipped a switch inside him, and everything became focused and clear.

That so wasn't happening tonight. For one thing, he wasn't riding alone. Her arms twined about his middle holding on tight enough he couldn't breathe freely. And her damn nails were digging into his stomach deep enough he could feel them through his shirt. *Jennifer.*

This entire night was one huge, screwed up disaster. Remy still couldn't believe Captain Hilliard made him chief babysitter for their brand new witness. Keep her safe, he said. Pump her, not in the fun way, but find out what she's hiding. Oh, yeah, Remy didn't have a single doubt she was hiding something. Beginning with who she really was. Jennifer Smith. Right. That wasn't a fake name, no siree.

Leaning the bike into the curve, he efficiently pulled into the gravel-lined driveway of his house, the one he shared with his *maman*. His grandmother. Bless all the saints, he'd never been happier she was out of town visiting her friend, Molly Connor, down in Boca Raton. He bit back a grin at the thought of his Cajun grandmother meeting Jennifer. She'd have every secret the woman possessed out of her within the first five minutes.

He let the engine idle, keeping the bike upright for a few seconds, before dropping the kickstand into place and cut the engine. Jennifer's nails still dug deep, her whole body trembling, even with the engine off.

"You can let go now, sweetheart." Her arms remained locked tight around his midsection, and she remained unmoving, her head still pressed against his shoulder. He had the impression she'd have crawled inside him if it were possible. He chuckled at the thought. Yeah, well he'd like to crawl inside her, but in a much different way.

"What?"

"We're here. Come on inside. I need to grab a couple of things before we take off." Her arms slowly unwrapped from around his midsection, and Remy was surprised that he missed their feel. It had been ages since he'd had a woman on the back of his ride, preferring that alone time, just him and his bike. When he was with a woman, he drove the POS Buick he'd bought off his brother, Max.

"This is your house?" Jennifer stood behind him looking at it, curiosity lacing her voice. He looked at his home trying to see it through her eyes. It wasn't a new house. His grandparents had lived in it for over fifty years, buying it shortly after they'd married. His mother and her sister had been raised in that house, only leaving when she'd married his father. He and Max had practically lived there as well, spending nearly as much time there as they had at their own place. This place was home to him. When his grandfather died a few years back, he'd moved in with his *maman*, intent on taking care of her. Instead, the feisty woman took better care of him than he'd ever done for her. And he let her because he knew taking care of him gave her a purpose, something to fill the lonely days and nights since his grandfather passed.

"This is my *maman's* house. My grandmother. I live here with her."

Jennifer looked over at him, then started toward the front porch. Both sides of the sprawling, whitewashed wooden porch were covered with lattice, and along each wooden frame cascades of honeysuckle blossomed, its fragrance perfuming the night air. The scent always reminded Remy of his grandmother and of home.

"I love it," she smiled and climbed the three steps onto the porch, "it's filled with charming character and shows it's been well-loved."

"Yes, it has." Jennifer's perceptiveness surprised him. Most people saw an eighty-plus year old house, and thought it run down and out of step with all the newer, more modern homes. But Jennifer saw deeper, noticing the telltale differences that made it more than the sum of its parts. It wasn't a house. In every sense of the word, it was a home. Maybe he'd underestimated her. She seemed to have surprising depths that in another place and time he'd love to delve deeper. Go beyond the superficial, and get to know the real woman. Maybe after everything was resolved and Dubshenko was behind bars, he'd get the chance to see what made this beautiful curvy woman tick.

"Come on, let's grab the stuff I need and hightail it out of here before Dubshenko finds us." Remy ushered her through the front door. He flipped on the wall switch and the room filled with light. Jennifer's indrawn breath had him focused on her. "What?"

"It's beautiful." She walked over to the sofa, running her fingers along the crocheted throw draped across the back. Made of thin cording, the delicate stitches wove lacy patterns of pinks and rose tones against the tan backdrop of the couch fabric. "This took a tremendous amount of work. Did your grandmother make it?"

"Yeah, she did. Most of the girly stuff in here is her handiwork. She's been doing stuff like that for as long as I can remember." Remy bit back a chuckle, but Jennifer caught it and raised her brow in silent question.

"When my mom was pregnant with my brother, Max, *maman* started embroidering all kinds of fancy sh—stuff to start a hope chest for the baby. When he turned out to be a boy she said it didn't matter, men needed hope chests too, so she kept at it. Tablecloths, napkins, pillow cases and sheets. All the things a daughter would need, she made for him. She presented it to him when he got engaged to Theresa."

"I think that's really sweet," She paused before giving him a cheeky grin, "so, do you have a hope chest, too, detective?"

Remy couldn't stop the heat flooding into his cheeks, and knew his face was red. He never blushed, but there was no denying this.

"Yep, I've got one too. Though she says she's still

working on it. I don't get anything until I'm engaged."

"Well, whoever the lucky woman is, I'm sure she'll appreciate it. This is beautiful workmanship. She must love you very much to want to make sure you and your future bride start your lives out with love and care from your family."

"I know. I'm a very lucky man to have *maman* in my life."

"Yes. That kind of love is special. Cherish it. Not everybody is that fortunate in their family."

Hmm. He knew about her brother, she cared deeply for him. But maybe she had other family she wasn't quite as close with. That might be a place to start.

"If you're hungry, go ahead and grab something in the kitchen. I'll just be a minute. Wait—on second thought come on back and let's see if I can find something for you to wear. That skirt won't be too comfortable for a long ride on the bike."

"Wait, what? I thought we came here to get your car. I'm not riding on that rattling death trap for hours. Nuh uh. No way, no how."

Remy didn't even attempt to hide his grin. He planned on taking the car, but couldn't resist getting a rise out of her. She looked so pretty when she got riled up.

"Sweetheart, we'll move much faster on the bike, and Dubshenko probably doesn't know I own it."

"Probably ain't good enough, Romeo. I am not getting back on that...that flaming rocket of destruction. I'll stay here. He won't find me."

Remy shook his head. "Jennifer, this is my home. It'll be the first place he'll look once he realizes you're not at the police station. He knows we've talked. He's not a stupid man, he'll know you are with me."

Jennifer paced back and forth in front of him, chewing on her thumb nail. He'd picked up on that habit of hers earlier in the interrogation room. Whenever she was deep in thought she nibbled on that nail, worrying at it.

"I still don't see why I can't go home. Dubshenko wouldn't hurt me."

"Right," Remy shot back, cutting her off. "He won't hurt you—you'll just disappear. Everyone who's ever crossed him, uttered a single word against him, has vanished without a trace. I will not see you become his next victim."

Grabbing her wrist, he towed her down the narrow hallway to his bedroom at the back of the house. It was a spacious room. When he'd moved back in with his grandmother, he hauled Max over and they'd knocked down the wall dividing the two smaller bedrooms, combining them into one large suite, complete with en suite bathroom. They'd spent a three-day weekend retrofitting and updating the bathroom to a hedonistic masterpiece.

"Through that door is the bathroom. You might want to make use of the facilities while you've got the chance. Once we hit the road, it'll probably be a while before we stop."

Jennifer stomped over and flung the door open. Her breath caught as she took in the dramatic upscale and luxuriously outfitted space. Remy knew he'd surprised her with it. Hell, he admitted, he wanted to impress her. Let her see there was more to him than just the cop who wouldn't let her leave.

"Wow. This is amazing." Her voice filled with awe as she spun around inside the bathroom.

"Thanks. I like the way it turned out."

"You did all this?"

"Sure did. Well, me and my brother, Max." He pointed toward the shower. "Steam shower, jacuzzi tub, heated floors, the whole shebang." Remy chuckled. "Trust me, in the wintertime, the heated floors are a decision I've never regretted."

Jennifer grinned. "I believe it. This is a dream bathroom. I hope I can update my…"

"Jennifer, you'll get to come back to your home and your life. Once Dubshenko is out of the picture everything will return to normal."

She shook her head, and he watched her turn away, stepping further into the bathroom. Turning to face him, she replied, "Detective, nothing will ever be *normal* again." With that, she closed the door, and the snick of the lock sounded as loud as a shot.

With a low growl, Remy stomped across his bedroom, yanked open his dresser drawer and pulled out clothes, tossing them onto the bed. He slammed the drawer closed, then flung open the closet door, snatching a backpack off the hook attached to the back. He shoved the few items into the bag and zipped it shut.

"I'll be right back," he snarled through the closed bathroom door. Dammit, he'd protect her, make sure she got her life back. He had no intention of letting Dubshenko win—again. Marching down the hallway, he threw open the door to his grandmother's room, going straight for her closet. Rummaging through the hangers, he found nothing he thought Jennifer could wear. He turned to the dresser and paused. Did he really want to be pawing through his *maman's* drawers? He really didn't want to see any of her unmentionables.

Right. Suck it up, big man.

He skipped the first two, starting with the third in the dresser. T-shirts. Those would work. A huge grin split his face as he read a couple of the sayings. Picking out two he knew would scandalize Jennifer, he put the rest back and went on searching. Bingo! The next drawer held yoga pants with drawstring waistbands. His grandmother was a couple of sizes smaller than Jennifer, but they were stretch material—they'd have to do for now.

Okay, there was no way on Earth Jennifer was wearing his *maman's* granny panties. He shuddered at the thought. She'd make do with the pair she wore now or go commando.

Rein it in, big guy. The thought of her bare from the waist down definitely got a rise out of him. Literally. Or maybe with her in those yoga pants with the string tied in an itty-bitty bow. One good tug and they'd pool around her ankles and…

"Detective?" Jennifer's voice behind him had him slamming the drawer, holding the two pair of yoga pants in one hand, along with the t-shirts.

"Here." He shoved a pair of the pants and a shirt at her in a jumbled mess, and she grabbed onto them before the hit the floor. "Put these on and let's get out of here. We've already wasted enough time. Dubshenko's already looking for us. You can change in here."

Stepping back into the hallway he closed the door, and strode back to his room shoving the extra shirt and pants into his backpack. He added his backup piece, a .38 snub nose and extra ammo. Grabbing up the pack and his keys, he headed for the living room. He gave a quick knock on her door and mumbled, "I'll be in the living room, let's go."

In less than a minute Jennifer crept into the living room tugging at the T-shirt. The clothes were tight on her as he'd suspected they would be, though the shirt was a halfway decent fit, especially across her full breasts. She definitely had a gorgeous rack. Luckily, the pants were Capri style, so they hit below the knee. Which was okay, nobody would look twice at that. Her bare feet, on the other hand, might be a problem.

"Crap. I forgot about shoes. Lemme see if *maman* has anything that might work. Wish I could take you over to Max and Theresa's place. Her stuff would probably fit you better." He kept talking while he rummaged through his gran's closet again. Luckily, there was a pair of decorated flip-flops, beaded with the gaudiest rhinestones and fake flowers he'd ever seen.

"Here you go." He tried to hide the smirk threatening to pull his lips upward, but it was a losing battle at the horrified look on her face. She quickly masked it, and fluttered her eyelashes at him in a blatantly exaggerated mock flirt.

"Why thank you so much, Prince Charming. What lovely slippers." She slid them onto her feet wincing a bit when the cuts met the rubberized soles, but never said a word. She'd been a real trooper about the whole thing, actually, Remy thought. Battered, bruised and bleeding when she'd come into the station, she'd never once complained about her own plight. She was too worried about her brother, Carlo. He spared a quick thought for him, knowing Captain Hilliard would do everything humanly possible to find him and keep him safe—if he was still alive—and that was a big if since Dubshenko was involved.

"I'm as ready as I'll ever be." She pulled her long hair back in one hand before adding, "Wait. Have you got a piece of string, or something I can tie this back with? If we're going to be on the motorcycle it'll be easier." Remy pulled open a drawer in the entryway table, and pulled out a leather thong, one he'd used on his own hair when it had been longer.

"Here. Use this."

"Thanks." With a quick flick of her wrist, her hair was bound back away from her gorgeous face, and Remy was struck by the unselfconscious beauty of her.

She doesn't even realize how beautiful she is.

Gabbing up his pack and keys, they headed outside. "I was kidding about the bike, Jennifer. We can take the car."

"No, I thought about it and you're right. They'll be more likely to look for a car than a motorcycle. Plus, we'll travel faster this way. I'm sure I'll get used to it— eventually," She chuckled before continuing, "if I can stay on the beast, that is."

They climbed on Remy's Ducati Diavel Dark, his pride and joy. Its black and chrome finish was polished to a gleaming shine, even in the darkness. He knew the bike inside and out, kept her in tiptop running condition and trusted her more than the car anyway. He strapped the pack on the back with bungee cords, tying it down tightly before motioning for Jennifer to climb on. His eyes were glued to her ass as she swung her leg across the seat, the dark yoga pants stretching to outline and highlight her luscious curves.

Get your head in the game, jackass. She's a witness, you're supposed to be protecting her, not lusting after her body.

He climbed on in front and hit the electronic ignition, waiting while she wrapped her arms snug around his midsection, fingers intertwined in front at waist level.

A last fleeting thought whispered through his mind as they drove into the darkness. *Crap, this is going to be a flaming disaster.*

Chapter Six

Around 3 a.m. Remy finally pulled into a motel where they could check in for the remainder of the night. Jinx had never been so happy to finally see a place with a bed and a bathroom. Her bladder had been protesting for the last hour, but she knew the farther away from New Orleans they got, the safer they'd be. Swinging her leg across the seat, she stood next to the black motorcycle. Or she tried to. Her legs resembled limp overcooked spaghetti, weak and not up to the job of holding her weight. *Well, crap on a cracker, this sucks.*

Remy's arm shot around her waist, keeping her from face planting onto the crumbling asphalt drive. Wouldn't that make a great impression on the night clerk? Heck, maybe he'd think she was too drunk to stand up on her own. Glancing down at her unique clothing choices, maybe he'd think she was a cheap hooker Remy had picked up. After all, the entire place looked like they rented rooms by the hour, not someplace you'd bring the family on the way to Disney World. Heck, for all she knew, the clerk probably had the local professionals on speed dial for easier customer service.

"Wait here and I'll get us a room." Remy strode toward the office and all Jinx could think was *A ROOM? One? Uh, oh. No, don't even go there. We're both tired, nothing's going to happen. He's keeping you safe. That's it. Of course we'd have to share a room. It only makes sense. Wait—I don't have anything to sleep in!*

She turned back to the bike and fumbled with the bungee cord, and unhooked the backpack. Sliding the strap across her shoulder, she paced beside the bike. Her thigh muscles ached from holding them at that angle for so long. Plus, she wasn't used to being on a motorcycle, so they throbbed, to say nothing of her butt. Talk about uncomfortable. She chuckled and whispered, "The vibrations were definitely a plus, though."

The office door opened and Remy met her halfway between there and the Ducati. "We're at the end, first floor. Let's go." Since it was such a short distance they walked, and he rolled the bike into the empty parking space two slots over from their room. When it was parked, he reached down and picked up a handful of dirt, and with a grimace smeared it all over the license plate.

"Why'd you do that?"

"Covers up the numbers from a distance. Somebody would have to be up close and personal to read them clearly. Just playing it safe." He wiped his hand down the side of his jeans before reaching for the backpack she had over her shoulder. With a shrug she slid it off and handed it over.

"You hungry? There was a vending machine in the office. It ain't much but..."

"No, thanks. I'm okay. I just want to sleep." Jinx followed him into the room. She waited a second while he flipped on the light. The rank smell of cigarettes, greasy fast food and stale sex permeated the room with their acrid stench. A king size bed dominated the space, its worn faded comforter a dull floral pattern of browns, oranges and a decidedly puke green color. A brown lamp with a lopsided, yellow shade sat in solitary splendor on the narrow nightstand to the left of the bed. Not even an alarm clock decorated its worn and scratched surface.

"Gee, you take me to the nicest places, Detective."

Remy grimaced and she felt bad about the verbal dig, but she was exhausted, worried about her brother and scared. Dubshenko was the unknown element in everything. The kind of monster you dreamt about in the darkest recesses of your nightmares, but happily faded into oblivion with the light of day. Only he wasn't fading away.

"Sorry." She sank down onto the corner of the bed, sitting on the verge edge, and absently picked at the bedspread. How should she approach talking to him about their sleeping arrangements? She got that they needed to stick together. But didn't they have a room with two beds? Then again, thinking about the kind of dump they were in, chances were good this was the penthouse suite.

"I know you're tired, Jennifer. Just know I'll do everything in my power to keep you safe." He tossed the pack onto the bed beside her and turned away. He walked toward the room's solitary window, its ugly green and yellow striped curtains doing nothing to disguise the cobwebs clinging to the curtain rod. They were clearly visible even with the light of only the single lamp in the room.

"I'm going to call Captain Hilliard, see if there's any

news about your brother."

She glanced at the cell phone he'd pulled out of his pocket. "Is it safe to make any calls? Can I use that when you're finished?"

"Burner phone." He replied.

"What's that?"

"Prepaid cell phone with no way to trace it. I'll only use it once, then get rid of it. It's not safe to have direct communication. Too easy for somebody with even minimal skills to hack into and track the GPS." He motioned toward the pack. "Why don't you go ahead and get ready for bed."

She headed toward the bathroom and within minutes was back out again, dressed in just the T-shirt she'd borrowed. It barely covered the edge of her panties. She tugged on the hem, and Remy caught the movement out of the corner of his eye. He turned back to the window, and she ignored him, instead staring at the bed.

He finished the call with Hilliard, removed the battery and smart card from inside the phone, and ground the plastic phone casing beneath his boot heel before he tossed the remnants of the phone in the trash, along with the battery. He carried the smart card into the bathroom. A quick flush took care of getting it out of the room and on its way to the local sanitation station. Good luck tracking it now.

# # # # #

Remy sauntered back into the room. Jennifer had already pulled back the bedspread and climbed beneath the covers, and pulled them up all the way to beneath her chin. Big blue eyes watched his every move, a blend of exhaustion and a tiny glimmer of fear readable in her gaze.

He hated this entire situation. Although they'd only spent a few hours together, from the time she'd walked into the station, he'd been instantly attracted to her. She reminded him a lot of Theresa. They had the same coloring, long blonde hair and a pale creamy complexion. That initial appearance of fragility disguising a core of solid steel. Under different circumstances, he wouldn't have hesitated to date her, bed her and move on. But these weren't the usual circumstances by anybody's definition. He was responsible for keeping her safe and out of Dubshenko's clutches, for however long that took.

Looking at her tucked up in the bed they'd have to share, he could only hope they arrested him pretty damn quick before his little head overrode all sense in his big head, and he did what he'd been dying to do ever since they'd left his house. Find out if her lips were as soft as they looked.

"Where are you going to sleep?" The softly voiced question brought his eyes zeroing back to her.

"Right beside you, sweetheart."

Jennifer struggled upright in the bed, keeping her death grip on the blankets. "Hell, no. I don't think so."

"Well, think again. Have you taken a good look at the carpet? There is no way I'm sleeping on that disease-ridden mess." He toed off his boots, and sat down on the edge of the bed to peel off his socks. Grabbing a handful of his shirt, he yanked it off over his head, and started to toss it onto the floor, stopping in mid-motion. He stomped over and folded it before placing it atop the backpack. Fingers flicked open the button of his jeans.

"Wait. Keep your pants on."

Remy turned around to face Jennifer, crossing his

arms over his chest. "I am not sleeping in my jeans. For heaven's sake, we're both adults. We can share a bed without pouncing on each other in uncontrolled lust." Although that sounded like a really good idea to him. It had been a long dry spell since he'd had a gorgeous blonde in his bed.

He unzipped his jeans and peeled them down his legs, smiling when he looked up and saw Jennifer's eyes squeezed tightly shut. Folding the jeans, he placed them with his shirt. Reaching inside the backpack, he pulled out his .38 snub nose and strolled over to the side of the bed closest to the door. *Which just happened to be the side she'd plopped her pretty little fanny on.*

"Move over, sweetheart. I need to be near the door."

With a huff she scooted over, still keeping her death grip on the covers. He slid underneath, punching the flattened pillow behind him and shoved the .38 beneath his pillow. With both their lives on the line, Remy wasn't taking any chances. While he was pretty sure Dubshenko didn't have a lead on them yet, it was only a matter of time.

"Try to get some sleep. We'll have to take off early to keep ahead of Dubshenko."

She turned toward him, braced her head on her bent arm and studied his face. "What did Captain Hilliard say? Was there any word on Carlo?"

Remy leaned forward and tucked a lock of her blonde hair behind her ear, marveling at how soft the skin of her cheek was. His groin tightened and swelled. Looks like the little head wanted to do the thinking after all. He needed to get a tight rein on things right now.

"There's no word on your brother yet. Cap's got everyone available out looking for any sign of him, but nothing so far. Dubshenko's limo was spotted at your house, but you already knew that. He thinks they loaded Carlo inside it after you took off, but there's no trace of him." He saw the tears welling up in her eyes, and he wanted to make everything better for her. He just wasn't sure how.

"No, don't think the worst. You talked to him. You know he was alive after he left your house. Carlo's smart, right? A fighter?" She nodded, and he heard her whisper, "You have no idea." He brushed it aside and continued.

"He's hurt, though we don't know how badly. Cap says there was some blood at your house. Not as much as you'd think for a gunshot to the chest, though."

"I've never been so scared in my life, and I've been through some pretty crazy sh—stuff. When Dubshenko shot him he stumbled backward, and blood spread across his chest." She paused and Remy could practically see the wheels turning in her mind, piecing together what she'd seen and heard. "I think he was more stunned than anything. You're right, there was blood on his shirt, but wouldn't a gunshot wound to the chest, especially one near the heart, have a lot of bleeding? Wouldn't it be pooling on the floor beneath him?"

Remy had thought the same thing after talking to the Captain. Things weren't adding up and this whole scenario stunk—like a set up.

"They didn't find any spent shell casings at your place. Can you remember anything else, maybe what the gun looked like?"

Jennifer glared at him, disbelief written across her face. "Are you kidding? No, I don't remember what the gun looked like. It was black. It was a gun. I was kind of busy looking at my brother, worried he was dead. Sorry to disappoint you."

"Dial it back, sweetheart. I'm just trying to piece things together. It's my job, remember?" He rolled over to face her, narrowing the space between them. His hand slid along her cheek, his thumb rubbing small circles on her soft skin. The movement was meant to offer comfort. He stared into her big blue eyes, which at the moment were glaring daggers at him.

"We need to get some sleep. In the morning we'll make some plans. I've got a few ideas of where we can head. You'll be safe, I promise. Shut off the light." She turned and flipped it off, plunging the room into near darkness. A faint sliver of light spilled through the split in the curtains, bathing the foot of the bed in a dim glow.

They lay side by side in the king-sized bed not touching, but both unable to sleep. Jennifer tossed and turned. Remy knew the instant she began crying, silent tears flowing. Sobs wracked her body even though she fought letting them escape. She turned on her side, facing away from him, as though trying to spare him the anguish tormenting her.

Remy rolled onto his side, scooting closer against her back, wrapping his arm over her and throwing his right leg across hers, pinning her body against his. She stiffened against his hold and started to protest.

"Shh, little one. Go to sleep. I'll take care of you." She gave a little hiccuping sigh and relaxed. Within moments she'd drifted off to sleep. Remy knew, with her body cuddled against his, it was going to be a long sleepless night.

Chapter Seven

Dubshenko glared down at the unconscious man lying on the floor. He'd had such high hopes for Carlo. Instead, he'd betrayed him. *Idiot.* Nobody crossed Vladimir Dubshenko and lived to tell about it. Carlo thought he'd been so clever letting his package get away. He drew back his foot and placed a well-aimed kick into his ribs. Too bad he wasn't awake to feel it. Not to worry, though, he'd make sure the bastard felt every ache, pain and bruise before he finished what he'd started earlier. Carlo didn't know it, but he was a dead man.

Dubshenko couldn't help but be impressed, though. Carlo had been smart enough to wear a vest. Otherwise, he'd already be dead from the shot to the heart. No way could he have survived a gunshot at that close range without protection. They'd found the vest soon after he'd been knocked out in the limo, once they'd left Jennifer's house.

Ah, sweet Jennifer. She'd held such promise. Such a meek, biddable woman. The perfect candidate for his special buyer. Long, golden blonde hair flowed past her shoulders in waves. Big, sapphire blue eyes that sparkled with life and joy. A figure most men would die to get their hands on. She wasn't one of these anorexic, stick figure women Hollywood and the press seemed to glorify. No, Jennifer would be the perfect handful of glorious breasts, and ample hips to grasp as a man rode her from behind.

Damn it. I wanted a piece of that before sending her on her way. Stupid bitch. If only she'd minded her own business everything would have been perfect.

He didn't normally sample the merchandise, but he'd have made an exception for her. There was something innocent and fragile about her, it brought out something he'd never felt before. He shook his head. It didn't matter now. Plans change and he'd adapt. He always did.

He'd shown her picture to a prospective buyer who'd been ecstatic. Her coloring and demure appearance came highly prized by certain connoisseurs. Fortunately, he'd worked with this collector before and convinced him to wait a few more weeks, take the time to prepare a special gilded cage for his latest acquisition. Maybe this whole debacle could be salvaged. Carlo'd better be able to tell him where to find his other little birdie who'd flown away, and he'd retrieve her before too much damage could be done. Taking Jennifer away from Carlo would be the ultimate punishment; the agony he'd inflict on him as he expounded in minute detail exactly what his beloved sister would suffer at the hands of her new *master,* the icing on the cake.

He'd put out feelers throughout the community. Nobody hid from him—not for long anyway. His contacts at the New Orleans Police Department hadn't reported in yet, but after the explosion the night before he wasn't surprised. They'd better not take too long, though. He didn't have time to waste.

Dubshenko glanced back down at Carlo, lying unmoving and prone at his feet. Before this was over, he'd basically kill three birds with one stone. Jennifer, sweet Jennifer, would make him a small fortune with her sale, and she'd disappear never to surface again to testify against him. Carlo would suffer greatly and die for his betrayal. And last but not least, Detective Remy Lamoreaux. The unrelenting thorn in his side; the boil on his posterior. It was time to eliminate the meddlesome cop once and for all.

Dubshenko laughed out loud at the thought. He'd take care of disposing of the good detective himself. After all, he'd sealed his own fate by making this personal.

Chapter Eight

One week previous

Carlo eased up to the interior wooden door, eyeing it with a jaundiced eye. He pressed his ear against it, and could make out voices—at least two. He'd seen Dubshenko and his bodyguard walk inside the abandoned warehouse less than five minutes before. He'd been following the pair for the last two hours, which was damned annoying. He'd rather be at his favorite hangout having a beer with his buddies, instead he was sweating his ass off following the Russian drug czar around. Still, he needed to be cautious, not lose his edge. If he wasn't careful they'd catch him and there would be hell to pay. The least of which his boss would nail his hide to the wall, and probably have his sorry butt tossed back into prison.

Lucky for him, Dubshenko didn't have a clue Carlo worked for the DEA and he planned to keep it that way.

He scanned his surroundings, up and down the narrow hallway, trying to find an alternative access to the office Dubshenko and his bodyguard currently occupied. Two doors on the opposite side of the hall, but no egress to the one place he needed to get into. Damn it! Who was Dubshenko meeting? It had to be important for him to be this secretive—and this cautious.

Carlo slammed his fist against his thigh, frustrated with the whole lousy situation. Why choose an abandoned warehouse? Dubshenko owned a half dozen buildings in and around the Greater New Orleans area, so why here? This was way outside his comfort zone.

Wait. He looked up at the ceiling. It was one of the acoustic tile drop ceilings most office building had, with metal grids and individual panels placed in row after boring row. One of the panels sat askew, a fissure of blackness peeking through the two inch opening. Could he somehow get up there without making any noise, or alerting anybody else to his presence? He was in pretty good shape, but hauling himself up by upper body strength alone—that would take some doing. Could he? Only one way to find out.

His fingertips eased into the opening created by the acoustic tile until he was able to grasp the edge, curling his fingers around and lifting up. He slid the tile along the metal grid until the darkened opening gaped like a maw, causing him to lose himself in the blackness. He wrapped his hands around the metal grid work, pulling downward to test the flexibility and strength. Would it hold up to his body weight? With a sigh, he wrapped his hands around it, as close to the center as possible, and pulled his upper body toward the opening. Biceps strained against his weight, the muscles burning as he shifted his weight, wriggling his body through the opening. It was a tight fit, but he finally popped through to the other side. His lungs sucked in a huge breath of air while he looked down at the floor. Some dust had fallen through the opening onto the concrete floor below when he'd worked his way through; hopefully nobody would see it and start investigating.

Fortune favors the brave because mercifully above the drop ceiling with its thin acoustic tiles, the ceiling joists were thicker, wooden slots well able to hold his weight. Easing along the wooden rafters, he made his way to his left toward the office where Dubshenko was meeting with someone. Who that somebody was seemed pretty damned important to Carlo since this was completely out of character for Dubshenko. *He* always called the shots. Meetings were always on his turf. Yet here he was at the bidding of somebody else. Anybody yielding that much power over the most feared mobster in New Orleans made him a definite person of interest.

With an awkward half crawl, have squat-waddle, Carlo made his way along the beams strictly by feel since visibility was nil. With a grimace when his knee hit a brace he wasn't expecting, he figured he'd crawled far enough to be directly over the office. Now, he had a new problem to contend with; could he move one of the acoustic panels aside without making any noise, or being seen? If they spotted him, he was a dead man.

He crawled further along the ceiling joist, having decided that moving a panel on the side of the room seemed more prudent than trying for one in the middle. It was nearly black as pitch up in the enclosed space, barely enough light to see his fingers in front of his nose. Carlo grabbed his cell phone out of his back pocket and slid his finger across the screen, and it spread enough light to illuminate the immediate area around him. With his right hand, he slid his fingertips around the edge of the tile, holding the phone face down against his thigh in case the small amount of light it provided showed up when he moved the panel aside.

He didn't dare move it much, though. It slid for a couple of inches. The tile made a little scraping sound against the metal groove of the grid, and he froze.

"What was that?"

Crap, they'd heard.

"Probably just rats, my friend." Oh, yeah, that was Dubshenko's voice. Carlo recognized it immediately. After all, he'd heard it enough times over the last several months.

Dubshenko snapped his fingers at his bodyguard. "Go check it out."

Footsteps echoed as the bodyguard left, and Carlo's breath caught in his throat. Damn it, had he put the ceiling tile back in place in the hallway? His frantic thoughts retraced his steps before he exhaled a sigh of relief. Whew!

He tried again to inch the ceiling tile a little further. A gentle slide like the caress of a hand against silken skin, easing the edges seamlessly one more inch. This close, the voices were distinct and clear.

"Is everything in place?" That was the voice of the stranger. Man, what he wouldn't give to see his face. His voice was vaguely familiar, but Carlo couldn't place where he'd heard it before.

"No worries, my friend. Everything is planned down to the tiniest detail. There will be no problems."

Something was wrong. Off kilter. It sounded like Dubshenko was taking orders from this stranger. *Who had that kind of juice on the Russian mobster?* He leaned forward and angled his head, trying to catch a glimpse of the mystery man. Dubshenko's distinctive blond head came into view. He faced directly toward Carlo, so there was no mistaking him. The other man's back was to him. Tall, impeccably dressed in an expensive navy blue suit even in the sweltering heat of a Louisiana summer night, especially inappropriate for a visit to an abandoned warehouse. Fancy black loafers. His dark brown hair was styled, one of those thousand dollar haircuts only the rich and fabulous could afford.

Carlo's gut instinct, the family knack of knowing when trouble was barreling head first into your path blared a warning, screamed at him—run! He couldn't. Whatever was going on directly beneath him was huge, maybe the big break in the case he needed to close it once and for all. This might be the single most important piece of evidence he'd ever get against Dubshenko. Carlo wanted this piece of dirt put away for the rest of his life.

He jerked at the vibration in his hand, almost losing his balance on the narrow ceiling joist. He'd forgotten all about his phone, since the screen had gone dark.

The phone!

It took videos. Why not tape the meeting taking place directly beneath him? The big wigs at the DEA had all that fancy equipment; they could analyze it once he got the hell out of there.

With the glide of his finger across the screen, he started recording.

# # # # #

Current day

Carlo took shallow breaths, fighting against the blackness that threatened to overwhelm him again. That sorry bastard Dubshenko and his bodyguard had discovered the bulletproof vest when they'd hauled him

74

out to the Dubshenko's limo. He knew he'd end up with a gigantic bruise from the impact of the bullet. That sucker hurt like hell, but at least he wasn't lying dead in a pool of blood on the living room floor. Things were looking up.

He bit down hard on his bottom lip to keep from crying out as he eased onto his side, and cracked open one eye. He didn't recognize the room where he lay sprawled on the bare concrete floor. The last thing he remembered was Dubshenko coldcocking him in the back of the limo, and then it was lights out. He tried to gauge where he might be from the sparse surroundings. With all Dubshenko's holding across the city, he could be just about anywhere.

There was nobody else in the room, but he knew guards wouldn't be far away. Dubshenko wouldn't leave him unguarded. It was too important for him to find out where his precious package ended up. *Fat chance.* He'd never tell that sorry bastard how to find the girl. She was safe—at least for the moment.

Every minute he'd worked for Dubshenko felt like a little bit of his soul died. He'd done a lot of crazy crap he wasn't proud of, but he drew the line at kidnapping and hauling an unwilling woman across state lines. Woman, hell, she'd barely been older than her mid-teens. No way in hell was he turning an innocent girl over to a twisted pervert like Dubshenko and his buddies.

Struggling to pull himself upright, he hissed at the stabbing pain in his side. Felt like a cracked rib, maybe two. His shirt was still ripped open from the search for the vest. He angled his back against the wall, leaning back against its coolness and looked at his side. Enormous black-and-blue bruises marred his side. Oh well, he thought, the good news is there's no ribs sticking out through the skin. *I've had worse.*

His eyes scanned the boxy room. Other than an old padded vinyl office chair, with a broken wheel and one handle hanging on by a rusty screw, there wasn't anything in the space. Nothing. No bed, no cabinets. A single, bare light bulb hung from an exposed fixture, its cord dangling from the ceiling. The dim light barely illuminating the space. No windows and only the one door straight ahead. A few roaches crawled up the wall near the corner, and he shuddered in disgust. *Real classy place.*

He eyed the chair again, determining the likelihood of using any part of it for a weapon. The metal swivel base would be hard to detach, and he didn't have the time to disassemble the whole thing. The handle might work as a club. Otherwise, he was basically out of luck and running out of time.

With one hand braced on the wall and the other on the hard floor, he heaved himself upward, groaning at the pain shrieking through his torso. He leaned over trying desperately not to puke up his guts. When the wave of nausea passed, he took a tentative step away from his supporting wall and staggered over to the chair. He rolled it backwards until the spine of the chair pressed against the wooden doorframe, to hold it steady while he wrenched the loosened arm free. *Metal and not plastic. That's good.*

He took a chance and tried the doorknob, turning it slowly and as silently as he could to the left and right. Yep, just like he thought, locked. He'd have to bide his time until one of the guards, or Dubshenko himself, came to check on him.

How much time had passed while he'd been out? Hours? All night?

What about Jinx? The last thing he remembered about her was Dubshenko rubbing it in that she'd been at the police station and a bomb had gone off. Please, don't let her be hurt. He was a stupid son of a bitch for bringing this danger to her doorstep, and he cursed himself for being a fool. Damn the FBI and the DEA for dragging him into this mess to begin with. They should have had a trained agent doing this, not some ex-con with an ax to grind.

He eased himself down on the edge of the chair after scooting it back from the doorframe. Barely five minutes had passed before he heard the murmur of voices growing ever closer. How many? He listened, trying to distinguish who was talking. Two males, right outside the door. Keys rattled and the doorknob jiggled and he rose silently from the chair, positioned in the space that would be behind and to the side of the door when it opened.

He'd only get one shot, so he had to make it a good one. The door swung open with a bang, and the talking stopped as the men strode into the room. They stopped in their tracks, obviously looking for him. Holding the chair arm like a baseball bat, he swung with all his strength, connecting with the skull of the closest man. The sickening sound of metal meeting bone echoed, but he didn't pause, didn't stop to think, he just acted. As the first man fell to the floor Carlo dove for the second guard, wrapping his arm around his throat, his forearm against his windpipe. Using his other arm as leverage, he exerted more and more pressure, cutting off the air. He flailed, struggling not only for air, but for freedom.

Carlo didn't relent, gave him neither. Time seemed to stand still, except for the jerking movements of the man, his struggles growing weaker as he was deprived of oxygen. Finally, he slumped forward, and Carlos turned him loose, letting his body hit the cement with a resounding thud.

He couldn't afford to wait and see if he'd killed either man. A quick frisk of both yielded two guns and a set of car keys. Perfect. Now if only he didn't run into anybody else, he'd get out of this dump and contact his handler. This whole situation had FUBAR written all over it. There wasn't a con big enough to dig his way out of this tar pit.

He stepped out of the room and turned right, heading down the hallway. Luck was on his side, it looked like the two goons were all Dubshenko had sent to handle him. The front door stood open and inviting, the cool air scented with the lovely fragrance of decaying garbage, stagnate water and pine trees. Yep, they were outside of New Orleans Proper, that was for sure.

Only one car was parked outside, and he hit the key fob. The lights blinked, and for the first time that morning Carlo smiled. It grew even bigger when he thought about Dubshenko's face when the bastard realized he'd escaped.

Yep, it was a good morning to be alive.

Chapter Nine

Jinx rubbed her face against the enticing warmth beneath her cheek. She was having the most incredible dream. Solid muscled arms trapped her against a rock hard body, holding her encircled in a cocoon of safety and desire. The slow glide of a hand up and down her spine, the roughened fingertips rasping against her naked skin tingled from the tip of her toes straight to her core. On the last downward stroke of that hand, it continued its sensual journey further, and grasped her butt, squeezing and molding it. She heard a throaty gasp and realized the sound came from her.

For the first time since this whole ordeal started she felt comfortable, and she burrowed closer to the mysterious stranger cradling her in his arms. It had been so long since she'd allowed herself to be this close to a man. The temptation was too much to resist. With a sigh she succumbed and snuggled against—a naked male chest, her head pillowed on his shoulder.

Her eyes flew open and the dream receded, replaced by the reality displayed in the early morning light peeking through the outer corners of the drapes. *Oh, crap*. Sometime during the night, while she slept, she'd become entangled within the arms of the sexy detective. The bed was narrow, but that was no excuse. She remembered starting out lying on her side as close to the edge as possible without falling off. Heck, she'd almost volunteered to sleep on the floor herself since he wasn't gentleman enough, but one look at the nasty stains and she'd changed her mind. Not even for a million bucks—who knew what had caused those stains—but she had a vivid imagination and that was just gross.

Every emotion seemed to pile on at once. She'd given in to the tears trying to cry without disturbing him, but he'd surprised her. He'd held her while she cried, his hold gentle yet firm. His fingers glided through her hair with a soft caress. Not in a sexual way, but more as a comfortable touch shared between friends. Before long, the tears had stopped and she'd slid into a dreamless sleep.

Until this morning. The dream started oh so slowly, but before long had turned into a carnal montage of passionate touches and kisses that warmed her from the inside out. Now the dream was shattered, and cold reality loomed in its place.

She blinked slowly, rising up enough to stare at his face. His eyes were closed as he slept, his deep even breathing steady and sure. Her arm was flung across his stomach, and one of his legs firmly wedged between hers. His thigh pressing up against her in a place where a stranger's leg shouldn't be pressing. Sliding her arm off his rock hard abs, she had a fleeting wish she could slide her fingers through the spray of dark hair curling across his chest. Lightly furred, but not too much. Which she really didn't like on a guy, his was just the right amount.

Her fingers itched to follow the narrowing trail from his nipples, down, down, down, until she reached...

Stop, don't go there, Jinx.

"Go back to sleep, babe." His arms dragged her up against him, snuggling closer, burying his lips against her neck. The leg between her thighs rubbed against her, and she felt wetness pool between her legs. She swallowed her moan. The fingers of his right hand cupped her breast and circled the nipple before squeezing it, and a bolt of need rocked through her.

"Um. You smell incredible. Want you."

She knew that voice, heard it in the erotic dream she'd just woken from. This couldn't happen. Not now—not ever.

"Detective, please move your hand. Now!"

Remy shot upright in bed and gaped at her, shock apparent on his face. She didn't even try to control her laugh. His hair stood straight up, and he had a crease in his cheek from where he'd lain on the pillow. He looked altogether too cute for her piece of mind.

"Damn. Sorry." He stretched and the blankets pooled around his waist, baring that sculpted chest she'd just been fantasizing about. "Forgot where I was for a minute. You get any rest?"

"Some. What happens now?"

Remy threw back the covers and slung his legs off the side of the bed. He stood and stretched, arms reaching toward the ceiling and Jinx couldn't help it, she looked. The man was seriously built. Not like a body builder, which wasn't her type anyway, but with a long lean torso and the well-defined muscles of a swimmer or a runner. His brown hair was longer than she'd expect from a cop, but then most of the cops she'd dealt with where uni's, not detectives. Apparently, they had a whole different set of rules. She wondered if the good detective would be doing so much to keep her safe if he knew how often she'd had dealings with cops in the past.

I thought that former life was over and done. It's not fair—I put it all behind me. Can't think about that now.

"Time for a quick shower, and then we're back on the road. You want to go first?"

"Thanks."

She rose from the bed, tugging down the hem of her t-shirt, praying it covered her big butt. Grabbing up the clothes from atop the backpack for him to wear, she laid them on the corner of the bed, snatched up the backpack and fled into the bathroom.

Remy swore softly as the bathroom door closed. He'd woken up horny with a gorgeous woman in his arms. Still half asleep he'd done what came naturally, and palmed her breast and snuggled in to kiss her soft skin, expecting to have a bit of fun before work. Instead, he'd woke to the icy voice of the woman he was supposed to be protecting.

Which was a shame, really, because he found her stunning. Just the kind of woman he loved. Heck, he'd never been picky about how a woman looked. He loved them all. Whether it was in a sisterly fashion, a motherly fashion or as a lover, women held a special place for him. His *maman* taught him and Max to always treat women with respect. But there was something about Jennifer that called to him. She was built like a nineteen forties pin-up. One of those calendar girls with lush full breasts, a trim waist and an ass that made you want to grab it with both hands and squeeze. The kind of body a man could ride for hours and never tire of. Yet he couldn't touch her. She was his job.

He walked over to the window and parted the crack in the curtain, looking around. Not sure about the time, but it probably wasn't much past dawn. Everything had that early morning look to it. Walking back to the bed he reached under the pillow and pulled out his gun, automatically checking to make sure the safety was on before flopping down against the headboard to wait for her to finish showering.

Wonder how she'd react if I went in and asked if she wanted to shower together? He laughed aloud knowing the answer. The ice in her tone when she'd asked him to take his hand off her breast—she'd freeze his balls solid with a glare—if she didn't take a knife to them.

Once they were back on the road they'd take a circuitous route toward Shreveport. Use back roads and stay off the main thoroughfares. He'd find a way to call Captain Hilliard when they made a pit stop. Hilliard had a burner phone he'd picked up before they'd split town, so it couldn't be traced. At least Remy hoped so. He'd also needed to get a message to Max about picking up a few more burners and getting them to Hilliard, so they'd have extras and he could destroy each one after a single call. Better safe than sorry. Not a problem, he knew Hilliard would trust any phones Max picked out since he'd worked with Max before, and knew he was trustworthy.

He heard the shower cut off, and his imagination took over. Closing his eyes, he pictured Jennifer climbing out of the tub and grabbing the threadbare towel hanging beside it. With an unconscious sensuality she'd rub the terrycloth against her porcelain skin, starting with her ankles and working her way up those mile long legs, wiping away the droplets of water with each sweep of the towel. Inching ever so slowly upward to dry her hips and her stomach, gliding the towel even higher, flicking it over the mounds of her breasts, the rough material causing her nipples to peak and harden as the abrasive cloth rasped against her skin. She'd drag out her sensual dance, her head thrown back, exposing the sexy expanse of her throat while she used little circular movements before stretching out first one arm and then the other, drying each inch of her body. Then, finally wrapping the miniscule towel around her lush curvy body, and tucking the fold between her ample breasts.

This was his daydream and he began fashioning it into a spectacular playground, morphing the images to suit his whim. He pushed open the door and she whirled around, gasping at his presence. When she started to speak he placed a fingertip against her lips, hushing her with a brief shake of his head. With a practiced ease his hand rose, flicking open the fold of the towel, watching it pool around her feet. His eyes swept up taking in her statuesque beauty. Jennifer had a body built for sin, and everybody knew Remy was not a saint. Her damp, blonde hair spilled across her shoulders. The ends brushed against the turgid tips of her breasts, and they tightened as the nipples peeked out from beneath the wet strands.

Remy dropped to his knees at her feet, lifted the towel and rubbed the already dampened cloth against her skin. Starting at her toes he paid exquisite attention to every detail, caressing each dip and curve of her legs. He heard her indrawn catch of breath when his hands skimmed up her inner thighs, closer and closer to her heated center. With each swirl of the towel against her flesh her skin flushed a rosy pink. He smiled at the scent of her arousal, spicy and sweet, knowing he gave her pleasure. Right here, right now, nobody and nothing else existed but the two of them. The rest of the world had faded away.

It took every ounce of inner strength he possessed not to lean forward and brush his lips against the dampened flesh between her thighs. He'd been pleasantly surprised to find her bare, the beautiful pink skin so close he wanted to dive forward and spread her wide for a taste. Instead, he continued his upward journey, the towel now forgotten, dropped to the floor as his fingertips skimmed across her pubic bones to her soft belly and upward to span her waist, gripping her when he leaned forward and pressed a soft kiss against her stomach.

He rose to his feet, his gaze ensnared with hers. His hands skimmed upward to cup her breasts. Mold them in his hands. Their abundant bounty overflowed his grasp, and he smiled when she ducked her head, a delightful pink blush staining her cheeks. His fingers encircled a nipple, tweaked it, rolled it, chuckling as it hardened even more beneath his touch.

"Remy?"

"Shh." He whispered, leaning forward, his eyes locked on her plump bitable lips. One kiss. Surely one kiss would quench the fire burning inside him. A simple brush of his lips against hers. So close. So sweet. So...

"Detective!"

Remy's head snapped up at the sound of his title. Jennifer stood in the open bathroom doorway, fully dressed, looking at him with her brow quirked. He felt the blush creeping up into his cheeks and sprang from the bed, taking a step away from her and toward the door.

"We need to hit the road."

She didn't say a word, handed him the backpack and marched past him. *Nope, can't let her go first*, he thought. *I need to check outside, make sure it's all clear*.

"Wait."

She froze, looking back over her shoulder, her hand on the doorknob. Crap, he hadn't meant to sound so abrupt, but he was still embarrassed. While having sexual fantasies about women was no big deal, nothing new to any red-blooded hetero male, he'd never had one about somebody he was working with. It was his job to protect her, not daydream about how hot the sex between them would be. And it would be scorching, peel-the-paint-off-the walls hot. He was convinced. He hadn't been this attracted to any woman in a long time. Love 'em and stay friends with 'em, was his policy. A couple of nights of raunchy, down-and-dirty, give 'em what they want sex without any strings. That he could handle. He wasn't so sure he could handle Jennifer though.

"I need to go first, make sure the coast is clear."

"You're right, I'm sorry. I didn't think." Jennifer gave him a chagrined little smile and a shrug. "Go ahead."

Remy pulled back the corner of the curtain and peered outside, looking to the right and the left before opening the door. He'd taken one step out when he froze, Jennifer running up against his back, she'd followed so closely.

"Get back inside. Now."

"Detective, what's wrong? Is it Dubshenko?"

Remy shook his head, a string of curses pouring from his lips. His booted foot connected with the doorframe, over and over. *Damn it!*

86

Jennifer leaned around him, staring out at the parking lot before turning her blue-eyed gaze on him.

"Um, I hate to ask, but where's your bike?"

Chapter Ten

The curses falling from Remy's lips painted a vivid picture of what he'd do when he found the person who'd stolen his beloved Ducati Diavel. She winced when his foot slammed against the motel wall, a mix of empathy and hilarity as he hopped around on one foot and the cursing began anew. They'd walked outside the room, so the solid concrete wall had to hurt like a son of a gun.

"Where do we go from here, Remy? Back to New Orleans?"

"No. That's out of the question. Damn it, let me think. We need another set of wheels. Gotta keep moving. But when I catch the son of a bitch that has my baby, so help me, his balls are gonna be hanging around his neck like a freaking bolo tie."

He scanned the parking lot, and Jinx remained quiet, though her mind was racing. *Had one of Dubshenko's thugs found them? Was that why the motorcycle was missing—to strand them without a way to leave until he could deal with them personally?* She hated to think what he planned for her. The little she knew about him and his activities kept her stomach tied in knots.

"Hiya, gorgeous." Remy's voice had her whirling around, ready to snap a quick retort not to call her that when she noted he wasn't talking to her at all. No, he'd walked a few doors down, where a tall, middle-aged woman hefted a khaki duffle over her shoulder, pulling the door closed behind her.

"You talking to me, handsome?" The woman replied, eyeing them both warily.

Jinx looked the stranger up and down. Long brown hair threaded through with silver strands, pulled back into a messy ponytail, topped with a baseball cap that read *Truckers Are In It For The Long Haul*. A black tank top showed off muscular arms and an enormous chest. She had to be at least a triple-D. Stocky build, though nobody would consider her fat, her legs were encased in jeans and she wore beat-up black sneakers on her feet with a hole where the little toe on her right foot showed through.

"I sure am, sweet thing. My girl and I were looking to catch a ride into the next town." Remy gestured toward Jinx, and she turned, looking for the girl he was talking about before realizing he meant her. *His girl?* He kept right on talking, ignoring her as she sidled up to the Amazon in blue jeans.

"I'm Randy and this is my girlfriend, Joyce. Look, this is really embarrassing, but my buddy and I and my best girl came out for a little fun last night, if you know what I mean." He smiled and waggled his brows, and Jennifer's mouth dropped open. *What the hell was he talking about?* "Anyway, things got a little—heated and Joyce decided she didn't want to play anymore, and my pal took off and left us stranded without a ride."

"What the…" Jinx started to say, but Remy flung his

arm around her shoulders, yanked her against his side and nuzzled his face against hers, whispering in her ear, "Play along. I'm trying to get us out of here before Dubshenko shows up."

"Randy, honey, you know that's not what happened. Tell the nice lady what your good buddy *really* wanted."

The stranger smiled, and shifted the duffle bag onto the sidewalk. "Yeah, Randy, tell me the real story."

Remy shut up fast, shooting daggers at Jinx. She knew he was trying to come up with a plausible alternative, but she couldn't resist yanking his chain.

"See, here's what really happened. Randy's pal, Joey, came along because he likes to party and he likes to drink. So, we're all doing shots last night, and Randy was getting all handsy and horny, and wanted to have a three-way." Jinx shrugged and flipped her hair over her shoulder like it was no big deal, and Remy rubbed his forehead as though he had a major headache building.

"Anyway, Randy gets my shirt off, and he's working on my pants, when Joey says he's all for having a three-way, only he don't want me, he wants him." She jerked her thumb at Remy, throwing a huge smile his way, and watched his hands clench into fists before he slowly uncurled his fingers. She'd bet he wanted to wrap those fingers around her throat and squeeze until she turned as red as a tomato and her eyes bulged.

"Baby, that's not *exactly* how it happened. You had an awful lot to drink; you're not remembering clearly."

"Aw, come on snookums, I wasn't so drunk that I couldn't tell that another guy was putting the moves on my man. Joey couldn't have cared less about getting into *my* pants—he was too busy trying to get into yours."

Jinx laughed and the other woman joined her as deep

red heat crept up into Remy's cheeks.

"So what happened next?"

"Maybe we could finish this in your car?" Desperation tinged Remy's voice with just enough persuasion to get them all moving.

"Ain't got a car," she answered.

Well, crap. Jennifer reached over and touched Remy's hand, a quick wrapping of her pinky finger around his before she let go. Just that bit of contact grounded her, kept her focused on the goal. They needed to get moving—and fast.

"Sorry to have bothered you then, ma'am. Honey, I guess we're gonna have to call your folks." Remy looked pained as if the thought of talking to her parents was an onus hardship or something. *Ha! If he only knew.*

"Hold on, fella. Said I didn't have a car. Didn't mean I don't got no transportation." She gestured toward the road and Jinx's eyes widened at the eighteen wheeler parked at the edge of the lot. Hallelujah! Dubshenko would never be looking for them in a big rig.

"Name's Ness."

Remy reached forward and shook her hand. "Ness, we'd be much obliged if you could give us a ride. Which way are you heading?"

"This run's up to Shreveport, but I've got about a half-dozen stops along the way to make deliveries."

Shreveport—right where they'd been headed. Far enough away from New Orleans and Dubshenko. Plus, he had a few other tricks up his sleeve once they got that far north. He smiled, feeling good for the first time since he'd walked out to the parking lot to find his baby missing.

"Honey, how'd you feel about heading on up to

Shreveport? Maybe we can find a nice little chapel up there and get hitched."

"H…hitched?" Jinx sputtered, barely able spit out the word. "Married? You want to get married?"

"Well sure, sugar, we've always said we would eventually. After last night, I need to get a ring on your finger ASAP. What do you say? Want to be Mrs. Randy?" Remy leered at her, waggling his eyebrows suggestively, and it took every ounce of restraint to keep from popping him smack in the middle of his pearly whites. Idiot. Didn't he realize Ness would want to come to the wedding? Then she paused—wait, he doesn't know any better—he'd never run a successful scam. He was a cop. Oh, well, they'd have a long spell on the drive where she'd come up with a believable story. After all, once a grifter, always a grifter.

"Oh, baby, yes!" She squealed, throwing herself into his arms and pressing kisses all over his face, studiously avoiding his lips. She kept her eyes on Ness's face over his shoulder and caught the brief glint of tears welling up in her eyes. Yep, Ness was an easy mark. Remy grabbed her and twirled in circles, spinning her around faster and faster, his laughter filling the air.

"Sweetheart, you won't be sorry, I promise."

The only one going to be sorry for this mess is you, ya big schmuck.

"If y'all plan on riding with me a spell, we need to hit the road. Gotta be honest with ya though, it ain't gonna be a straight shot. Like I said, I've got half a dozen stops along the way for deliveries." Ness turned away from them, and sauntered over to her truck, an impressive site as her triple-D's led the parade. Jinx squinted against the early morning sunlight thinking Ness looked exactly how she'd picture a female trucker to look. Tall, strong, the kind of woman who wouldn't take crap from anybody.

Ness swung open the passenger side door before she continued around to the driver's side, hitched herself up into the driver's seat, tugged the ball cap further down and slipped on a pair of aviator sunglasses. Remy turned to Jinx and held out his hand.

"Coming, sweetheart?" He grinned and she slapped her hand into his, wincing at the tight grip when he crushed her fingers in his grasp.

"You are so going to pay for this, cop." Jinx pasted on a saccharine sweet smile and waved at Ness as they started across the parking lot.

"Now, honey, is that any way to talk to your fiance? The man of your dreams?"

"Don't you mean the man of Joey's dreams, sweetie?"

Jinx stole a glance at him from beneath her lashes, surprised when he let out a belly laugh and hugged her against his side when they got to the truck. He seemed a lot cheerier than he'd been just a few minutes ago when he'd discovered his motorcycle missing. She took a deep breath and the humidity struck her like a blow to the solar plexus. Even though it was early morning the heat had already started climbing, and would probably be in the nineties again by late afternoon.

Remy leaned in closer, his lips against her ear and whispered, "You don't have a thing to worry about. Joey can't hold a candle to you." His lips brushed against her cheek as he pulled back, helping her into the truck's cab with a boost, his hand landing a distinct slap against her ass. The skin tingled and burned where he'd touched it. Had he done that on purpose, or was it an accident?

"Perv."

She climbed between the seats into a small sleeping compartment behind them, and Remy plopped down into the passenger seat, tossing a smile over his shoulder as he buckled his seatbelt. Within minutes they were on the road, headed north and away from New Orleans. Jinx realized she hadn't once thought about Dubshenko, Carlo or the mess they'd left behind. Though she felt guilty about leaving her brother, a deep-seated feeling of freedom soared within, something she hadn't felt in a very long time. Not since breaking away from her family. That spark of creativity, the urge to go with the flow and see where life led, kindled and fanned the flame of adventure.

Today was the start of a brand new day and she couldn't wait to see where she landed.

Chapter Eleven

Captain Ronald Hilliard sat beneath the green and white awning of Café du Monde, a steaming hot cup of coffee nestled between his large-boned hands. A plate of untouched beignets sat before him, flakes of the white powdery sugar floating around in the slight breeze stirring the already warm morning. A bead of sweat trickled down the side of his face and he wiped it away. *Where was Max? Why isn't he here yet?*

Max Lamoreaux, Remy's big brother, called asking to meet him for breakfast. Called him at home before the ass-crack of dawn. This had to be about Remy, he knew it. He'd obviously heard from his brother and needed to pass along a message. Damn, he hoped Remy had gotten the girl outta the city before Dubshenko heard they were in the wind. With her protected, at least for now, the biggest job he had was trying to find Carlo. This had to be handled off the books, too, since no official crime had been committed. Unofficially, he had a couple of guys that he mostly trusted out looking for Mr. Carlo Marucci.

He'd done some research into the mysterious Carlo, Jennifer's brother. Jennifer had finally given them her real name along with her brother's. Giancarlo Marucci had a record. He'd been arrested for a string of petty crimes as a juvenile, nothing big. Shoplifting, joyriding, one arrest for possession of marijuana. Penny ante stuff. At eighteen, he'd been popped for robbing a liquor store and pled no contest, even though he hadn't actually been in on the actual liquor store holdup. He'd been in the car when the police pulled it over in Bossier City. Made him just as guilty as the one's who'd actually help up the place. Sentenced to five years. He'd been assigned a public defender who'd done a piss-poor job of advising his client. Still, from what he could tell he'd kept his nose clean in the joint, eligible for parole at 3 years, but was denied and served out his full sentence. He'd wandered around after he'd gotten out, moving from place to place.

About a year ago he'd moved to New Orleans and lived with his sister, Jennifer Marucci, or as she'd called herself at the station, Jennifer Smith. *Yeah, right. Like he'd never heard that one before, although the Jennifer was a nice touch—they usually went with Jane Smith.* Hadn't been long before Carlo got pulled into Dubshenko's ring of illegal activities. The Russian mobster bought a brand new eighteen wheeler, and Carlo had driven supply runs. Never caught hauling anything not listed on his paperwork, and he'd been pulled over a few times, usually to yank a knot in Dubshenko's tail when he got too complacent.

Was he dead? His sister claimed he'd been shot smack dab in the center in the chest, had seen the blood. There wasn't any blood at her house, though there'd been evidence of a hasty cleaning effort. Funny thing, there had been a few drops of red on the floor, but it hadn't been blood. Not real blood, anyway. Synthetic, the kind used for movies and for the wanna be Goth groupies on the vampire tours down in the French Quarter. Unfortunately, they wouldn't be getting another chance to check out Jennifer Marucci's house. It had burned to the ground sometime after midnight last night.

Hilliard glanced up as Max slid into the seat across from him.

"Want coffee?"

"Is the pope Catholic? Of course, I want coffee. It's too damn early in the morning for this clandestine crap. Either that or I'm just too old for this spy stuff." Max signaled and a fresh cup of hot black chicory bliss was placed in front of him. He waved away the offer of beignets.

"Have you heard from him?"

"Last night." Max passed across the brown paper bag he'd been carrying, sliding it across the table. Hilliard glanced at it, but didn't open it. "There's a half dozen untraceable burner phones in there. I've labeled them one through six. Keep 'em handy. He'll contact you when he can. One call per phone, then yank the sim card and destroy it and the phone. I've disabled the GPS on all of them, but with Dubshenko's team of computer geeks, you can't be too careful."

Hilliard slid the bag onto his lap, picked up his coffee and took a large swallow. "Remy's got you looking for the brother, doesn't he?"

Max nodded, not saying a word.

"Found anything?" Hilliard hated asking, but knew Max was the best private investigator in the city, hell, probably in the state of Louisiana. If Carlo Marucci could be found, Max would find him. If he couldn't, chances were good Max's pretty wife would give it a shot.

"Talked to the girl's neighbor. He saw three men get into the limo parked in front of her house. Never saw the driver, though. So, total of four. Stopped for gas in Metairie before heading toward Lake Pontchartrain. After that we lost them."

"Dammit, that's a hell of a lot of ground to cover. Parts of St. Tammany, Orleans, Jefferson, St. John the Baptist, and Tanginapahoa parishes all border that area. Lots of places to disappear—or hide a body."

They sat in silence, mulling over the possibility Dubshenko had disposed of Carlo, the same way he'd done to most people who crossed him. They'd never found proof, though, and he still walked the streets a free man.

"I've set up an encrypted e-mail for Remy to use in an emergency, and I'm the only one with access. It's alerted, so if he uses it, I'll know immediately." Max waited a beat. "You think this girl really has enough to put Dubshenko away—or is my brother putting his life out there on a hunch?"

Hilliard ran his hand across the top of his freshly shaved head, his dark caramel-colored skin gleaming with sweat. Mid-morning and the temperature had already climbed up to the high eighties, and would be mid-nineties by lunchtime. He blew out a heavy breath before meeting Max's steely gray gaze.

"I'm gonna tell you something and you cannot repeat this, not even to your wife, got it?" With Max's nod, he continued, "She has some information, that's true. Whether it's enough to put Dubshenko away, I hope so. Problem is, I don't think even she knows whatever it is

Dubshenko wants—but we'll find out. Your brother will dig until she doesn't have any secrets left. But there's another reason I had Remy take her on the road instead of putting her in a safe house in the city."

"You've got a leak in the department." Max finished for him. Hilliard stared at him unblinking, and Max grabbed up his cup and drained it. "Dammit, I owe Theresa a hundred bucks."

Hilliard laughed, breaking the tension. "Never bet against your wife, son. Even when you're right, you're wrong. When the wife is a card-carrying psychic, you're just asking to get your ass handed to you on a silver platter."

"Before Remy called and said he'd be going out of town, hell, even before the bad pizza bomb thing, she mentioned she thought there was an information problem with the N.O.P.D. Got any ideas who it might be?"

Hilliard shook his head. "Right now, the only other person at the station I completely trust is your brother. Everybody else—much as I like and respect them all—nope, everybody's a suspect."

"Anything I can do?"

"No. Just be there for Remy, and keep looking for Carlo Marucci. I've got a feeling he's the key to this. Somehow if we can find him, if he's even still alive, he's gonna be the straw that breaks the camel's back and puts Dubshenko away, once and for all."

Max stood, his eyes scanning the early morning crowd at the landmark bistro. "We won't be able to meet or even talk in public again. Dubshenko's probably got all the phones at the station bugged, and though I've check my house and office, he's probably got ears on me, too. If you need to get word to me, leave a message at

Theresa's shop. She'll get it to me."

Hilliard stood and held out his hand. Max gripped it firmly, one former cop to a fellow brother in blue. "Be safe, my friend. Dinner's on me when Remy's back home safe and sound."

"I'm counting on that, Captain. Good luck."

Chapter Twelve

Riding in an eighteen wheeler sounds like fun in the abstract. Crowding three alpha personalities into one confined space made for some very tense vibes. They'd ridden in relative silence for the last half hour. Ness's gaze strayed in his direction again, as the crackling static of the radio filled the cab of the truck. Jennifer lounged in the sleeping area, legs crossed and her back against the wall. She was thinking about Carlo; concentrating so hard he could almost read her mind. Damn, he wished he could call Cap, or Max, get word on what was happening back home. Instead, he was playing babysitter/fake fiance/sexual pervert if Jennifer's story was to be believed.

He bit back a chuckle. She really had jumped into that story with gusto, embellishing it like a pro. Then again, maybe too much like somebody used to telling whoppers. Hmm, maybe he needed to rethink everything he knew about Ms. Marucci.

When Carlo was on the phone, before the explosion, he'd called her Jinx. What kind of nickname was Jinx? He'd said it with lots of love and affection, but still…

"So, Ness, what kind of stuff are you hauling?" Jennifer finally spoke up from her perch behind the seats.

"Supplies for convenience stores, nonperishables like paper products, cleaning supplies, stuff like that. Mostly for smaller, non-chain stores. Mom and Pop shops mostly." Ness glanced back, smiling at Jennifer before giving Remy the side-eye again. Obviously she liked Jennifer a whole lot more than she liked him.

"Small stuff, huh? This is a great rig, by the way. I always preferred a Mack myself. My brother drives a Peterbilt, mostly long-distance hauls." A hint of sadness threaded beneath her words. At least she'd still spoke about her brother in the present tense, Remy thought.

"Years," Ness answered. "I did the long distance stuff for years. It's a tough gig, being away from home for such long stretches. Money's good, but going home to an empty house ends up not being worth it after a while."

"Where's your first stop, Ness?" Remy asked, trying to determine how far off the major highway they were headed. Riding with her had been a stroke of genius. There was no way in hell Dubshenko would look for him or Jennifer in an eighteen wheeler delivering goods to merchants.

"About another fifteen to twenty minutes, outside Opelousas. Decent folks, been delivering to them for about five years. Steady customers, pay their suppliers on time." Ness gave him the side-eye again, before focusing back onto the road. "Then I'm headed further north to Marksville."

Remy was good with that. Good choice staying off I-10 or I-20. Small towns worked. If they played things right, got in and out with minimal fuss, Dubshenko wouldn't get a bead on them any time soon. He had a pretty good idea where they could head, a place he could take Jennifer and keep her safe, with the added bonus of some additional help from men he knew and trusted. A win-win.

"Can I help unload or gas up the rig or anything when we get there?"

For the first time since he'd climbed into the front seat, Ness relaxed and smiled. "Naw, I'm good. You and your fiancee stay in the cab. Get a few minutes of private time. First stop shouldn't take more than half an hour max."

"But, we can help." Jennifer piped up from the back.

"Don't worry about it, hon. I've got this down to a quick in and out, all organized. I appreciate the offer, but y'all would just slow me down."

The truck sped along the asphalt, and a companionable silence settled over the trio. Being a cop, even when relaxed, Remy stayed constantly alert, checking the side mirror for anybody who might be following. Just normal traffic as far as the eye could see. *Good.*

"Ness, if you don't mind my asking, you've got a very unusual name. I like it, but, I'm wondering if it's a nickname or a shortened version or your full name?" Jennifer's question had Remy looking toward the driver, and he noted the blush creep up into her cheeks. Oh, ho, so Ness wasn't her real name. He grinned.

"Um…"

"Never mind. I didn't mean to embarrass you. Trust me, I know all about embarrassing nicknames." Now it was Jennifer's turn to blush, he noted. Maybe now would be a good time to find out about that nickname her brother used on the phone.

"No, it's okay. I've lived with my—unusual name all my life. My mother was a big movie fan for as long as I could remember. She named me after her favorite movie star when I was born." Ness cleared her throat. "My real name is Princess Grace Fagenbaum."

Remy pinched his thigh hard to keep from laughing. Oh, man, he'd thought his name was bad, but when his father got to pick Max for his first born son, his mother demanded she get to pick the name of their next child. He'd ended up with the moniker Remington, but everybody called him Remy. Her first choice had been Winchester. She had an almost morbid fascination with anything and everything western; art, guns, even John Wayne. At least his father had convinced her not to go with her first choice. Knowing Max, he'd have ended up being called Whinny. Or even worse, he could have been teased growing up with My Little Pony. Yeah, that sounded like something big brother Max would've come up with. Remy shuddered at the thought. He'd happily stick with Remy.

"Oh, I loved Grace Kelly. She was so beautiful and elegant and classy." Jennifer's kind comments seemed to ease Ness, and she chuckled before glancing in the mirror, meeting Jennifer's eyes.

"I'm kinda used to it now, but growing up it was a pain in the butt. Kids can be cruel little buggers, and with a name like Princess, well, let's just say I grew up tough. Most of the boys in my third grade class had bloody noses or black eyes at some point during the school year. By fourth grade I was taller than most of 'em, and could beat the snot out of the boys and the girls, so the teasing pretty much stopped. At least until high school. That's a whole different story."

She stared through the windshield, a faraway look on her face. "My baby sister couldn't say Princess when she was little. It came out Ness, so I've been Ness ever since." Her full blown laugh filled the truck's cab and Remy wondered what she found so funny.

"Mom loved her movies and was fascinated by the actresses and all that old Hollywood glamour. Little sis didn't make out much better than me in the name department. She's Marilyn Monroe Fagenbaum-Gillingham now."

Jennifer leaned forward and placed her hand on Ness' shoulder. "Trust me, I get the whole nickname thing. In my family, I'm known as Jinx." Remy coughed into his fist, fighting the words wanting to spill out. He desperately wanted to ask why her own family would label her with such a hurtful name.

"What in the world did you do to deserve something so mean?" Thank goodness, Ness asked the question before he blurted it out.

Jennifer's cheeks turned a lovely shade of embarrassed pink again, and Remy was intrigued by the laughter twinkling in her big blue eyes.

"Well, I'm not really the luckiest person in the world, you know?" She looked at Remy, her gaze locked onto his, sending a silent message for help. He shrugged, not opening his mouth but cocking his brow. He couldn't wait to hear this. With a huff, she resumed talking.

"Some of my family is a bit—colorful—in their extracurricular activities. Aw, hell, they run cons. Confidence schemes. They're all grifters, and damn good ones most of the time."

Remy straightened in his seat. *Wait a minute! Was*

this why she hadn't given her real name when she'd shown up at the N.O.P.D.? Did she have a record? Or worse, was she wanted by the police?

"My family always works together for the more elaborate grifts. Single short cons, no brainers we called them, only took one person. The more complicated the scams, the more people needed to pull it off. When I was younger they tried to train me, bring me into the family business. Not their wisest decision." She got a hangdog expression, and glanced down at her crossed legs, the yoga pants stretched tight.

"Let's just say I wasn't very good at it. Every single time they'd get the mark set up, and all I had to do was one little job. Only, I obviously didn't inherit the family gene that makes a good grifter. No matter how well planned, or how many times we'd practice, I'd screw things up and the whole job would fall apart. Every. Single. Time."

Ness tsk'd, keeping her eyes focused on the long stretch of asphalt. "Nothing to be ashamed of, hon. You seem to have a sweet nature, probably wouldn't have bilked people out of their hard earned money even if you'd wanted to."

"I think that was the heart of the problem. I didn't want to. Heck, even when I wasn't part of the con, and had no clue what game they were running, I'd somehow stumble into the middle of things and screw it all up. They said I jinxed things. So they started calling me Jinx, and it stuck. Now, it's a term of affection. I can't remember the last time my brother called me Jennifer."

Jennifer slapped her hand across her mouth, realizing at exactly the same time Remy did what she'd said. *Why had she used her real name?* Dammit, she'd gotten too comfortable talking to Ness,

And now she'd blown everything with one lousy word. She turned to Remy and mouthed, "Sorry."

"I thought your name was Joyce?" Ness turned her steely-eyed stare on Remy. "Let me guess, your name isn't Randy, either, right?"

She slammed her foot on the brakes, steering the huge eighteen wheeler to the side of the two lane blacktop with a loud squeal of brakes.

"Get out."

"Ness, I'm sorry, it's all my fault. Please. If you'll just take us to the next town, we'll leave and…"

"My own fault. Should've listened to my first instinct and never picked you up. I can't abide liars and that's all you've done since you opened your mouths at the hotel, ain't it?"

Jennifer looked ready to burst into tears, and Remy knew he had to do something to diffuse the situation before it exploded. The last thing he needed was two screaming hysterical women ready to start a brawl on the side of the road. Or worse, two crying ones. The problem was, how much could he tell Ness without putting her directly into the crosshairs of Dubshenko?

"Ness, if you'll start driving again, I'll tell you the truth." Remy had to wing it, think on his feet, but they couldn't afford to be stranded on the side of the road with no transportation and no ID. They'd left every scrap of identification behind at *maman's* house. No way could they be caught with any. That would have been an automatic death sentence. The first rule of flying under the radar—no ID.

While the engine idling, and the scratchy static from the radio filling up the otherwise silent truck, Ness

107

tapped her fingers against the steering wheel, deep in thought. With a jerky nod, she threw the truck into gear and eased back onto the roadway. Remy heaved a sigh. One crisis averted.

"Part of what we said at the hotel was true. We really were stranded. Sometime during the night somebody stole my Ducati out of the parking lot. I didn't hear a damn thing." Which still irritated the heck out of him. He was a trained professional and he'd slept right through a grand theft auto. Didn't that make him feel all warm and fuzzy? If the guys at the station ever found out, his ass was grass.

"My real name is Remy and this is Jennifer. I'm a cop from New Orleans."

"A cop? That explains a lot." Ness grimaced, the corners of her mouth turning down.

"You have something against cops?"

"Nothing personal, dude, but from my experience I haven't met any that were all honest and forthright, if you catch my drift?" Ness gave a distinctly unladylike snort. "Driving a truck doesn't endear me to the local yahoos who patrol the back roads, much less the highway cops."

Remy nodded, sympathizing, but still, he was a good cop. Always dealt with his perps fairly and solely within the limits of the law. Well, except for that stunt he pulled with Mickey Trejo—but that had been for a good cause. Trejo was a confessed serial killer who preyed on the homeless men throughout the state of Louisiana and had even ventured into the surroundings states of Arkansas and Mississippi. Getting information to aid in his confession and help in capturing his sadistic partner, while rescuing a kidnap victim—he'd not only tiptoed into the shades of gray area, he was damn lucky Captain

Hilliard hadn't fired his ass.

"I get it, Ness, I really do. But I'm a detective not a street cop looking to fill his ticket quota—and you didn't hear that from me. There's no such thing as a quota." Everyone laughed, knowing that for the B. S. it was.

"Jennifer is a witness in an ongoing investigation into illegal activity going on in New Orleans. And, no, I can't go into details, but I've taken her out of the city to keep her safe until she can testify." Remy watched Ness closely reading her body language, and knew the bare facts he'd given her had piqued her interested. Bait the hook and drop it in the bayou. Now to be patient, and watch the fish take the bait.

"So, she's in witness protection—like on the television shows?" Awe filled Ness' voice and it was all Remy could do not to roll his eyes. TV shows had ruined good police work. People expected everything to happen exactly like their favorite shows. Most of the time, actually ninety-nine percent of the time, it was nothing like television. It was a lot of hard, boring, tedious work, slogging through mountains of paperwork. Sitting on your backside waiting, just to have the district attorney show up and say there wasn't enough evidence to get an indictment.

"Yep, just like on the TV. I had to get her out of town fast. We stopped to rest for a couple hours, and bam, my bike's gone. That's when we ran into you this morning." Remy put on his hangdog face and batted puppy dog eyes at her.

Man, she's eating this up.

"Sorry for not telling you the truth, but I'm outside my comfort zone, and can't trust anybody. You get that, right?" Remy heard a stifled laugh coming from behind his seat. He didn't dare turn around. If he looked at Jinx right now he'd bust his gut laughing, and they'd be out on the side of the road with their thumbs in the air, praying that the next car wasn't Dubshenko's.

And when did I start calling her Jinx?

"Sure, I mean, I guess so. But exactly where do I fit in this witness protection thingy? Are they gonna come after me, since I helped you?"

"Oh, no, Ness, Remy would never let that happen." Jinx piped up, reaching forward and placing her hand on Ness' shoulder. "I haven't known him long, but he's been nothing but trustworthy. His captain told me he'd trust Remy with his life, and that I could trust him with mine." She paused and looked over, meeting Remy's gaze, her blue eyes shiny with tears. "I do trust him. You can, too."

Ness looked over her shoulder at Jinx before turning her gaze back to the road. Without a glance at Remy, she asked, "So all that fancy talk about proposing, that wasn't real? You're not in love with each other?" She shook her head slowly from side to side, tutting. "Seems a real shame. You ask me, you two are perfect for each other."

Remy blanched at the thought—perfect for each other? Oh, hell no. He was footloose and fancy free and had no intention of changing that status any time soon. He loved women—and the thought of being tied down to just one for the rest of his life, nope he didn't think so. There was plenty of time for that later. Thoughts of Max and his beautiful Theresa gave him pause. They were happy and so in love it hurt sometimes to be around them. His cousin, Connor, and his wife, Alyssa, too. They'd made their own miracle, reconciled and were happier than he'd ever seen them.

Maybe...Nope, not gonna think about that. Can't think about love, marriage or happily ever after until I've broken up Dubshenko's syndicate of terror and the rat-bastard is behind bars for the rest of his life.

"You just keep driving, Ness. We'll figure out our next step along the way.

Chapter Thirteen

Dubshenko walked around the metal folding chair in the middle of the otherwise empty room. It was currently occupied by a skinny, stringy-haired man of indeterminate height, indeterminate weight, and definitely indeterminate intelligence. Right now, there was a gag in his mouth, and a trickle of blood ran in a river of scarlet along the right side of his face, down his cheek and dripped onto his filthy shirt.

"Remove the gag." Dubshenko waved his hand toward his prisoner, and his guard rushed forward to do his bidding. Ah, yes, he thought. I love how quickly fear or money can accomplish more in a few seconds, than months of negotiations and politicking.

The bound man's eyes flashed wildly as the cloth was untied from around his face. The second it came lose a scream erupted, its shrill high pitch making Dubshenko wince.

"Shut up." The authoritative command in his voice had the shrieking immediately cease.

"Much better." He walked around the chair stroking his chin, and took in every minute detail of the man seated before him. "I have a few questions. If you answer them truthfully, we should have no problems, *da*? Nod if you understand me—do not speak." A vigorous nodding of the man's head was his response.

"Excellent. Do you know who I am?" Again a vigorous nod. "Then you know better than to lie. We begin." Dubshenko stood directly front and center of the seated man, peering down at his helpless captive. He smiled, but it never reached to the icy blue of his merciless eyes.

"What is your name?

The man sucked in a shocked breath before responding, "Stanley." So, Dubshenko thought, the greasy monkey was named Stanley. How fitting.

"You were found with a two thousand and thirteen Ducati Dravel Dark motorcycle. Where did you obtain it?"

"Motel outside Openousas."

"Exactly how did you come to possess this motorcycle, Stanley?"

"Guy gave it to me." Sweat beaded along Stanley's forehead, mixed with the streaky blood oozing from the open cut on his scalp.

Dubshenko tsk'd. "Really? How very generous of this person. Did you know this guy, Stanley? Was he perhaps a friend of yours?"

"Yeah, sure. He gave it to me because he owed me some money. Said I could have it until he got flush, then he'd pay up and get it back."

Dubshenko tugged at the cuff of his white dress shirt, visible beneath the sleeve of his jacket. Even in this intolerable heat, he felt it was important to always represent total control, and dress to impress. With a quick jerk of his head, he stepped back and his bodyguard's fist shot forward, slamming into Stanley's stomach. A loud oomph filled the room.

"Would you like to rethink your answer, Stanley? The truth this time or I'll let my friend here—persuade you."

"I stole it!" He screamed, leaned back against the chair as far away from Bubba as he could get. Dubshenko started to chuckle when he realized he'd referred to his bodyguard as Bubba, the nickname that Carlo had given him in the limo not so long ago. When he'd shown such bravery in the face of his imminent demise. He realized he kinda liked the nickname. Bubba—maybe he'd keep using it.

"Good answer. Now tell my good friend and I, did you see the owner of the motorcycle before you stole it? Was he alone or was there someone with him? Or her?" He decided to throw that last question in to see if maybe Remy was smarter than he thought, letting the enticing Jennifer take his beloved Ducati and head out on the open road away from New Orleans. No, Mr. Boy Scout would never let the damsel in distress ride away alone.

"Yeah, I saw 'em. Man and a woman. Checked into the place middle of the night. She was a real looker, too. Much better looking than the usual hookers who work the place. She was real upscale, ya know what I mean?"

"Ah, Stanley, I know exactly what you mean. Describe them for me, please. Exact details. This is very important; do not leave out even a single fact. You might say your life depends on it."

Dubshenko watched Stanley's Adam's apple bob as he swallowed, sucking in huge lungsful of air through his mouth. Penny ante crooks. They were all the same.

Show them who's the boss and they'll roll over and present their bellies every time. This hadn't even been much of a challenge.

"Um, dude had dark hair. Kinda longish. He drove the bike. His whore was a blonde with big tits. Really stupendous rack. Filled out her t-shirt fine, and wore stretchy pants that hugged her ass tight. Little too big in the hips for me, but some guys like a gal with some meat on her bones. And she was a looker. Oh, yeah, she had flip-flops on her feet with some kind of flower things on them."

"I see you paid much more attention to the lady than to the driver. Fortunately, for you, I believe they are the couple I am looking for." Dubshenko paused and then turned away from Stanley before pivoting and backhanding him across the mouth.

"Do not ever refer to her again as a whore." He checked his hand, noting no broken skin, no blood. Excellent. It was rare that he personally did the dirty work anymore, but it felt good to put this little pissant in his place.

"Make sure Stanley gives very precise directions on locating the motel where our friends were staying, then turn him loose. You might want to emphasize the importance of keeping his mouth shut about our little conversation tonight, too." He instructed Bubba.

With those final words, Dubshenko walked out of the room, closing the door behind him with a silent snick. He done well, having put a state-of-the art tracking device on Lamoreaux's motorcycle a few months before. The good detective loved that useless pile of metal with an unhealthy obsessiveness. At the thought, he laughed, amused and delighted with this unexpected turn of events. After all the grief Lamoreaux caused him lately it seemed only fitting that he exact a little sweet revenge—even if it was against an inanimate object. The cop's favorite mode of transportation would be a pile of rubble and ash before the night was through. Rubbing his hands in glee, he climbed into the back of the limo and pulled out his phone. There were plans to make.

The chase was on—and he intended to win—at any cost.

Chapter Fourteen

Carlo pulled his stolen car into the parking lot of a strip mall and killed the engine. He'd driven a couple of hours west, getting as far away from New Orleans as possible. Dubshenko's men had to have been discovered by now, meaning he knew Carlo was free. He'd be gunning for him, that was a given. First things first, though, he needed to ditch the car. While he'd love to douse it with gasoline and strike a match, all that did was send a flaming beacon to Dubshenko. He might as well post a flashing neon arrow directly over his head and have it point, "Here I am, come and get me."

He tossed the car keys under the driver's side seat, leaving it unlocked and all the windows down. If some enterprising thief happened upon it before the Russian mobster's goons did, well...

The parking lot was deserted, except for a homeless guy sleeping in one of the store's doorways. No help there, guy probably didn't have a dime to his name at this time of the morning. But he was nearly out of options himself. No phone, no cash and no connections in this town. Going to the local cops was out of the question.

He didn't trust cops. From prior experience, he knew facts could be manipulated and circumstantial evidence quickly amounted to years in the state penitentiary. Been there, done that.

There was a gas station down the street, not one of the major franchises, but that worked in his favor. He took off at a brisk clip, headed that way. The lights from the strip mall cast the entire area with a dismal pall. All those lights would be off soon, and the empty parking spaces likely to stay exactly the same—empty. Prosperity had obviously bypassed this section of town. Reminded him of his life—prosperity had pretty much bypassed him, too.

First things first. He needed to get to a phone. Unfortunately, pay phones were practically nonexistent any more, except in larger, heavily populated places like airports and shopping malls. In a small town like this—not a chance. So he'd have to see if the gas station attendant would let him make a call. If he was lucky, the guy would have a cell phone, where the long distance charge wouldn't show up right away. He needed to call his boss—that was call number one. Second and more important call—find out about Jinx.

Dubshenko's vivid description of exactly what he had planned for his baby sister made his skin crawl. That sick, perverted son of a bitch was going to pay for every scratch, every heartache his sister endured because of him. Maybe the cop, the one Dubshenko seemed so worried about, was keeping her safe.

Jinx was his whole world. The family all called her Jinx, and Carlo couldn't help smiling at the funny nickname. She'd hated it at first, even though they called her that in love. The girl was a walking bad luck magnet. Every single time the family had planned a big score, down to the last minute detail, Jinx somehow found a way to screw things up without even trying. She hated that the family made their living pulling cons. It never bothered him much. He'd just cruised through life, did what his folks asked him to do. Figured he'd join the *family business*, maybe pull the big heist and be rolling in dough. Not Jinx though. She wanted no part of any of it. She'd barely been eighteen when she'd moved to the city all on her own, got a legitimate job and put the *art of the grift* behind her. Kept in touch with the family, still spent holidays and birthdays with everyone, but refused to have any part of their shady lifestyle. They knew Jinx loved them, never doubted it for a second, but she had her life and they had theirs, and they didn't mesh.

He'd never told her how proud she made him. Wished he'd had her guts to turn his back on the easy mark and walk away. She was his inspiration, made him want to be a better man. Instead, he'd ended up doing time because he was with the wrong crowd at the wrong time. Oh, well, water under the bridge.

Finally, he thought, strolling across the concrete pad with its gas pumps and trash cans. Looking through the glass doors, he spotted the clerk behind the counter. Hot damn, he was in luck. It was a woman. She looked to be just this side of thirty. Her bored expression was evident even from a distance. He smoothed out his rough appearance, running a hand through his hair and checking his breath in his hand. Ugh, bad enough to knock down a full grown buffalo, but he hadn't exactly had access to a toothbrush or mouthwash in the last several hours. He'd make due.

"Hey, sugar." He pasted what he hoped was a sexy

smile on his lips, and gave her a wink. Flipping through the pages of a magazine she'd barely glanced up when he'd sauntered through the door, but at his words she peeked in his direction. She looked back down at her magazine before her head bounced back up, and her eyes ate him up from his head to his toes in a slow, lingering survey. Once she reached bottom, her smoldering gaze started the reverse trip. He practically felt her hands moving across his skin, caressing as they roamed.

"Hey, yourself, stranger." She slid the magazine off the counter onto a shelf below, resting her breasts on the countertop as she leaned forward in what he assumed was her take-a-good-look-at-my-assets pose. "You look like you've been rode hard and put away wet. What happened?"

Damn, he forgot about the cuts. "No big deal. Car broke down and I made it as far as the strip mall. When I lifted the hood, I whacked myself in the head. Bled like a stuck pig, too. Walked the rest of the way here when I realized I'd forgotten my phone. You wouldn't happen to have one I could borrow, would you?"

Her hand slid beneath the cash register and pulled out a cell phone in a neon hot pink case. *Why do women always wrap their phones in that hideous color? Why?*

"You are a life saver, babe."

"Sure, no problem. Just put your digits in there before you make any calls, 'kay?" Jeez, the only thing missing was her popping bubble gum to make her a walking, talking cliché, but what the hell, he needed to make those calls.

"Planned on it, sweet thing." He glanced around the empty convenience store/gas station. "Not real busy, huh?"

She shook her head before leaning back against the cigarette rack behind here, placing her hands on the counter, causing her breasts to jut forward. He gave them an appreciative once over, knowing she needed the confidence boost. Plus, he needed to stay on her good side. Didn't need her calling the cops—at least not yet.

He nodded to the phone in his hand. "Thanks. I'll get it right back to you." He walked a few feet away and dialed a number from memory, praying that his boss answered. It was picked up on the first ring.

"Branson." Yep, even the sound of his dulcet nasal tones set his teeth on edge. Damn he loathed the S.O.B. *Jackass.*

"It's Marucci. We've got a problem."

"This isn't your secure number, Marucci. What's happened? The whiny tone disappeared, all business now, any trace of sleep erased the minute he'd mentioned a problem.

"Dubshenko's on to me."

"How'd that happen? Didn't you make the scheduled run like you were supposed to?"

"Yeah, well, there was a—complication."

There was dead silence on the other end. Seconds ticked by, and sweat beaded along Carlo's forehead. He worked for the giant pain in the neck, had for the last year and a half, but he didn't like the guy. Not one iota. Something about him had the hairs on the back of his neck standing at attention every time they were face-to-face, and Carlo learned the hard way to always trust that instinct. It had saved his skin on more than one occasion.

"What the hell happened, Marucci?"

"I lost the package."

"What!" Carlo pulled the phone away from his ear at

the exclamation from the other end.

"Not my fault, boss man."

"Dammit, this is unacceptable. We've waited months to get enough intel to take down Dubshenko and his organization, and with one screw-up you've blown everything to dust. Tell me you at least found out what the package was, please? Gimme that at least."

Carlo debated for about ten seconds before answering. "No clue. You know I'm not high enough on Dubshenko's food chain to be trusted with that kind of info. The only reason I even had a chance at delivering this package was because Jimmy the Snitch got arrested right before the run. You have anything to do with that?" He looked up at the girl who was twirling a curl around her finger, and she gave him a coy little smile, waving at him with her little finger. He waved back.

"No, that wasn't us. FBI picked him up for something entirely unrelated, but we didn't interfere, thinking it was a good opportunity for you to move up in the ranks—which you have. Where did you lose the package anyway?"

"Fell out of the truck somewhere outside Houston. I picked it up from Ivor, right on schedule. When I checked the load before the Louisiana state line, it was gone." Carlo felt no remorse about lying to his boss. There was something else going on here, something he wasn't privy to. He damn sure wasn't saying anything else about the girl, A.K.A. the package, without knowing what was really going on.

"How, Marucci? How did everything go FUBAR without you having a clue?"

"Not sure, but it gets worse."

"Worse than losing the best chance of putting

Dubshenko away for good, putting a giant dent in the Russian mob in New Orleans? Oh, I can't wait to hear this."

"My cover is busted all to hell and back. Dubshenko knows."

Curses burned Carlo's ear and he again pulled the phone away. He held it out at arm's length, knowing the girl behind the counter could hear the yelling, but couldn't make out any of the words. Well, maybe she'd figure out some of the really bad words. He chuckled softly, not wanting the jackass to hear him.

"He knows you're DEA?"

"Well, I think the bullet to the middle of my chest was pretty much self-explanatory, don't you, boss? Good thing I had my vest on, or I'd be in the morgue right now."

"Son of a bitch. You're telling me he shot you—wait, let me get this straight. Did Dubshenko himself actually pull the trigger? That's great. We can get him on attempted murder of a federal agent."

"Not yet. There's more going on than we know. I'm going to ground. I'll call you when I have more intel, but until then I'm off the grid." Carlo ran his hand across his forehead feeling the bump and the sticky dried blood. He really could use an aspirin or eight right now.

"Wait. You need to come in, debrief. Maybe we can salvage something from this cluster—"

"No can do, Chief. By the way, this isn't my phone. I borrowed it from this nice lady. Don't bother sending anybody to get me, I'll be long gone. I'll keep you posted, though. *Ciao*." He ended the call with the push of a button.

Taking a chance, he made one more call, brief—only

a few words. He just hoped it was enough.

With unhurried steps he walked back to the counter, handing the phone to the clerk. The gleam of light reflecting off of a car pulling up to a gas pump reflected through the windows, and he stepped back into the shadows pretending to peruse the shelves. A tall man dressed in a polo shirt and a pair of dress pants walked straight past the pump and through the front door of the store.

"Ma'am, I'm looking for somebody, a man who might have stopped in here within the last thirty minutes or so. He's a friend. I was supposed to pick him up. Tall, dark hair, blue eyes. Might be a bit banged up." At his words, Carlo peered around the corner of the shelf he'd positioned himself behind and got a good look at the guy at the counter. Yep, it was one of Dubshenko's men from earlier. He'd obviously changed clothes and was out looking for him.

The clerk's eyes grew round with the man's words, her gaze darting around the aisles. Carlos put a finger in front of his lips and shook his head no, begging her silently not to give him away. A barely perceptible nod was his answer.

"Sorry, mister. There hasn't been anybody in here for the last two hours. Really slow morning." She snapped her gum and cracked a big smile. "At least it was until you showed up."

Dubshenko's man looked her up and down, taking in the tight t-shirt and even tighter jeans, before turning to do a cursory sweep of the store one more time.

"If you happen to see him, give me a call." He handed her a business card out of his pants pocket. "Especially since my friend had car trouble, I really need to find him." He hesitated before pulling out a folded piece of paper and slid it across the counter.

"I'm also looking for this woman. She's my baby sister. Her name's Jennifer. This other guy's her abusive ex, and the family thinks he's kidnapped her. Everybody is really worried. There's even a reward, so if they happen to stop by please call me. I'll make it worth your while."

Every muscle in Carlo's body seized up at the mention of Jennifer's name. Damn, Dubshenko had the goon squad out looking for Jinx. The good news, it meant she hadn't been injured in the explosion at the police station. The bad news, Dubshenko had his network of lowlifes searching for her. Jinx was good at taking care of herself, but she wasn't a match for Dubshenko alone. Hopefully, the cop she was with was wicked smart and street tough.

"Sure thing, honey. I'll keep my eyes peeled. Maybe I could give you a call, even if I don't see 'em?" She batted her eyelashes and ran her index finger down the cleavage exposed by the low cut t-shirt.

"Now, I'd like that. I'd like that a whole lot." Without a backward glance, Dubshenko's hired thug walked out to his car and drove off. Carlo stayed behind the shelf filled with potato chips and greasy fried snacks for another minute, making sure he'd really left.

"You can come out, he's gone."

Carlo sauntered over to the counter and picked up the paper he'd left. It looked like a wanted poster. The kind you'd see in the post office. Jinx's picture on the left side, and a dark-haired stranger opposite. He'd never seen the guy before, but it was better she was with this guy than alone. As smart as Jinx was she didn't stand a chance against Dubshenko's underground network. The Russian had his fingers in every kind of illegal racket out there, and Jinx didn't have a clue how to disappear, to get off the grid and stay hidden.

"Listen, sugar, this girl sure as shootin' ain't that clown's sister and this guy didn't kidnap her. Do not under any circumstances call him. Unless you have a death wish."

The store clerk's mascara-caked eyes widened at his words before she narrowed her gaze at him, assessing him more thoroughly than she had when he'd walked into the convenience store.

"Why should I trust you instead of him?"

"You shouldn't. Don't trust either one of us. But if you call that number, Vladimir Dubshenko will be in your face before you take your next breath." She visibly paled at the mention of Dubshenko's name. "I see you know who I'm talking about. You do not want to get involved with him or his men. That is the nastiest kind of business, and you'll be the one who pays the price. Is your life really worth risking for a few measly dollars?"

Carlo knew he was being harsh, but she needed to know the score. The minute she made that call, her life wasn't worth one thin dime. She'd be the next nameless, faceless body found by the side of the road—if her body was found at all. In the parishes around here, it was easy for somebody to disappear—permanently.

"You better hit the road, fella. I ain't calling nobody. I sure as hell didn't see your friends or you. Got nothing to say. But you get gone, pronto. And don't come back."

That suited Carlo just fine. He'd done his job, called his boss at the DEA, and warned the little clerk to keep her mouth shut. All in a day's work lately.

He crossed the cracked concrete by the gas pumps, skirted around staying out of the open space between them and the roadway and kept to the shadows. Chances were good he'd be thumbing his way for a bit.

Some days, he thought, *it just doesn't pay to get out of bed.*

Chapter Fifteen

Ness had been right, it hadn't taken long for her to
get the pallets unloaded from the back of her eighteen
wheeler at her first stop. Remy tried again to help her,
but she'd said he'd be more hindrance than help, so he'd
stayed in the truck's cab, while Jinx went inside to use
the facilities.

She'd been a real trooper about everything so far, but
he still couldn't get a good read on her. She was like a
chameleon, changing to suit the situation. She'd been the
shy, timid sister, reporting a crime when they'd been at
the police station, sweet and demure in her skirt and
blouse. Even with the signs of wear and tear, the dirt and
tears in her clothing, she'd carried herself in a manner
befitting the role that she played. And he was convinced
it was a role. That hadn't been the real Jennifer. Last
night at the hotel she'd been too exhausted to do more
than sleep, even though she'd protested sharing the bed
with him. When she'd finally capitulated and agreed to
share the space she'd slept like a baby, while he'd barely
closed his eyes all night.

Then this morning, she'd been flirtacious and funny,

her smile bright and carefree. That curvaceous body stoking the fire that hadn't been quenched since he'd first laid eyes on her. In the stretchy yoga pants that fit her like a second skin and the t-shirt clinging to her magnificent assets, she had the body of a nineteen-forties pin up queen. The kind servicemen had drooled over for decades.

"We've got about another thirty minutes or so before the next stop." Ness' voice sounded through the cabin, rousing Remy from his musings. Jinx had remained seated in the little alcove behind them, strangely silent since they'd left the small mom and pop store where they'd made their first delivery.

"You okay back there, Jinx?" Remy swiveled in his seat as much as the seatbelt would allow, noting the strained look on her face. She gave a little smile and nodded, tucking an errant strand of hair behind her ear.

"I'm good. Just wondering about Carlo." Turning to Ness, she continued, "Carlo's my brother. Before we left," she waved her hand between herself and Remy, "he'd gotten himself into some trouble with the wrong crowd. I hope he's okay."

"Why don't you call him?"

"I—can't." Jennifer stopped talking, and Remy knew she was afraid to say too much. They'd given their new friend the basics of why they were on the road without transportation, but couldn't risk giving her too much information. The less she knew, the less trouble she'd get into.

"I'll try and find out how he's doing at our next stop." Remy made the rash promise, knowing full well they needed to stay incommunicado. Dubshenko had an entire team of computer hackers who wouldn't have the slightest difficulty tracking any movement on Hilliard's phone or Max's for that matter. Silence was golden when you were on the run—and he'd just promised to basically throw their safety out the window—to satisfy the aching heart of one beautiful woman.

"Best thing would be to find an internet café, but a library or hotel might work. As long as we can get internet access I can contact my brother. He'll know what's going on with Carlo."

"Internet?" Ness piped in, glancing first at Remy then Jennifer. "You can use my cell phone, if that'd help." Remy shook his head.

"Thanks for the offer, but it'll be safer all around if we keep things out in the public arena. It would be too easy to trace the calls back to your phone within a matter of minutes, and I won't do anything to put you in danger, Ness. You've helped us out, and that would be a really piss-poor way of saying thanks."

Ness chortled. "Okay, fine. Appreciate it. But how about you use the cell phone to Google and see where the local library or internet whatchamacallit it might be, so we can get you to it ASAP."

"Great idea." Remy took her phone and handed it back to Jennifer. "Her you go, hon, why don't you start checking?" Maybe looking up the info would keep her busy for a while, and get her mind concentrated on something besides her injured brother.

He and Max had set up an e-mail account years earlier when Remy had transferred from homicide to vice. The chances of him going to ground during one of his undercover investigations made the possibility a reality, and they'd wanted a line of communication only they knew about. They didn't use the account for anything except extreme emergencies. Remy assured Max before they'd left New Orleans he'd check the account regularly.

He'd also instructed Max to give Captain Hilliard several untraceable burner phones with instructions to keep one on hand at all times, plus the order of the numbers he'd call them in, if everything went from shine to shinola. Those numbers were in an encrypted e-mail Max had forwarded first thing.

"Do you really think he's going to come after me, Remy?" Jinx's softly whispered question floated from the back of the truck's cab.

"I'd love to tell you he'll forgive and forget, but Dubshenko's not the forgiving type, hon. Plus he's got a long reach. We have to stay one step ahead of him until they arrest him and make sure it sticks. My job is keeping you safe until that happens."

"There any way I can help with that, big fella?" Ness reached over one-handed and squeezed his shoulder. "I've got a lot of connections with other truckers. We can keep you moving up and down the interstates for hours, if not days, if that's what it takes."

Remy felt a lump rise in his throat. Sometimes the kindness of strangers surprised him. Working vice, he didn't see it all that often. Working with the nastiest lowlifes you tended to forget there was generosity and decency in most people. When things were at their lowest, the inherent goodness of folks tended to show up when it was least expected.

"Thanks, Ness. Appreciate it. But the longer we stay with you, the more likely it is you'll become a target. I can't let that happen. You've been more than generous to two complete strangers, and I won't forget it. But right now, just get us to a place with Wi-Fi. When I get more information, then I'll be able to make concrete plans for our next step."

The rest of the trip was quiet except for the occasional chatter of the radio, but the three in the truck didn't talk. They drove past the city limits sign, and Jinx pulled up directions to one of the larger chain hotels not far from where Ness had to make her next delivery. Remy emphatically stated he'd help unload the next shipment, which he knew from their earlier conversation was one of the bigger hauls in the back. He'd snuck a peek at the inventory sheets at their last stop.

Pulling up to the back of the convenience store, Ness left the truck idling while she and Remy began stacking the pallets of goods. They hauled each loaded hand truck through the back employee's entrance and into the large refrigerated storage area.

Once they'd unloaded their last pallet of goods, they headed toward the manager's office. He hoped it wouldn't take long to have the manager sign off the receipt of goods, so they'd get moving again. Staying in one place, knowing Dubshenko was always one step behind him, Remy felt like there was a large bulls-eye painted smack dab in the middle of his back. At least a moving target was harder to hit.

"Hey, why don't you run inside and grab a couple of sodas or coffee before we head out?" Ness nodded toward the open door leading to the store's interior. "I'll get his signature, and we'll hit the road."

"Sure thing." With a jaunty little salute, Remy headed in and grabbed several bottles of soft drinks and walked to the register. Placing the items on the counter, he reached for his wallet, but paused when he noted the clerk staring at him before looking down at a paper in his hand. He looked at Remy again and quickly shoved the paper face down on the counter.

"That be all for you, sir?" The clerk's voice didn't squeak, but his Adam's apple rode up and down in his throat and he swallowed several times, a sure sign he was nervous—or anxious. *What the hell?*

"Nope, that's it."

"Okay, that'll be three ninety five." Remy passed across a five dollar bill and grabbed up the drinks, while the guy fumbled with the keys on the register.

"Keep the change." Remy stated as he slid the sheet of paper into his hand along with the bottles. "Have a good day."

"You too, sir." The guy's voice did squeak then, and Remy hurried back out. Something was definitely wrong, and they needed to get moving—now.

Ness met him at the manager's office door and they hustled their way out to the truck where Jinx waited. The minute he slid into the seat, he pushed the drinks toward her, and opened the paper he'd stolen from the clerk. And stared at his own face—and Jennifer's.

Dubshenko definitely played dirty. He'd made out wanted posters on them, claiming that Remy was an abusive ex-boyfriend and Jinx was Dubshenko's daughter. The flier stated Remy had abducted Jinx and Dubshenko was offering fifty thousand dollars for any information leading to the apprehension of the monstrous abuser and return of his sweet baby girl.

He heard Jinx gasp as she read over his shoulder. "That son of a bitch!" She snatched it out of his hand and growled.

"What's that?" Ness leaned across the center console

trying to get a good look. Jinx handed it across and Ness's indrawn breath on seeing their faces on the flier stabbed at Remy. He watched her read the unflattering and utterly false accusations against him, and the offer of reward. Her eyes widened at the amount before she handed the sheet back.

"So, where to now, Remy?" Her calm acceptance without any questions swept over him like a wave.

"Don't you have any questions? Demands to know if this," he waved the paper, "is the truth?"

She snorted in a most unladylike manner. "Heck, I don't need you to tell me that's a big fat pile of dog poop. I've only know y'all a couple of hours, but you haven't once raised your voice, much less your hand, to this woman. Plus, I'm a good judge of people and you are good people." She grinned. "Like I said, where to now?"

"Just head toward your next stop. We need to get moving out of this place fast."

Putting the truck in gear, bumping and chugging from behind the store, they pulled into traffic and hit the road. Remy knew chances were good the clerk was on the phone with Dubshenko right that minute, and they needed to get as much space between where they were and where they needed to be before Dubshenko caught up to them. If that happened, all three of them could kiss their asses' good-bye.

Chapter Sixteen

Jinx felt blindsided by the accusation. What made Dubshenko think he could get away with any of this? But, he probably could. Most people outside of New Orleans didn't know Remy. Wouldn't realize he was a police officer of the highest integrity. They certainly didn't know she wasn't the man's daughter—although her parents could attest that he hadn't sired her—or raised her. The last thing she needed was to bring them into this—they'd use it as an excuse to try to extort money from Dubshenko, and right now the way her luck was holding…well, let's just say it was bad enough Carlo was up to his eyeballs in Dubshenko's illegal affairs. Add her family into the mix and you might as well invite the four horsemen of the apocalypse to the party.

She and Remy had hightailed it away from New Orleans and headed for the more isolated, less traveled back roads. Even Ness said she usually took smaller roadways to avoid the congested traffic and unending construction of the major throughways, but now seemed a good time to get from point A to point B without delay.

"I think we need to separate." Remy's voice echoed

hollowly in the cab.

"What? No, it's safer to keep moving, stay ahead of this monster." Jinx couldn't hide the tremble in her voice. Darn it, she wasn't a mouse. She was a strong, independent woman who'd gone out and made a life for herself, yet everything she'd worked and struggled for was slipping through her fingers. *Jinx strikes again.*

"Not you and me—we need to let Ness get on with her job. Besides, I've got a plan." Remy looked back at her and winked, a quirky grin tugging at his lips. *Oh, man, I love that little smile of his. Wait, what? When did I start thinking about his smile? No, no. Danger Will Robinson! Attempted murder. Bombs. No thinking about handsome hunky cops with cute smiles.*

"Don't you think it's better to stick with me and keep going?" Ness voiced the question and Jinx nodded again in agreement.

"Unfortunately, Dubshenko or one of his guys is probably dealing with the store clerk right now. I know he recognized me. Dollars to donuts, he was on the phone before I hit the back door. When they question the manager, and trust me they will, they'll put two and two together and figure out we've been riding with you." Remy took a swig from his bottle of water, and she watched the muscles in his throat as he swallowed. Dang, even his neck was sexy. Or she was just feeling extra horny this morning. Sheesh, after a really long dry spell now was not the time for her libido to raise its ugly head.

"Once we reach your next stop we'll split up. There's a place we can head, some guys I know who'll keep us off the radar for as long as we need to stay lost. Plus, you'll be safer if we're not around. Tell them we ditched the truck when you stopped for gas."

"Which way are you headed? I mean you say you got friends to stay with, but how'll you get there?" Ness downshifted as three lanes became two and a trail of red taillights blinked off and on in front of her, as traffic slowed to a crawl. Must be getting close to town, Jinx thought. Construction backups always snarled traffic outside of the big towns. It was an inevitable fact of life in the South.

"It's best if you don't know which way we're going, Ness. Dubshenko will know if you lie. I doubt he'll hurt you for giving a ride to two strangers, but stay as far away from him as you can."

"I've heard about him. I doubt there's anybody in Louisiana who hasn't. Never had dealings with him though, and don't plan on it. But I'm gonna worry. Will you at least take my number, call me when everything's cleared up and he's behind bars and you're both safe?" She shrugged, trying to act like it wasn't a big deal, but Jinx knew in the short time they'd known Ness she cared about her a great deal. Apparently, Ness felt the same. She got on her knees, on the bunk behind Ness' seat and reach forward to give her a hug.

"We can do that, right, Remy?"

"Yes. I'm also going to leave my brother's number with you, as well as my captain's name and number. If anything happens to you—if Dubshenko tries anything—you contact them. They'll keep you safe." Remy tore off a scrap of paper from the paper sack which had held their fast food breakfast, and jotted down Max's and Hilliard's names and numbers before handing it to Ness. Without giving it a glance, she folded it and tucked it into her cleavage.

Well, that's as good a place as any to put it, I guess.
Jinx looked down at her own not inconsiderable assets,
pushing them out and up. While she hadn't been given
the triple D's that Ness sported, being a curvy woman she
definitely had more than a handful. Remy caught her
movement and glanced down at her breasts before
meeting her eyes. She smirked and shrugged one
shoulder. *What the heck, when you've got it, flaunt it.*

# # # # #

After another twenty minutes of stop-and-go traffic,
they pulled into the outskirts of Harrisburg, the biggest
city they'd come upon since leaving New Orleans, where
there should be plenty of places with internet access and
hopefully a computer. Remy needed to get into his
secure e-mail account, get the phone numbers to contact
Hilliard. Max was on top of things, he'd have handled
getting the phones to Hilliard at the butt crack of dawn,
knowing him. New Orleans was probably plastered with
the wanted posters Dubshenko was spreading throughout
the state. How in the hell did he expect people to believe
Jinx was his daughter, when he was known to have no
children? Now, telling people Remy was an abusive ex-
boyfriend might work on several levels. People around
the state would believe that in a nanosecond. Folks
tended to believe the worst case first until proven
different. That was just human nature.

One of the larger chain hotels loomed down the block
from where Ness had dropped them off. She'd protested
the entire time. She had demanded they stay with her,
despite the danger, but no way was Remy putting another
innocent bystander in the path of Dubshenko's bullets.
Lately, he tended to shoot first and worry about the
repercussions later. Too bad he seemed to be Teflon and

nothing stuck—no matter what charges the district attorney brought against him, he always walked.

Finally, walking through the hotel lobby, they headed for the concierge's desk. She was a tall, pretty woman with a pleasant smile and efficient manner. Within a few minutes, he'd charmed his way into the lounge and bar area and a borrowed laptop.

"You want some lunch while I'm checking things out back home?" Remy smiled at Jinx, watching as her fingers tapped on the tabletop in a nervous gesture. Her manicured nails no longer held the sophistication of polish and shine. Instead, they were chipped and ragged, the dark pink polish peeling and scuffed.

"Why don't you grab a menu from the bar and we'll eat. Bet they've got some pretty decent food here." Fortunately, he had a wad of cash divided between the backpack and his pockets, so money wasn't a problem—yet. His fingers flew across the keyboard accessing the password protected e-mail account, grinning at several messages already from his brother. Max was a lot of things—patient wasn't one of them.

Jinx came back and slid onto the barstool, menu in hand. "Anything in particular you feel like?" Her soft voice sent a zing through him. Yeah, there were a lot of things he wanted, he thought, looking at the gorgeous woman before him. Even after the last twenty-four hours she'd been through, watching a shooting, being in a bombing, running from the Russian mob, she still had an innate beauty that shone through. Her baby blues twinkled with a *joie de vive* most women took for granted.

"Burger and fries. Bacon, extra pickles, no onions."

"Okay. I'll place the order at the bar while you finish

up." She stood and walked back to the counter, and Remy's eyes focused on her ass hugged tight by the yoga pants. Damn, those pants never looked like that on his *maman*. Ugh, wipe that vision complete out of his brain or he'd have to bleach his eyeballs. Jinx's body was all luscious curves, and she moved with a relaxed confidence that said she was aware of her body and made no excuses for knowing she was attractive. That self-assuredness was one hell of a turn on.

Without access to a printer, he had to write all the phone numbers down by hand, making sure to note the exact order for each. Always prepared, Max knew what he needed to stay viable off the grid, at least as much as possible in this modern age of electronics, social media and closed circuit TV cameras everywhere.

"Our order will be up in a few minutes."

"Great, thanks." Remy didn't look up from his notes, staring at the laptop screen.

"Crap." He slapped the pen on top of the paper, leaning forward to search the screen.

"What's wrong, Remy?"

"Dubshenko's pulling out all the stops. He's taken out media coverage, print as well as radio. Damn it, there are pictures of us across the entire state." He stood, snapping the laptop shut with an audible click. He gathered up the papers and shoved them all under his arm, and Jennifer jumped out of her seat, grabbed her purse and waited.

"We've gotta move now. With this kind of money on the line anybody seeing us will call. We're sitting ducks out here in the open. Let's go."

Within seconds they returned the laptop to the concierge's desk, and strolled out of the hotel's front door and onto the sidewalk. Traffic zoomed past on the busy street. Remy looked both directions before turning right, one hand wrapped around Jinx's waist, her fingers digging into him. He hated running. The adrenaline pumping through his veins, the spike zinging through his system, if he'd been alone he'd deal with Dubshenko one-on-one like he always did. But priority number one was keeping Jinx safe and out of Dubshenko's hands. Dammit, he wished he knew what Dubshenko thought she had, and why it was so important.

"Yep, that's what we need." He pointed further up the street in front of them.

"What—where are we going?" Jinx kept stride with him as best she could with the borrowed flip-flops on her feet. Then again, pretty much everything she had on didn't belong to her.

"Drug store, about half a block up. We need some supplies."

"Supplies?" Remy could practically see the wheels turning in her mind. He knew when she realized what he meant.

"No! Tell me you aren't talking about dyeing my hair."

"Sugar, there are pictures of you with a fifty thousand dollar bounty on that pretty little head of yours. Long blonde hair and big blue eyes and that gorgeous face— every person who sees you remembers you. Until we can get far enough outside Dubshenko's reach, we need a disguise and a big floppy hat isn't going to cut it."

"But color—"

"Would you rather cut it, because that's the other option we've got." Please say no, he silently pleaded. He loved her long hair, remembering how it looked last

141

night spread out over her pillow. While she'd slept he'd wrapped a single curl around his fingertip, savoring the silken feel of it against his skin.

Jinx sighed and ran a hand across her face. "This son of a biscuit is going to get a severe butt kicking before this is all over. I hope he rots in prison for the rest of his life." She laid the back of her hand against her forehead, doing a perfect imitation of a swooning Southern belle. "I declare, sir, you do request the most outlandish things of me. All kidding aside, let's get it over with." She grinned and it was so infectious Remy couldn't help smiling back.

"I've always wanted to be a redhead. What do you think? Can I pull it off?"

Remy's groin tightened at the sudden picture of Jinx with long red hair, dressed in a black leather bustier and thigh high boots with four-inch heels. He swallowed the sudden lump in his throat and willed down the tightening in his groin. *Where the hell had that thought come from anyway? Sweet, mild mannered Jennifer decked out as The Dominatrix?*

"Uh, yeah, red will be good."

They walked into the drug store and Remy grabbed a hand-held basket, pointed Jennifer toward the hair color aisle while he decided to pick up a few other necessities they'd need. He met her at the front of the store and took the two boxes of hair color, a t-shirt, shorts and canvas shoes from her and added it to the stuff he'd grabbed. Naturally, he paid cash and they hightailed it out of the store without a backward glance. He glanced toward the clerk, but didn't see him pick up the phone, so maybe they'd caught a break and he didn't recognize them. Be kind of nice to get a few minutes reprieve.

"Okay, first thing, we need to find some hole-in-the-wall motel. Won't be up to your standards, sweetheart, but we're not gonna be there long."

"What do you know about my standards, flat-foot? I've roughed it a time or two in my day." Jinx's retort made Remy grin. He just bet she'd seen her share of less than stellar accommodations, after hearing a bit about her family. He'd pictured her as more the tea-and-crumpet set, but he was getting a kick out of finding out how wrong his misperceptions were. Jinx was an enigma and he was more than ready to unravel some of her layers, figuratively and literally.

"Let's find a rent-by-the-hour place, change our appearances the best we can, and hit the road." Since they were in the business area, it took a bit of walking before they'd reached the seedier section of the city. Littered with paper, empty bottles and cans, the sidewalks were cracked and jagged, sticking up in places, making walking a hazard. Remy felt sorry for Jinx, in her flip-flops. They weren't the best fit to begin with, and whoever designed them hadn't intended them for long-distance walking.

Finally, a two-bit fleabag motel came into view. Remy wanted to tell Jinx to wait outside the office, but one look at the vagrants lying in wait right outside the doorway of the first room had him rethinking that plan. The desk clerk openly smirked at Jinx's outfit, the too tight shirt and the black yoga pants stretched across her delectable backside. Remy wanted to pop him in his face, but refrained with effort. Couldn't' afford to draw any more attention their way. Dubshenko's hunters were on their trail, and the first item on the agenda was to disappear. For that to happen, they needed to look different.

Within minutes, and after the exchange of way more money than a dump like this should charge, he had their room key. Catcalls and rude gestures flew when Jinx started past the yahoos lounging against the open doorway. Remy expected her to walk past, head held high, ignoring the idiots. Instead, she put a little extra sway in her caboose, flipped her long blonde hair over her shoulder, gave the men a saucy little wave and walked on past. Remy's tongue nearly lolled out of his mouth at the sight of her sweet ass in front of him. Focusing on it made it easier to stroll down the hall steps behind her, instead of beating the living crap out of the trio of imbeciles shouting suggestions and offering payment for services. Instead, he flipped them the bird and kept walking.

About halfway down the row was their room. Opening the door with an old fashioned key, not one of the electronic key cards, but a real metal key which took a little jiggling and finagling before the lock finally opened. Remy was doubly convinced they'd overpaid for the room. Even working vice, he'd stayed in better rattraps than this dump.

"Oh, you really know how to spoil a girl, big guy." Jinx grinned over her shoulder at him as she moved further into the room. The one queen-sized bed dominated the center of the room. Its hideous dark blue bedspread was a solid color. Heaven only knew what kind of stains decorated its surface. A single wooden chair with uneven wobbly legs sat beside an equally sad what-used-to-be-white plastic table that probably hadn't been used in decades, even when it was new.

Plus, he definitely didn't want to take his shoes off

and walk barefoot on the carpet, which was a multitude of variegated colors ranging from putrid orange to I've just been thrown up on brown. Nope, quick in and out, not even sitting down if it could be avoided.

"Best I could do. You need help with the dye?" Not that he knew the first thing about hair color, except that it looked pretty good on most women. But applying it—well he could read instructions.

"I think I can handle it. How are you planning on changing your appearance though? Didn't see you picking up any color."

"Pretty much a ball cap and sunglasses. Stop shaving. Not a terrific disguise, but most people don't notice the guy anyway when there's a beautiful woman around."

He watched the rush of pink in her cheeks. Good. Let her know he found her attractive. Not that he'd make a move on her or anything, not while she was under his protection. But still, he had eyes and she was a whole lotta woman with a body any breathing man couldn't help but notice. Sure, some men went for a stick figured chick. Not him. He loved having a real flesh-and-blood full-figured woman in his arms and in his bed. She was exactly the kind of woman he found attractive—and she was totally off limits.

"Go ahead and get started, we'll need to hit the road again pretty quick. I've got a feeling Dubshenko's men aren't far behind us, so we need to keep moving."

Digging in the plastic sack, she pulled out the two boxes of hair dye, along with the shorts and T-shirt she'd bought and moved with an elegant grace into the bathroom. The door clicked between them with a soft snick of sound. Mere seconds, yet he already missed her quick wit, her outgoing smile. Oh, boy, at this rate he was going to be in so much trouble. He couldn't afford to let himself be distracted from his goal by a gorgeous woman. One thing, and only one thing, was important. Getting Dubshenko off the streets of New Orleans once and for all. To do that he needed to keep Jennifer Marucci safe, and discover what she knew or what she had that Dubshenko felt was worth killing over.

He emptied out the contents of the plastic bag onto the table, rifling through the remaining items, making sure he hadn't forgotten anything. Small denim backpack, check. Baseball cap, check. Sunglasses, check. Deodorant, toothbrushes, toothpaste. Basic necessities he could easily replace if needed.

The last item on the table drew a muffled curse. Box of condoms. Check, dammit. This case took precedence before anything else, but he was human and a guy. He knew the dangers of being out in the field with a member of the opposite sex, the long hours confined together. Emotions became clouded and better judgment flew out the window in the face of unbridled lust. Better safe than sorry. Besides, *no glove, no love*. That was one chance Remy never, ever took.

Repacking everything else into the pack except for the cap and glasses, he paced the room. How long did it take to color hair anyway?

Through the bathroom door, he heard movements, though they were muffled. Then the shower kicked on. She had to shower? Oh, wait, probably the fastest way to rinse all the junk out of her hair, and easier than the tiny sink he'd spotted in the nasty bathroom. But she was in there, and the warm water sluiced over her naked skin.

Stop. Danger. Do not go there. Remy turned away,

his back toward the bathroom door. Instead, he jogged across the filthy carpet and eased back the corner edge of the drapes, peering into the parking lot. If he leaned just right, he could see the three guys still lounging outside the doorway of the room next to the office. The rest of the parking lot was empty. Good, meant they still had a jumpstart on Dubshenko's men.

The creaking of the bathroom door had Remy whirling around. The sight of Jinx in her new outfit had him practically swallowing his tongue. The shorts came to midthigh, so they weren't indecent or Daisy Duke's, but the woman had fabulous long legs with thighs he wanted wrapped around him while he pounded into her. The t-shirt was plain cotton, a deep blue that brought out the startling sapphire of her eyes. The clothes definitely fit better than the makeshift outfit he'd put together for her out of his grandmother's closet.

But still, damn.

She rubbed the towel through her hair, still damp from the shower. The startling change in its color made him pause, and he studied her closely. It might work. The new darker color gave her a different appearance, the auburn color making her eyes look even bigger and brighter than before.

"Sorry, but it has to stay wet. They don't have a blow dryer here. It should dry pretty quickly in this heat, anyway. Think this will fool anybody?"

She twirled before him in a slow spin, and he studied the effect. Taken as a whole, she did appear unrecognizable from before. More exotic in an indefinable way, which might or might not be a good thing.

"You look great. Sorry about the lack of amenities.

You ready to go?"

"Let me grab the other clothes out of the bathroom and I'm set. Wait. Where's the bag? I need the shoes I bought." Remy pointed to the end of the bed where he'd placed them when he'd packed everything into the backpack.

"Okay, great. I'm so ready to lose the flip-flops. They might be cute, but they were not made for walking." Within a minute she had all her stuff together, and slid her feet into the canvas shoes. Clothes shoved into the bag, Remy checked the window again, before giving the all clear.

On leaving the room, they headed to the right, away from the office, and cut across the parking lot. Hopefully nobody spotted them, and Remy had them back on the street and headed north. He thought about calling a cab, at least to get them out of the city, but they were still too close to New Orleans. On the off chance they were spotted, they didn't want to leave any trail for Dubshenko's trackers to follow. They'd taken too many chances already.

"Where are we heading now?" Jinx asked while they continued walking.

"I figured we'd find out where the nearest bus station is, ride for a while and plan our next move." Remy watched her shoulders slump, and felt like a pig, but they didn't have a choice except to keep moving.

Because if they stopped, they died.

Chapter Seventeen

Hilliard reached into his desk drawer and pulled out one of the cell phones Max gave him the day before. He was so tempted to call Remy, make sure his best detective and their star witness had gotten away clean. Remy he trusted with his life, and the life of their victim/witness; otherwise, he wouldn't have risked everything letting them walk out the door.

When the big brass found out he'd probably lose his stripes anyway, maybe even his badge, but what the hell, Dubshenko had enough people in his pocket when they made this move against him, he'd probably be out of a job anyway.

A roar of voices echoed down the hall, and he slid the drawer closed, turning the key to make doubly sure nobody got to the phone. There was a hard rap against his door before it swung inward, and a sea of bodies invaded his sanctuary.

Reporters. Great. As welcome as a root canal without anesthetic.

A second look and he groaned inwardly, but slapped on his business face. *Politicians.* One rung on the ladder closer to hell than reporters. Wasn't this just the cherry on his sundae?

"Gentleman, what can I do for you?"

A tall, well-dressed man stepped forward, hand outstretched. The flashes of cameras clicking photos and microphones shoved forward followed the man. Hilliard recognized him immediately, and strove with every ounce of fortitude to remain civil. The jackass was a thorn in his side, had been ever since he'd announced his candidacy for lieutenant governor of this great state. Jonathan Caine was an up-and-comer in political circles, having a meteoric rise throughout the ranks from city councilman to mayor. Now he had his eye on a bigger prize. Too bad Hilliard couldn't stand the man.

"Captain Hilliard, I'd like to offer any assistance I can toward finding and convicting the perpetrators of this horrible, unjust attack against the fine officers of our fair city of New Orleans. This brazen attack against our finest, the men and women who put their lives on the line every day protecting our citizenry, will not go unpunished." Sincerity oozed from the man's lips, and Hilliard didn't believe a single word he uttered.

Unfortunately, Caine's opponent for the lieutenant governor's slot was also in the cavalcade of bodies invading his office, and he stepped forward as soon as Caine finished talking, ingratiating himself before the cameras and mics.

Also tall, dark and charismatically appealing, Daniel Delaney was cut from the same ruthless cloth as Jonathan Caine. Ambition drove him on his path toward power and prestige. Hilliard felt about him pretty much the same way he felt about Caine. Couldn't stand either one of 'em, but he had to play nice with the politicos before the news media, show no favoritism.

Not that he gave a rat's patoot who won. One bad choice competing against another bad choice. As far as he was concerned, there were no winners in this race, and the losers were the good people of Louisiana. Then again, what did he know or care about state-wide politics, he liked being in his section of the state. The people were down to earth, and you knew the good guys from the bad guys, at least most of the time.

"Captain Hilliard, let me echo the sentiments of my colleague. We want this scourge of society caught and dealt with as quickly as possible. We cannot and will not allow the citizens of our magnificent city to be terrified by outlaws roaming our streets with impunity, wreaking havoc in their wake. Tell us, Captain, do you have any leads in apprehending the mysterious bomber?" Delaney stepped back, smoothing a hand down his tie. His visage of concern directed toward the many video cameras recording the scene for posterity, and the five o'clock news.

Damn, I hate politicians. If I wanted to broadcast the fact that we're basically sitting on our hands without a friggin' clue that I'm willing to share, I'd have called my own press conference.

"Ladies and gentleman, we are currently investigating several leads into the bombing here yesterday evening. Although we have one suspect in custody, all avenues are being thoroughly explored to ensure the safety of all the citizens of New Orleans. The attack appears to have been targeted directly to this precinct, so people should go about their business exactly as they always have, without fear. We believe this was an isolated incident. That's all I have to say. We'll keep you informed as new information is available. Thank you."

Within minutes the room had emptied of everyone except the two candidates, who remained behind. He'd have preferred they'd left with the vultures, instead they pulled up the chairs in front of his desk. Looked like they were hunkering in for a prolonged visit. Great.

"Off the record," Caine started, leaning forward in his chair, "what can you really tell us about what happened here?" Delaney nodded, though he remained relaxed in his seat, a causal picture of restrained power.

"Gentleman, there really isn't anything more to tell. It was an isolated incident. An individual came into the precinct carrying a vinyl food container, stating he had a pizza delivery. Inside the carrier was a pipe bomb which subsequently exploded." Hilliard sank down into his seat behind his desk, his fingers steepled beneath his chin. He stared at the men seated across from him, but neither so much as flinched. Funny, now that he saw both men together it was remarkable how alike they looked. Both were just over six feet tall, dark haired, with a wiry muscular build. Similar coloring, similar haircuts. Was there some kind of factory churning out candidates for office, like an assembly line? Or maybe a Chinese restaurant. Choose one candidate from column A and another from column B?

Delaney tugged on his cuff, before speaking. "My sources tell me you suspect Vladimir Dubshenko is behind the bombing."

"Exactly. Dubshenko targeted one of your detectives, isn't that correct?" Caine added.

"Where did you get your information?" Damn, Hilliard knew they had at least one leak supplying info to

Dubshenko, but did these two jerks have spies in his department, too?

"Where isn't important, Captain. Is the information accurate is the real question." Caine nodded at Delaney's rebuff.

"All I will say—off the record—is Vladimir Dubshenko is a person of interest in the incident, along with a multitude of other suspects. Now, gentleman, if you'll excuse me, I have work to do and a city to protect."

In other words, get the hell outta my office.

Within minutes, both men were gone, and Hilliard had just added another problem to his growing list. Thankfully, they hadn't asked about Remy specifically. He'd hate to lie to them, but he'd have done it in a heartbeat before confirming Dubshenko had targeted his finest detective.

Priority number one—find the leaks and plug 'em. Immediately. As much as he wanted to call Remy, he'd refrain. He was a grown man, fully able to take care of himself and his female companion. Hurt like hell though. Remy was like his own son, and he hated he was out there with no backup, nobody to turn to if things went south. With Dubshenko hot on his heels, things needed to get kicked into high gear. Find the leak—and find Carlo Marucci.

Marucci had been with Dubshenko at the time of the phone call, right before the bombing. Chances of him still being alive were slim to none. Though if Dubshenko was smart, and nobody ever considered Dubshenko a fool, he'd keep Carlo as a bargaining chip for the sister. He'd wanted to keep Remy's brother, Max Lamoreaux, totally out of the picture, but they needed to find Carlo

Marucci and get him out of Dubshenko's hands. A bullet to the chest should have killed him, but as long as he was alive, there was a chance he'd flip on Dubshenko.

Turning the key, he slid open the desk drawer and pulled out the burner cell phone Max had given him earlier that morning.

Whether he liked it or not, the Lamoreaux brothers were his best shot at taking down Dubshenko. He exhaled a deep sigh, knowing what needed to be done. Instead of calling Remy—he dialed his brother, Max.

Chapter Eighteen

They'd walked for hours. It had to be hours, her feet felt like giant flaming balls of lead at the bottom of her legs. Each step forward almost more effort than Jennifer could muster. If they didn't find shelter soon she might just lie down in the middle of the dusty dirt path and erect a big flashing sign telling Dubshenko to come and get her.

Sweat pooled between her breasts and trickled down into her midriff, only to be soaked up by the knit waistband of her new shorts. If she never saw another pair of yoga pants for the rest of her life it wouldn't bother her one little bit.

"Hang in there, Jinx, we're nearly there." Remy glanced over his shoulder, and smiled encouragingly. Fat lot of good that did; she wanted to smack him upside the back of his head. Nearly there—he'd been saying that for the last half hour at least, maybe longer.

"How near is near, big guy? If I don't sit down soon…"

"Right there." Remy pointed to the left of their nearly invisible path, between the trees. There stood the most beautiful site she'd ever seen. Little more than a shack, at least there were four walls and a roof, with a wooden deck surrounding the entire thing.

"Amen, hallelujah, and woot woot!" Jennifer laughed and felt a surge of energy rush through her, and she sprinted past Remy headed for that little piece of heaven on Earth. Blessed shade, maybe a working bathroom, indoor plumbing. All the comforts of home. The only thing better would be if it also had food. Right now she'd wrestle one of the crocodiles they'd spotted earlier for a peanut butter and jelly sandwich.

"Jinx, hang on a second." Remy grabbed her by the upper arm, stopping her in her tracks. "Give me a sec— let me make sure there's nobody else around first."

Yeah, right, dummy. Just like you to leap first and pay for your rashness later, she thought. She nodded, and stayed where she was while Remy eased forward skirting around the lush green bushes, dead leaves from seasons past crunching under his steps. He silently approached the dilapidated shack. The porch creaked beneath his added weight as he snuck closer to the front door. Pulling the gun out of his waistband, he leaned forward and peeked into the dirty, cracked window. *All clear*. With a stealthy gait he headed toward the screen door. Time stretched by, the seconds ticking like a wind-up clock in her brain. He pulled open the door an inch at a time, and she listened for the expected eerily loud screech of rusty hinges. There was nothing but a quiet swoosh of sound as it swung outward, and he jiggled the handle of the inner wooden door.

"Damn." His whisper floated up to where Jennifer stood, and she watched him start scouring the porch, obviously searching for a key. The heck with this, she thought.

She eyed the dirt and detritus around her feet, finally deciding on a fist-sized rock. Its jagged surface dug into her hand as she balled up her fist and carried it directly to the porch.

"Use this." She handed it to Remy, and he quirked his brow before chuckling.

"Cupcake, I'm a cop. We tend to frown on breaking and entering."

She snorted in an unladylike manner. "So if you find the key, we're only entering, right? Forget it." Taking careful aim, she tossed the rock through the window. The tinkle of breaking glass was abnormally loud in the quiet of the bayou.

"I did the breaking in. Want me to do the entering, too?" She caught the twinkle in his eye and couldn't help herself, she laughed. It was a moment out of time, where they were in perfect sync and it felt good.

"I think I can handle that, sugar." She'd never admit it, but she loved all the nicknames he called her. He probably didn't mean anything by it, but they made her feel—special. Heck, he probably called every girl he met some special name, that way he didn't have to actually remember their names. As gorgeous as he was he probably had women climbing out of the woodwork to be with him. He had his choice of all the beautiful, sexy women in New Orleans, and here he was stuck with Jennifer the Jinx.

Remy knocked the rest of the glass out of the window frame, letting it fall inside the shack, and eased his long toned body through the opening. Within seconds the front door swung inward, and he stood there with a big smile.

"Come on in, darlin'. Looks like nobody's home and hasn't been for quite a while."

He turned away, heading for the kitchen, opening cupboards looking for food. Canned goods lined the shelves, their bright and shiny labels a godsend to her. Her stomach chose then to rumble, and her hands flew to cover her middle, embarrassed. Maybe he didn't hear that? He didn't turn around or comment, and she sighed in relief.

"Looks like this is somebody's fishing cabin, and it's been stocked pretty well. We've got plenty of staples here. He strolled across and opened the refrigerator, closing it quickly as a rancid stench filled the space.

"Yep, just what I thought. No electricity. They stocked the shelves, but didn't clean out the fridge. Nothing cold, I'm afraid."

Jennifer started pulling down cans, checking labels. There were boxed crackers, dried beans, oatmeal, and even some grits. Enough she could make a decent meal.

"Think the stove works? Looks like it's a gas one."

"Lemme check." Remy pulled open a couple of drawers before he found what he was looking for—a box of matches. Striking one, he turned the knob on the stove and held the match to the burner. A whoosh of sound accompanied the flame that shot up, and he grinned, yanking his hand back.

"Gas is working."

"Yes! I'm going to fix us some dinner, and we can figure out what our next move is."

The sweltering heat from outside permeated the kitchen, the tin roof reflecting some of the sun's merciless rays. But with the temperature in the upper nineties she was hot and uncomfortable, but mostly starving. Figuring soup and crackers would be fast and filling, she wiped a layer of dust out of a pot and dumped three cans of soup in, placing it on the burner. Grabbing down two bowls and some silverware, she turned to the sink, and turned on the faucet. Orange-colored and smelling stagnant, water sputtered and chocked its way through the pipes into the sink. She let it run for several long minutes until it ran clear, and washed the dishes and silverware they'd use.

"Dinner's almost ready."

She turned and realized Remy was nowhere to be seen. Where'd he go? "Remy?"

The swishing sound of the screen door opening had her spinning around, her hand planted against her stomach. Fear roiled in her belly at the thought Dubshenko had caught up with them. Instead, Remy strolled through with their pack and slung it down onto the wooden plank floor.

"You scared me half to death." Jinx inhaled a shaky breath, and turned away hoping he didn't see the trembling of her hands. She picked up the spoon, gave the soup a quick stir and felt arms wrap around her from behind.

"I'm sorry, sweetheart. I didn't mean to scare you. Just wanted to take a quick look around outside, make sure nobody was around." Without thought, she leaned back into his embrace, relishing the feel of his arms encircling her. It had been such a long time since she'd been held. Too busy working, trying to get ahead in her career and stay on the honest, straightforward path, and not fall back into the habits ingrained in her misspent youth. She'd rarely dated and hadn't been seriously involved with anyone for more than two years.

"When I couldn't find you, and heard the door, I thought maybe he'd found me." One shuddering breath betrayed everything she'd been holding inside, and she carefully laid the spoon atop the stove, afraid she'd drop it. Remy leaned his head forward, resting his cheek against the top of her head. A whisper of touch against her cheek before his fingertip trailed downward along the nape of her neck, sliding lightly against where it met her shoulder. His left arm wrapped around her waist, pulling her closer against him and she let her head fall back against his shoulder, submitting willingly to his exquisite touch.

"I promised you, babe, I'll keep you safe. Haven't I kept us one step ahead of him this whole time? Tomorrow, at first light, we'll head out. Get a car somehow and head over to Superstition, Texas."

"Where? I've never heard of it."

"I've got some friends who live there. It's a small town in East Texas. We'll get to their place and you'll be safe. Between the four of us, nobody will touch you. They're all former military, so they know what they're doing and know their way around weapons. Plus, they are all mean sons of bitches. Dubshenko or his goons show up there, well, let's just say it'll be the last mistake he ever makes."

Jennifer straightened stepping away from him, and picked up the spoon idly stirring the soup. Darn it, she'd felt comfortable in his arms, wanted to stay there and rest in the glorious feeling of warmth and safety that oozed from Remy. But if there was one thing her family had taught her it was that you can't rely on anybody but yourself. Somebody tries to help you out—use 'em and lose 'em. When this mess was all over and done with that's exactly what she'd do. Staying too close to Remy was dangerous—not just physically, but emotionally.

"Give me a minute and I'll have this ready to serve. Do we still have any of the bottled water left? I don't think you want to drink the stuff coming out of the spigot."

Remy looked at her, really looked at her, and Jinx forced herself to look away from those piercing brown eyes. He saw too much, like he peered all the way to the depths of her soul. She already felt raw and exposed. He didn't need to know how much his closeness and his touch called to something in her like she'd never experienced before.

"I'll check, but I think we do."

"Great. Let me serve this up and we can eat." She poured the soup into the two bowls, giving Remy the larger portion, and grabbed the crackers off the counter where she'd put them earlier. She'd hoped they weren't too stale to eat. A feast fit for a king. Well, the king of the bayou anyway.

Okay, so far so good. The soup was hot and tasted amazing after the long morning and afternoon they'd spent. Food hadn't been a priority—surviving Dubshenko's assignation attempt topped the list. Now, filling her belly with something as simple as a bowl of canned soup felt like one of life's little pleasures. Plus, the crackers hadn't been stale, either. She chuckled.

"What brought that on?" He looked up from his own bowl at the sound, and she saw that it was nearly empty.

"Just thinking about today, and how far we've come. That a simple meal of canned soup makes the mental highlight reel."

"Yeah, I get it. This was good, thanks for fixing it."

"It's not like I cooked a gourmet meal or anything." She scoffed at this thanks. "Dumping a can into a pot and putting it over a burner isn't exactly rocket science." She got up and went to the stove, lifting the pot. "There's a bit left, want some more?"

"Nope, I'm good." Remy rose and gathered up his dishes from the table, carrying them to the sink.

"Leave those, I'll take care of them."

"You don't have to," he protested. "You cooked, I'll clean up." She shrugged. A few dishes weren't worth fighting over.

"I'm going out on the porch for a few minutes, before we lose all the light. Want to join me?" She slid the screen door open and sidled onto the wooden porch out front, leaning against the railing that ran its length. The sounds of abundant life filled the air, heavy with humidity and heat. Perspiration trickled down between her breasts, always a problem for her. Being a curvy gal, there were certain places on her that seemed to be natural crevices, and her cleavage definitely fit the bill. Summertime was the bane of her existence. Being full-figured as people euphemistically called it, was a hard cross to bear when the weather heated up. She loved her body, wasn't ashamed of it, but she'd learned dressing for comfort meant keeping more covered than not. No matter what the fashion magazines and Hollywood might spoon feed the public, she'd had learned men gravitated toward a woman with a little extra oomph.

Bikinis became a no-go unless she desired a ton of unwanted attention. She wasn't fat by any means, her curves had been described more than once as luscious. She looked damn good out of her clothes as well as in them. Unfortunately, sometimes people lost the ability to reason when 38 double D's were tastefully on display. It became easier to dress conservatively whenever she was out and about in public. Now, in private...well that was a whole different story.

Sexy lingerie. Her weakness. Her kryptonite. Skimpy lacy bra and panty sets trimmed with ribbons with peek-a-boo detailing in every color of the rainbow. Seemed like every time she'd start saving up money, putting it aside for something important like a vacation, her favorite shop would call and tell her about an exclusive sale, and all her disciplined saving went out the window. Having to dress like a stuffy businesswoman in tailored suits and low heeled pumps wasn't her idea of attractive, but she felt alive and free and just a wee bit provocative knowing she had some scandalous naughty bits on beneath the pin stripes and pearls.

Too bad she hadn't been able to pack for this little unexpected excursion. She'd like to model a few of those ensembles for Remy. Maybe he liked lush curves, too. At least a girl could dream, right?

The screen door squeaked as Remy joined her on the porch. The briny scents from the nearby water along with an occasional splash from one of the bayou creatures filled their companionable silence. Standing side by side, Jennifer wrapped her arms beneath her breasts, before turning to face Remy.

"So what's our next step? Dubshenko's not going to give up. We're barely staying a step ahead. We got lucky this morning avoiding those two before they spotted us, but I'm afraid my nickname is about to rear its ugly head..."

"Don't. You're not jinxed. None of this is your fault. Besides, I like your nickname." He grinned. "Though I still want to hear the whole story of how you got it."

She snorted. "Keep dreaming, cop."

Remy moved to stand behind her and rested his hands on the railing, caging her body, his front pressure enticing against her back and buttocks. Jennifer suppressed the little stutter in her stomach at the brush of his skin against hers. Stop it, she told herself, silently cursing her suddenly overactive libido. This is so not the time to be thinking about anything but running as fast and as far away from Dubshenko as you can get, not jumping on the sexy stud of a detective. Even if he is tall. And handsome. And has dreamy eyes. And…just quit it. Remy's hands skimmed lightly up and down her arms, raising goose bumps at his sensual touch. *He's only trying to comfort me, not turn me on. Though, oh my stars, his hands on me feel so good. So right.*

"In the morning, we'll hike back to the road and find someplace with a pay phone. I'm going to try and get hold of my friends in East Texas, see if one of them can meet up with us and drive you back to their ranch. You'll be safe there."

"Don't you mean we'll be safe there?"

"They'll take care of you, keep you safe." Remy pulled back slightly and Jinx spun around, clutching at his upper arms.

"No! You promised you'd stay with me, keep me safe until your captain arrested Vladimir. I'm not going off with strangers…"

"Jinx, honey, you'll be safer at their ranch than anywhere else I can think of. These guys are my friends, plus they are all former Navy SEALS. Nobody, and I mean nobody, steps foot on their ranch without them knowing about it."

Jennifer shook her head vehemently. "Absolutely not. You're planning on going back to New Orleans, aren't you? Confronting Dubshenko. You can't do it, Remy. He'll kill you this time and won't shed a tear over it. You're the pesky fly that keeps buzzing around him and he's the type to pull out a .357 Magnum rather than a flyswatter to take care of the problem. I…what would I do without you?"

She lowered her head, resting it against his shoulder as she wrapped her arms tightly around him. Sorrow and pain rocketed through her as the image of Remy dead and gone shimmered behind her closed eyes. No, she couldn't, wouldn't let Dubshenko win. She wasn't sure when it happened, being on the run for their lives, staying one step ahead of Dubshenko, but somehow she'd come to care about the big lug standing before her. Was it love? She didn't know, but it was something she'd never felt for anyone ever before. Maybe it was too soon, but she wanted the chance to explore these feelings, find out if maybe they'd have a chance at something special if Dubshenko wasn't in the picture.

"Shh, sweetheart, it's okay." Remy's hands glided down her back in a soothing motion. Up and down, then back up, over and over again. "He's been trying to get rid of me for a long time, and I'm still standing."

"But you weren't with me before, Remy. He's deadly serious about getting his hands on me, and he won't hesitate to go through you to do it. People don't achieve and maintain the position of power he has without sacrificing their soul somewhere along the way, and Dubshenko lost his a long time ago. When I looked into his eyes after he shot Carlo, there was nothing left there vaguely humane, only pure evil. He won't stop until he's got me in his possession." She shuddered at the thought of Dubshenko's hands touching her the way Remy's were right now. Remy's touch thrilled her, made her think of warm nights and satin sheets, and bodies entangled in passion. Dubshenko's touch evoked nothing but fear and loathing.

"I promised to keep you safe, so I'll stay with you. Somehow, when we get to Texas, we'll find a way to set up some kind of trap to draw Dubshenko to us and take him out once and for all. If Captain Hilliard hasn't come up with a plan by the time we reach the ranch, well... I'm not above bending the law a bit to get Dubshenko out of our lives for good. Don't worry, babe, everything will be fine."

The daylight had faded, and they stood in the dusk. Jinx snuggled deeper into Remy's embrace. Warmth and comfort flowed from him, things she desperately needed—but she wanted so much more. She leaned back and stared up into his gorgeous whiskey-brown eyes, loving the tiny golden flecks sparkling in their depths. A circle of darker brown rimmed the lighter color giving them a depth of hues that reflected his moods, something she'd noted the longer she'd spent time around him. Right now, they reflected an emotion back at her she was all too familiar with—lust.

Wow, he wants me! Well, I want him too. So much. I want to spend tonight in his arms, making love—no wait, having sex. It can't be love. Love is for foolish people who expect a happy ending. I'll settle for what I can get and surrender in his embrace, and worry about tomorrow when Dubshenko's out of the picture. Until then, I'm going to live for the here and now, and that's with Remy—in Remy's arms and hopefully in Remy's bed having the best sex of my life.

She took a step back and raised both hands, gently cupping his face between them. Tilted her head back, raised on her tiptoes and lightly brushed her lips against his. Once, twice, the barest whisper of lips touching before Remy's control broke and he took command of the kiss. And what a kiss. His arms encircled Jinx and she gave a little shiver, never breaking contact. Oh, wow, could the man kiss! No soft, gentle exploration but a full on frontal assault. Lips, teeth, tongue, everything went into making this kiss—THE KISS.

As first kisses go between two people who've never shared that intimacy before, on a scale of one to ten, Jinx would rate this one a solid twenty-five. After that, she stopped thinking and started feeling.

Chapter Nineteen

Jinx couldn't believe she was standing here, in the middle of a swamp, in a fishing shack with no electricity, barely working plumbing, and didn't give a flying fig about any of it. The only thought in her head was the amazing man holding her in his arms and kissing her like she was the only woman he'd ever wanted. Things had gone to hell in a hand-basket earlier when Dubshenko's goon squad had caught up with them, but they'd escaped. Now, the adrenaline rush was past and reality had set in—and she didn't care.

Everything within her was focused on the man holding her, kissing her. She'd wanted him almost from the moment she'd met him, but everything had conspired to keep them apart. Tomorrow might be another day just like today, and they'd still be running for their lives. Tonight, right here, right now, she planned to live life to the fullest, and that meant spending the night wrapped in Remy's arms.

She broke the kiss gasping for breath, her head tilted back. Remy's lips trailed along her jaw and down her throat, dropping nibbling kisses along the exposed skin.

Her heartbeat thundered in her ears, faster and faster with each touch of his lips against her skin.

"It's gotten pretty dark," she whispered on a sigh as Remy's fingertips skimmed along the collar of her shirt, rubbing erotically against the exposed skin above her breasts. "Um, we should probably head inside. Otherwise, the mosquitos are going to eat us alive." *Oh, my stars, did I actually say that out loud?*

Remy chuckled softly as he straightened. *Yep, I guess I did say that stupid mosquito bit aloud.* "Let's go inside." His hand slid into the curve of her spine and meandered lower, cupping the cheek of her ass and squeezing.

She yanked open the screen door, anxious to get inside and continue what they'd started. There was only one bed in this sorry excuse for a fishing shanty, and she planned to make the most of it. Remy had barely made it back into the cabin and closed the door before she flung herself toward him, wrapping her arms around his neck and locking her lips against his. He clasped her to him, hungrily devouring her mouth. She silently thanked her lucky stars and friendly gynecologist that she was currently on her birth control shots, and didn't have to worry about missing any pills. Kind of hard to think about things like that when the Russian mob puts a price on your head.

"I'm on the shot, so we don't have to worry about birth control—as long as you're clean. I mean, I got a clean bill of health a few weeks ago, um, that is if you want to…"

"Oh, I definitely want." Remy's lips cocked up in a cheeky grin, the twinkle in his eyes backlit by the golden glow in the room had Jinx realizing he must have lit the kerosene lamp before he came outside. He really was a boy scout, she thought. "I have a condom in my wallet, and several more in the backpack. Picked some up when we got the hair dye. I'm clean, too. And I have never had unprotected sex, ever. We can use them, if it would make you feel better. Double protection is better than no protection."

Jinx bit her lower lip, nibbling at it with her teeth for the few seconds she thought about it. Like him, she'd never had unprotected sex. She'd only ever had two previous partners, and she'd insisted they always use condoms. But something about the thought of being totally skin-to-skin with Remy seemed different, exciting yet—more.

"I want to feel you inside me, Remy. All of you with nothing between us."

Remy groaned at her words, reached forward and grabbed the bottom of her t-shirt, pulling upwards until it was off. He tossed it across the room, and it landed in a heap on the floor. She stood before him in the stretchy knit shorts riding low on her hips and a lacy confection of pink and white. The frilly corset-like bra lifted her breasts up and made them look amazing, another reason she always loved sexy lingerie. She was a big woman with ample breasts that needed firm support, but firm didn't have to be ugly. Judging from the hunger in Remy's eyes, he appreciated her personal indulgence, and her taste in undergarments. His fingertips traced across the ruffled lace that edged around the top of each cup, where her breasts mounded. The roughness of his hands was a direct contrast to the softness of her skin. A shiver of awareness skittered down her spine, and she felt the moisture pooling between her thighs. Oh, she wanted this man—knew he would fulfill her every desire. She was counting on it.

Remy reached for the front closure of the mini-corset. He slipped each hook-and-eye fastener free, spreading it wider when the last one slipped from its catch. Her breasts spilled forth. Her nipples were pebbled and hard, aching for his touch, and he didn't disappoint. Both breasts were cupped and lifted in his strong hands, mounded as he gently massaged the undersurface while staring at her. His tongue slid across his lips as his eyes took in the bounty held within his grasp.

"Amazing. You are so beautiful."

"I know I'm not shaped like most women…"

"Stop right there." Remy interrupted. "I've never judged any woman on the way she looks, or how big or small she is. I'll tell you the truth—I love women. All women. Ask my brother or any of my friends, they'll tell you. Size doesn't matter, unless it bothers the woman. Truth be told, I prefer a woman with curves, who isn't ashamed of how she's built. I've watched you and how you carry yourself. You've never given off the impression that you're concerned about your God-given curves, which are absolutely gorgeous, by the way." Remy chuckled.

Jennifer grinned at his words. "You're right and I wasn't going to apologize about my shape, either." She shook her head scoldingly. "I was about to say that I'm happy with my body and the way it looks. Sometimes, I dress more conservatively for my job because it's expected and I don't want or need the extra attention, but never for one minute am I ashamed."

Remy stared into her eyes, reading the truth in her words. "This body," he pointed at her by raising one finger, though he didn't release either breast from his massaging hands, "is truly amazing. Gorgeous breasts I'm aching to taste, generous hips I'm planning to sink my fingers into while I'm pounding into you. I love having something to hold on to besides skin and bones. Hell, half the time I'm afraid I'm going to break them if I get a little too…enthusiastic."

Jinx burst out laughing, and Remy's eyes shot straight to her breasts as they jiggled within his hands. "Oh, yeah," he whispered, "do that again." She playfully swatted at his chin.

His thumb flicked one nipple and it beaded beneath his touch. She inhaled sharply as pleasure zinged through her. Before she could catch her breath, the hard texture of his tongue slid across her other nipple. She moaned his name, thrusting forward into his mouth a little deeper. The hand on her opposite breast squeezed, and she bit back a cry of pleasure as he tweaked the tip between his finger and thumb. He exerted just the right amount of pressure before he laved it with his tongue, circling the distended bud. Her head flung back as exquisite sensations bombarded her, and all he'd done was touch her breasts. Much more of this and she'd have an orgasm before they ever made it anywhere near the bed. Heck, she was still fully dressed from the waist down.

Remy pulled away from her breast with a soft popping sound. He walked her backward until her knees hit the mattress. She eased herself down onto the bed while Remy stood staring down at her, his gaze filled with a blazing need that she knew was reflected in her own eyes. Thankfully, she'd taken off her shoes before going out onto the porch, so there was no impeding his hands when they swiftly pulled the stretchy shorts along with her panties down her legs and off, tossing them onto the floor beside the bed.

"You're overdressed. Get naked." She whispered, reaching up. Remy stepped back one step, just out of her reach while she was reclining on the mattress.

"Let me look at you."

"That's not fair," she protested. "If you get to look, so should I."

Remy shook his head, but reached for the bottom edge of his shirt, swiftly yanking it upward and over his head, flinging it down onto the floor with the rest of her clothes. He toed off his shoes before reaching for the snap at the top of his jean, popping it open, but leaving the zipper all the way up. Jennifer's mouth curved down in a frown when he stopped undressing. *He'd just been getting to the good stuff!*

"Why'd you stop?"

"I need to touch you. If I'm naked, it will all be over before it really gets started good."

Inhaling deeply, she let out a sigh and plopped back on the bed, arms outstretched on either side. Her breasts jiggled with the movement, and Remy's eyes immediately focussed on them, his heated gaze making her feel beautiful. She jerked her chin in his direction.

"Maybe you need to get busy then."

Remy reached forward, brushing his fingertips across the curve of her stomach, which was gently rounded outward. She knew she didn't measure up with the size twos in the world, but she wasn't ashamed of anything about her body, and he seemed really pleased with everything he saw.

"You're so soft, and you've got the most amazing

curves." He grasped her hip and gave it a quick squeeze, his fingers digging into her ass. She sucked in a startled breath, and then chuckled. *Looks like he's definitely an ass man.*

"Please, more. Touch me, Remy."

Her plea seemed the impetus he needed. His knees hit the floor and he spread her thighs wide, fitting his body between them. His hands sliding up across her soft skin to her breasts, playing with them again. Sensation shot from her nipples to her heated core the second he touched her. She was so close to the edge the second he touched her clitoris she'd go off like a rocket.

"What do you want from me, Jinx?" The gravel-laced whisper caught her by surprise, and she raised her head off the mattress to stare down her body to Remy's brown-eyed stare. His pupils were enlarged, the blackness nearly obscuring the whiskey hue, until only a small rim of golden amber encircled it.

"Everything. I want everything. Nothing is out of bounds, off limits. For tonight, there's nothing and nobody else around. No bad guys chasing us. No running for our lives. There's just you and me. Let's make this a night to remember."

"That works for me, babe."

"Then kiss me, Remy."

"My pleasure." With blinding speed, so fast she barely saw him move, Remy sprawled beside her on the bed. He rolled pinning her beneath him. She gasped at the sudden movement, welcoming him when he lowered his mouth to hers, slowly leaning in. Gentle lips found hers in what started out as a sweet, tender kiss before morphing into something...more. Forceful, taking her breath away, he deepened the kiss, cupping her jaws between firm fingers. Pulling back, he stared intently down at her, and long moments passed with his hungry gaze focused solely on her.

Jinx decided to telegraph her message loud and clear. Grasping his cheeks in her hands, she leaned upward, sealing their mouths together in a savage meeting of lips. Sinking into the sensations of heat spiraling up her spine. Remy's lips answered hers in a marauding journey of exploration. Tongues swirled around each other, moving in and out in a synchronized dance, mimicking what she wanted his body doing to hers.

Biting back another moan, she gulped in air, her face burrowed into the juncture of his neck and shoulder. Her tongue snaked outward, licking a trail up his nape to below his ear, taking a teasing nip at his earlobe.

"Make love to me, Remy. I need you." The words left her mouth before she realized she'd voiced them. It was true, though. She needed him. Her body yearned for his touch, desire and lust roiling deep inside. Though she wasn't a virgin, she hadn't been promiscuous either, but none of her other lovers ever made her feel this way with just a single kiss. She ached to feel Remy deep inside her.

"Oh, I plan to, sweetheart. But we've got all night and I've always been one to savor my meals." He ran a fingertip down, starting at the hollow of her throat, teasing oh so slowly. A puckering of her nipples answered his sensuous touch. They tightened nearly to the point of pain, their stiff peaks evidence of her desire. Remy's eyes blazed, nearly scorching her with the desire burning within their depths. "I'm going to make a banquet out of your body."

Jinx whimpered at his words. Remy's hands resumed

their downward journey, tracing an erotic pathway down her body. He propped up on his side with his head braced on his bent arm, watching as his fingertips traced over the mounds of her breasts. She couldn't hold back the shiver of excitement his touch evoked. *Soon*, she thought. Anticipation built as he continued lower, his finger dipping into her belly button, before continuing oh so slowly toward the ultimate prize.

When his hand cupped her mound, she nearly bolted upright on the bed. His hand pressed lightly, and a zing shot through her at the incessant push against the bundle of nerves directly beneath his palm.

"Like that, do you?"

"Umm...yes." Was that her voice? Had that deep, sexy sound come out of her?

"Me too, sweetheart. Let's see if you like this." He sat up beside her and his hand reached between her spread thighs, sliding into the slick wetness at her center. She was soaked and dripping for him. Spreading her wide, he slid a finger around her clit. Her back bowed off the bed, she arched into his touch.

"More. Remy, give me more." Desperation laced her words, need clutching at her.

"Oh, baby, do you know how badly I want to be inside you? I've wanted you since the moment I laid eyes on you, with your torn blouse and hair falling out of that fancy up-do. You were gorgeous then, but nothing compared to how I see you now.

She raked her nails up his arms before burrowing them in his hair, tugging him back to her lips for a kiss. Everything she felt poured into the kiss. Heady with the power, the lust rolling through her, she led his mouth back to her nipple.

Remy's mouth at her breast felt better than any sex she'd had before. Everything paled in comparison with what this man could do with his mouth. He was a virtuoso playing a concerto, and her body was his instrument. Her body thirsted for something more, a sexual fulfillment she'd never shared with anybody else—and she wanted to share that with Remy.

Fingers played through the wetness between her spread thighs once again, tapping against her clitoris. Jinx moaned, her body clenched against the rising tide. She needed to come, but wanted Remy deep inside when she exploded.

"Remy." Her voice trailed off as she felt his hard length poised at her entrance. He was big and long and thick, and she wanted every inch of him. She sighed at the slight burning sensation as he pressed forward. It had been a long time since she'd been with anybody. She groaned at the feeling of fullness, seated so deep she could barely breathe.

"That's perfect." Remy's voice echoed beside her ear, his body stretched out atop hers. He grabbed hunks of her hair, licking up the side of her neck, and tingles rocked through her. She gulped, her gaze locked with his. A wicked ball of tension began to build, twining itself inside Jinx, as Remy plunged deep within her, only to pull nearly all the way out. He rocked his hips urging her to move, faster and faster.

"That's it, baby." His words were rough and low, and Jinx's arousal built higher. Desire coiled through her building higher and higher, nerve endings sparking to life she hadn't known existed. Her body was poised on the edge of explosion like a ticking bomb.

"You are so sexy, hon. The look in your eyes—it's

like you want to eat me alive. It's one hell of a turn on."

Her body clenched around him, as he rode deeper within her. The thought that he found her sexy, to hear him say the words, ratcheted her closer to the pinnacle. Their rhythm seemed in perfect sync, like they'd been lovers forever and knew exactly how, when and where each touch increased the other's pleasure.

"I want you to come with me, Jinx." Remy growled the words as he rocked his hips faster and harder. "Come now." An intense orgasm spiraled her world out of control. Remy made one more deep powerful thrust and roared as his release filled her. She plummeted from the summit spiraling into a sea of bliss, knowing Remy had joined her in a mind-blowing, earth-shattering release.

Long minutes passed, the only sounds in the room the ragged breaths as their heartbeats returned to normal. She didn't protest when Remy turned her on the mattress, and gently covered her with the threadbare blanket. He brushed the hair back from her forehead, gently tucking it behind her ears, and smiled down at her before placing a quick peck on the tip of her nose.

"I'm going to do a quick check, make sure everything's secure for the night. Be back in a few minutes." He strode naked from the bed, straight out the front door and onto the porch. Jinx snuggled deeper beneath the blanket and plumped up the flat-as-a-pancake pillow beneath her head.

This changed everything—yet changed nothing. She couldn't afford a man in her life, not while Dubshenko relentlessly pursued her. Remy was the best thing to ever happen to her, but if he knew the real her, the life she'd led before, would he want anything to do with her? More importantly, would he want *her*?

It didn't matter. The odds weren't in favor of her surviving Dubshenko and his goon squad anyway. Time was running out, and she knew no matter how good a cop Remy was he wasn't a match for the all-encompassing power of the Russian mobster. His life was in danger the longer he was with her, and she knew she'd never forgive herself if he ended up dead because he'd chosen to help her.

The snick of the front door closing drew her eyes back to Remy, his naked golden skin glowing in the faint light from the kerosene lantern spilling across his amazing body and painting him in hues of golden bronze deliciousness.

They had tonight, and she'd take every minute of it, and store up memories of this place and time with this very special man.

Pasting a smile on her lips, she leaned forward allowing the blanket to drop and held her arms open wide in welcome. *Laissez le bon temps rouler.* For tonight, let the good times roll.

Chapter Twenty

Carlo couldn't hold back his grin as his ride rolled across the Texas state line. He'd called his buddy, the one who was holding onto the *package*. Try as he might, he hadn't been able to figure out exactly who she was, or why Dubshenko was chomping at the bit to get her back into his clutches. Carlo was just as desperate to make sure the Russian never laid a finger on the poor girl.

When he'd picked her up at the drop, Ivor Gregorski had roughly shoved her into the back of the truck, threatened him with dismemberment if Carlo even thought about touching her and ordered him to deliver her as soon as possible to the boss.

Of course, Carlo being Carlo, he'd done exactly the opposite. How the hell could he turn an innocent young girl over to a monster like the Russian? She hadn't spoken any English, other than to say no and cry every time he even smiled at her.

Thank heavens Foster spoke some Russian. Maybe not as fluently as others, but he trusted Foster—as much as he trusted anybody. They'd worked together on and off for the last few years for the DEA. Although, now they had different supervisors and operated out of different states. Texas got a lot more action than Louisiana, but drugs were drugs no matter where the scum-suckers smuggled them from. Unfortunately, as fast as they shut down one dealer, three more sprang up to take their place.

Foster said he had a hell of a lot to tell him, so maybe the girl had talked. He hoped so—she was another chink in Dubshenko's armor, a major component to taking down Dubshenko once and for all. The bastard needed to spend the rest of his life rotting inside the same prisons where his former dealers currently resided. Of course, he deserved the death penalty, but chances were good he'd hire sharks for representation. People like him never seemed to pay for the havoc they wrought on others, just profited from it.

Mile after boring mile rolled by, the scenery never changing, the unrelenting heat of the Texas summer turning the grassy medians a dull brown. In a state with severe drought conditions, water had been at a premium for the last several years, so landscaping took a back seat to surviving the hundred plus degree heat.

Thirty minutes later the nondescript sedan pulled into a strip mall parking lot, and Carlo emerged from the backseat, thanking the strangers for picking up a lone hitchhiker.

He spotted the payphone exactly where Foster said it would be and strode purposefully toward it, not hesitating. Reaching into the change compartment, he pulled out the folded piece of paper stuffed inside. Unfurling it, he read: Walk around to the back of the building and wait. Don't talk to anyone. Your ride will be there at 1:00 p.m. *Cool.* He didn't' have long to wait.

He paced back and forth, counted the steps from one metal door to another, pivoted and counted again, only to start over.

A black Italian sports car slid around the corner, its engine a quiet purr. Carlo ducked down beside the dumpster, holding his breath at the stench to keep from gagging. The car eased slowly along the alleyway, and rolled to a stop beside where Carlo squatted out of sight. The driver's window lowered.

"Mr. Marucci?" A voice Carlo didn't recognize called out his name. Should he answer? Was it a trap—had Dubshenko found him after all?

He stood, brushing his hands down along his jeans.

"I'm Marucci."

"Foster sent me. Get in, please."

Carlo stared at the driver, trying to read him. Short blond hair, cut in a stylish fashion. The dark gray jacket encased a body that looked like it saw a gym and weight room regularly. A moneyed vibe oozed from every pore.

Who the hell is this guy and why'd Foster send him?

"Who're you? Carlo walked around the front of the car, running his hand across the hood. The car was gorgeous and had to have cost a bloody fortune.

"A friend. Foster told me you're in a bit of a bind with Vladimir Dubshenko." There was an accent there, pretty well hidden beneath a Texas twang, but Carlo caught the occasional undertone of carefully pitched diction. British maybe?

"Foster obviously needs to keep his big mouth shut."

The stranger laughed while Carlo buckled in, and hit the gas as soon as the catch clicked. Carlo expected him to floor it, show off the horsepower under the hood.

Instead, he eased along the alley's broken and pitted pavement. He paused at the end before pulling out into the parking lot, driving past each storefront.

"What do you know about Dubshenko?" Carlo couldn't bite back his curiosity at what Foster might have revealed to somebody outside of the agency. Things were spiraling out of control, with Dubshenko at the eye of the storm. He wanted this over and done. He rubbed at the bruise on his chest. Remembered the gun pointed directly at his head. The flashback played through his head like a full color video—his sister Jinx's scream, his frenetic wrestling with Dubshenko over the gun and the fiery explosion of pain at the bullet's impact.

Jinx—wherever she was, he prayed the cop was keeping her safe. Carlo's sole purpose coalesced into a single-minded focus, taking down Dubshenko and keep his plans for his beautiful, naïve baby sister out of his control. Dubshenko's taunts about raping Jinx and selling her to the highest bidder—well that would happen over his dead body.

The long silence after his question to the stranger driving the car had the hairs on the back of his neck itching with suspicion. Why hadn't he answered the question?

"Dubshenko's only the tip of the iceberg, Marucci. Taking him down may be important to you, and I'm praying you bury him beneath the prison, but once he's taken out of the picture, there are a dozen more just like him to take his place. He's dirty, nasty and evil, but the people pulling his strings are the bigger picture here. That's where I come in."

"Yeah? What's your angle?"

"Not important. Right now, let's get you to Foster

and your little friend."

Damn, he knew about the girl? That wasn't good.

"Who are you?"

"Samuel Carpenter." Carlo's brow rose at the name. Samuel Carpenter, A.K.A. The Ghost, was infamous throughout the DEA grapevine. He'd been the rising star, on the fast track to the highest ranks, until a botched operation derailed his career. He'd left in disgrace and basically disappeared off the governmental grid. Instead, he'd become the biggest playboy of the western hemisphere, money and parties, women and decadent excess overflowing.

"Okay, I'll bite. What's your interest in this whole thing, Carpenter?"

"Foster contacted me. I knew him from my days with the DEA. We'd worked a couple of cases together. He knows I speak fluent Russian, and asked me to come and talk with your friend."

Okay, that made sense. Foster couldn't have gotten in touch with Carlo anyway, since he'd been flying under the radar, trying to stay one step ahead of Dubshenko. Still, bringing somebody else into the picture complicated things.

"She able to tell you anything? Last time I talked to her, all she could say was no and cry. A lot."

Carpenter stared ahead through the windshield, a cold dark expression clouding his face. Carlo knew he never wanted to find himself on the wrong side of this stranger—that was one scary dude.

"Can't really blame her. She's barely fifteen, kidnapped from her home and smuggled out of her country. All she wants is to go home. A couple of bastards walked right into her exclusive boarding school and snatched her up before anybody knew what had happened. She was then taken aboard a private plane to an island off the coast of Alaska, where she was put on a boat."

"Damn, poor kid. I knew something bad was going on. Dubshenko's got a real hard on to get his hands on her." Carlo's mind whirled at the possibilities. The girl was obviously important to somebody, or Dubshenko wouldn't have a use for her. But who?

"Any idea who she is?"

"You want the bad news or the really bad news? Her name is Isabella Sokolov. Her father is Anatole Sokolov."

Carlo groaned. Might as well stick a gun in his mouth and pull the trigger. If Sokolov thought he had something to do with snatching his baby girl, Carlo knew before he finished with him, he'd pray for death.

"No way. Even Dubshenko wouldn't be that stupid. Kidnap the daughter of the head of the Sokolov syndicate? Think he's got a death wish?" As he said the words, Carlo knew this was exactly something a manipulative bastard like Dubshenko would try. His overinflated sense of entitlement as a big fish in New Orleans had obviously given him delusions of grandeur.

"My sources say Sokolov has kept this quiet. Nobody outside the immediate family is aware the girl is missing. But he'll be in the United States in less than 24 hours, and all hell will break loose the second he's wheels down." Carpenter's hands tightly gripped the steering wheel while he spoke, his grip causing the black padded leather encasing it to creak, and Carlo grimaced.

"I need to think. Dammit, how do we diffuse this situation with minimal bloodshed, without creating an international incident and dragging this half-assed kidnapping all the way to the front door of the White House?" Carlo scrubbed his hand across his face, grimacing as he encountered the stubble of beard. Things were spinning out of control so fast and furious he wasn't even sure what day it was anymore.

"Foster said you're DEA, right?"

"Yeah, undercover at the moment." Dammit, Carlo needed to have a serious talk with Foster. He thought the guy knew how to keep his trap shut. One word to the wrong person, and chances were good Carlo really would be floating face down in the bayou.

"Who's your boss?" Carpenter swung right onto a barely paved road, with live oaks creating a dense canopy overhead. Rutted holes pockmarked the drive, and Carpenter cursed when his Italian baby scraped against the rock-strewn asphalt.

"Branson." Carlo answered, holding onto the armrest, and Carpenter swerved sharply to avoid another huge hole smack dab in the center of the road. He jolted forward when Carpenter hit the brakes before throwing the car into park. He swiveled around in the seat, his gray-eyed stare boring into Carlo.

"Do you trust him? Don't think about it—gut instinct—yes or no?"

"No." Carlo answered spontaneously, realizing it was the absolute truth. Throughout the entire time he'd been assigned to Branson for the Dubshenko case, he'd had an instinctive dislike for him. He couldn't put his finger on it exactly; the guy seemed squeaky clean. The men working for him never spoke ill of him, in fact they sang his praises about what a great and fair boss he was.

"Think you could trust him with something as big as

Sokolov's missing daughter?"

Carlo didn't even pause before he answered. "Hell, no. I wouldn't trust him to baby-sit my cat, if I had one. I don't have any reason not to trust him—but something's always been a bit off."

Carlo watched as Carpenter pulled out his wallet, extracting a business card from inside. He raised a brow in question, but remained silent.

"Your instincts are probably right. Branson's department has been under investigation for a while and we're pretty sure he, or somebody in his upper echelon, is dirty. Case is ongoing, nobody has enough evidence to move them—yet." He flicked the business card with his finger before handing it to Carlo.

"Here's the number for a friend with the FBI. Give him a call and tell him what you know. Everything about Sokolov, his daughter, Dubshenko, and especially Branson." Carpenter chuckled before putting the car back in gear and easing forward, veering to the left to avoid still another pothole.

"Of course, that would mean you'd have to trust me to be helping you and not setting you up to be exterminated the second we drive up to the house— which is right around the next corner. So think fast and make the smart choice."

Taking one hand off the wheel, Carpenter leaned forward and flipped open the console in the dash, and pointed to the Browning nestled atop a stack of papers.

"Grab that—you probably need one."

Carlo reached forward toward the open dash, fingers outstretched toward the weapon, and gently flipped closed the door with a soft snick. He leaned back against the soft upholstered leather, sinking deeper into its buttery depths, and he smiled for the first time in what felt like days.

"No thanks," he replied. "I've got my own."

Chapter Twenty-One

Damn, dawn came much too early in the heart of the bayou. The sounds of wildlife penetrated the walls of the sorry excuse for a cabin. Remy wanted nothing more than to bury his head between the sumptuous breasts of the goddess next to him, and let the world outside wait. Instead, he stretched and climbed out of the narrow bed, the same bed he'd spent such a wonderful night with the woman currently occupying it. He debated whether to wake her, deciding against it when she burrowed beneath the cotton sheet, her arm stretched forth across the spot he'd vacated moments earlier.

Instead, he walked to the itty-bitty excuse for a bathroom, and quickly took care of business, thankful that even though it was tiny, at least it was indoors. He'd always despised having to use those outhouse bathrooms. Something about them just gave him the willies. Ugh.

First things first, he thought. Coffee. Please, by all that is good and holy, let there be a coffee pot in this shack. Quietly opening the cabinets one by one, in the third one he hit pay dirt. An old-fashioned, but usable coffee pot. Next step, coffee. He'd spotted a can on the upper shelf the day before, when checking out the supplies. At this point, he didn't care how old the stuff was, he'd drink it.

Once it was on the stove and gurgling away, he scratched his belly, and surveyed the contents of their limited pantry. Wasn't much, but they wouldn't starve before they made it back to civilization. Two arms twined around him from behind, and a soft curvy body pressed against his. A naked curvy body. He turned within her hold, smiling down at the tousled auburn curls and pillow creased cheek. Amazing that without all the artifice of makeup and hairstyling, she still looked gorgeous. Her big blue eyes reflected the smile curving her lips, and he couldn't resist leaning forward and kissing that appealing mouth.

"Mmm. Good morning, sunshine." He said after the kiss ended.

"Hello yourself, handsome." Jinx's husky, just-woke-up voice whispered back.

"I've got coffee on. We really need to get moving pretty soon. Should make it back to town in a couple of hours, and I'll call the guys." He moved back and spun her around, giving her a gentle tap on the butt, and a nudge toward the bathroom doorway. "Get dressed and I'll have breakfast ready when you get done."

Within minutes she was back, seated on the edge of the bed and putting her shoes on, then finger-combed her hair into some semblance of a style. She joined him in the kitchen when he started pouring the coffee into two mismatched ceramic mugs.

"Sorry, it'll have to be black. I couldn't find any creamer or sugar."

"That's okay, I'll make do." She took a sip and made

a face at the bitter brew. Remy tasted his and scowled. The stuff was horrible.

"Are you sure you want to call East Texas? Involve more people in this walking disaster I call a life?"

"I promise, Jinx, they'll watch over you, keep you safe."

"No. I told you before—if you don't come with me, I'm not going. They may be the best trained military experts in the country, but I don't know them. I know you—I trust you. If you're not staying, I'll find my own way back to New Orleans and confront Dubshenko. I'll—"

"No. There's a price on your head, and the son of a bitch has everybody in the state looking for you. Hell, we barely got away from those two yesterday. The second he gets his hands on you, you'll disappear, and nobody's ever gonna see you again. Is that what you really want? Think about it. What about your family— what are they going to do when you've vanished off the face of the earth? Or Carlo? If you're not around, there's no reason for Dubshenko to keep him alive." Remy hated throwing the harsh words out at her, but she needed to face reality. Vladimir Dubshenko was a powerful man in New Orleans and the surrounding parishes. The minute Jinx got within a hundred miles of New Orleans he'd snatch her up, and she'd be gone. Like every other person who stood in Dubshenko's way. The thought of her in the clutches of a power-hungry sociopath like the Russian churned in his guts. He couldn't do it—couldn't let her make herself a target.

"Fine. You win. We'll call and have my friends pick us up—both of us. I'll stay until we hear from Captain Hilliard or Max that Dubshenko's been taken care of and it's safe."

"Thank you, Remy." She flung herself into his arms and Remy pulled her tight, enjoying the feel of her soft body pressed up against him as she hugged him, her cheek on his shoulder. Leaning forward, he pressed a soft kiss to her temple, inhaling the fragrance of her. No artifice, no fancy perfumes or lotions—she smelled like soap and skin and woman. A unique blend of scents that was hers and hers alone.

He didn't know when it happened, or even how it happened, but somehow she'd wormed her way beneath his defenses and into his heart. He loved her. No more denials or evasions. In just a few short days she had come to mean everything to him, and he'd be damned if he'd lose her before they even got a chance to see where things might go.

"Drink your coffee while you can," he said with a smile. He tugged on a lock of hair, his fingers rubbing against the silky softness. "We're out of here in five minutes and it's a long walk."

Remy sauntered out onto the front porch, taking a look around. Dawn's light colored everything in shades of pink, orange and yellow as the sun rose over the left side of the treetops. A fine mist engulfed the waterways as the evening's chill gave way to the early morning heat. Spanish moss dangled from the branches, and the smell of salt water permeated every breath. To anybody else the portrait of a Louisiana bayou in the early morning light might be an eerie sight, but to Remy it was home. He'd been born and raised here and if he had any say in it, when he breathed his last breath, he wanted it to be Louisiana's one-of-a-kind sights and scents that carried him home.

He focused on the pathway leading up to the fishing shanty they'd spent the night in, checking for any sign Dubshenko's men might have tracked them here, but didn't see anything. Good. They needed to stay one step ahead until Cap had enough to throw his ass under the prison. Remy knew between Max and Cap, they'd find that chink in his armor, and burrow deep until they got him. But, damn it, he'd been working to arrest Dubshenko forever, and the Russian had thwarted him at every turn. He wanted to watch Dubshenko's face when he was confronted with the evidence.

A sound from inside the cabin had him smile. Then again, he thought, let Hilliard arrest him. As long as it kept Jinx safe and sound and in his arms, he'd be a happy man.

# # # # #

Jinx didn't think she could walk another step. At least she'd picked up canvas walking shoes when they'd grabbed supplies, and wasn't wearing those horrible bedazzled flip-flops. They'd never have lasted through the last day's activities. But these shoes were new, and even with socks, were rubbing blisters along the backs of her ankles. But she didn't dare complain. Remy'd immediately stop and let her rest, and they didn't have time for that. They needed to keep moving. She could live with blisters, but she wouldn't survive a bullet to the brain. Yeah, putting it like that, her feet didn't hurt quite so much anymore.

They walked in the opposite direction they'd come from the day before. Remy remembered there was a small town not too far down the road; he'd visited it before when he'd used the cabin for a fishing trip years ago. He still planned to call his friends in East Texas. A shiver of unease skittered down her backbone. He promised she wouldn't have to go alone to their ranch, and she trusted he'd keep his word, but knew taking down Dubshenko and nailing his sorry hide to the prison wall conflicted with his need to keep her safe.

"Not much farther, babe." Remy smiled over his shoulder, checking on her, since she was lagging behind.

"Great, again with the not much further. How long will it take your friends to reach us?"

"Once I get hold of 'em, probably three to four hours. Their spread isn't too far outside Longview. So it's maybe one-hundred and eighty to two hundred miles."

Remy pointed forward, and Jinx's gaze followed the direction he'd indicated, noting a small cluster of buildings in the distance, lining either side of the two-lane blacktop. Must be the barely-a-dot-on-the-map town Remy'd been talking about. It sure didn't look like much. The small barely-there town reminded her of places she traveled through years ago with her family. No fond memories evoked at the remembrance of the havoc her family had caused the decent, upstanding but gullible people who embraced the small town lifestyle. Though they were by no means stupid, they were naïve and trusting toward strangers—a fact the Marucci's preyed upon without a single thought to the consequences or devastation they left in their wake. She surreptitiously crossed her fingers behind her back, hoping this wasn't one of the places they'd "traveled" to during her formative years. Try as she might, blacking out the memory of the cons and grifts her family pulled still filled her with shame.

It turned her stomach she'd willingly participated in that lifestyle. Growing up, she hadn't known better—it was the life she'd been brought up in—trained from the cradle to believe it was better to grab what you want because nobody was gonna hand it to you on a silver platter.

Now, she knew better. Each day she tried to make up for every person she'd hurt, directly or indirectly, but the list seemed unending.

"Come on, let's find a phone, and grab a few supplies. You deserve a short break. Me, I'm dying for some ice cold water."

"Heck, no. You wanna bribe me, cop, you're gonna have to do better than that." Jinx grabbed his hand, twining her fingers through his and squeezing. "I'll give you a hint. It's dark brown and sweet and comes wrapped in shiny foil paper—and it's in a bar form." She laughed, before tugging on his arm, speeding up the pace. "Get the picture?"

"Ah, ha, so you're a chocolate lover? Good to know in the event future bribes are required. Any more secrets you want to share, my dear?" His teasing tone had her mind winging back to the people she'd been thinking about, victims of her family and their scams. She'd hinted at her past before, but thankfully he hadn't asked for more details, and she hadn't volunteered any either. She loved her family. Marucci's had been in and around Northern Louisiana for generations, sometimes traveling east to Mississippi, north to Arkansas, and even into East Texas, but never staying too long in any one place. Peopled tended to look down on them because of the way they dressed, or the ramshackle caravan they drove. Heck, she was the first person in her family to own her own home. They'd always moved around so much, rented houses wherever they could and if there wasn't a handy spot around, they lived out of their car or van.

"Jinx?" Remy's voice stirred her out of her thoughts and she gave him a half-hearted smile.

"Sorry, no secrets to share today."

"Okay." They stopped in the middle of the narrow roadway, devoid of traffic. Barely more than packed dirt with deep culverts down each side overgrown with weeds. It consisted of potholes and gouges from years of use and abuse. He held out his hand. With a sigh, she placed hers within his confident grip and matched his steps until they crossed over into the town. Wooden and aluminum buildings housed a small general store with one lone gas pump out front, the aluminum sign proudly proclaiming the price per gallon. Faded red and white paint on the wooden siding reflecting how long it had been since it had seen a rejuvenating facelift. Some industrious soul had filled two barrels sawed in half with soil and planted flowers, but with the unrelenting and unseasonable heat of the last few weeks their vibrant colors seemed faded and brown tinged around the edges of the petals.

A bait and tackle shop sat cattycorner from the general store, the hum of an ice machine loud in the surrounding stillness. A few cars were parked beside the buildings in a higgledy-piggledy fashion, with no rhyme or reason. No fancy parking lots with uniformly lined spaces here. It was more come-as-you-are parking.

A bit further down a brightly painted sign seemed incongruous amidst all the faded glory of its sister buildings. Bright red, white and blue sparkled like a newly polished diamond amongst the costume jewelry, its setting eerily out of place and time. The vibrant lettering above the striped awning proclaimed it Pop's

Diner. Remy looked at her and quirked his brow in silent invitation. Why the heck not, she thought, and nodded.

Walking inside, it felt like she'd stepped back in time. Jennifer looked at the square four-seater tables covered with red and white checkered tablecloths, little vases of flowers centered precisely in the center of each. Several Naugahyde booths lined the back wall, their gleaming seats appeared brand new, as though they'd hardly been used. A large lighted jukebox sat in place of pride in the back corner, and an old fifties tune pumped out of the speakers, filling the air with long-forgotten songs.

Jinx had a soft spot for old diners, had loved them since she was a kid. Some of her fondest memories from childhood were those few hours spent with her granddad at the old counters, sitting on the spinning stools, eating an ice cream and having some alone time, just her and her Pop-Pop. Whenever she passed one, she had the urge to stop in, even if it was for a cup of coffee. She inhaled. Dang, even the smells were the same homey and comforting.

Remy led them to one of the booths in the back, and she slid in across from him. The place was eerily quiet, except for the music playing in the background. No shouting of orders back in the kitchen. Certainly no kids screaming or complaining, or even laughing. A lone man dressed in jeans and a white t-shirt with a pack of cigarettes rolled into his sleeve sat on one of the round stools in front of the long Formica counter, sipping a cup of coffee, digging into a plate of pancakes drowning in syrup.

The waitress finished her conversation with the gent at the counter and ambled over to their table, her considerable bosom leading the way. Her brassy red hair was piled atop her head in a messy style, a pencil tucked into the topknot. Wearing a button-front shirt tied into a knot at the waist, a rolled up pair of jeans and a pair of Mary Jane's. She blended seamlessly into the place, enhancing the authenticity of the diner. Plunking down a couple of menus, she smiled, her pretty blue eyes sparkling in the morning light.

"Morning, folks. Welcome to Pop's. Can I start you off with some coffee?"

"Oh please, yes." Jennifer's hands clasped in a prayerful display earned a chuckle from both the waitress and Remy. Great, she thought, let's get this morning off to a good start.

"Sure thing, hon. Be right back."

Within seconds the waitress was back carrying two cups of steaming dark heaven in a cup. Remy sipped his straight from the cup, black, but Jennifer doctored hers, adding both sugar and creamer. She took a sip and closed her eyes in bliss. *Oh, yeah, that's the ticket.*

"You folks ready to order? I can recommend the breakfast special if you're really hungry. Three egg omelette, bacon and sausage, hash browns and your choice of toast or pancakes. Darryl's a real good cook, so you won't be disappointed no matter what you order."

Remy glanced at Jennifer, who shrugged. She didn't care what they ate, as long as it was good and there was plenty of it. She was starving.

"Sounds great, two specials please." Remy's quiet voice placed the order and he took another drink of his coffee, while Jinx smiled at the waitress. She remembered the days of standing on her feet, serving customers. Dealing with a happy customer first thing in the mornings was a heck of a lot easier, to say nothing of nicer, than dealing with a grouch.

"Sure thing, sugar. Have it right out to ya." With a snap of her gum, she hurried back to the kitchen to get their order placed.

"Remy," Jinx watched him put down his cup and look up at her before she continued, "Do you find it strange that nobody else is here? I know it's still fairly early, but it's a Saturday morning. Lots of people eat breakfast out on the weekend."

"Funny, I was wondering that myself. Lemme ask." With a wave of his hand, Remy motioned the waitress back over to their table, inquiring about the lack of customers.

"Yeah, it's pretty slow this morning, but we expected that. Today's the annual fishing tournament. Most of the places here in town are closed today. Heck, you're lucky we're even open. I'm planning to close the place up in a couple of hours and head over to the festivities myself. Ain't that why you folks are here?" Jinx heard the curiosity behind her words. Yep, living in a small town meant dealing with local gossip, especially with strangers. They always wanted to know who you were, why you were there, how long you were staying. But being a nice southern girl, the waitress wouldn't just blurt out the questions. No, that wasn't the way you did things in the South. You eased your question into the conversation, steering it in the direction to get all the answers you wanted—in a most gentile fashion. She bit back a snort of laughter. Yep, she knew exactly where the waitress's questioning style came from. She'd used it herself a million times. After all, you get more flies with honey—isn't that what they always say?

"Actually, we heard mention of the fishing contest,

so we thought we'd check things out. Can you tell us a little more about the celebration?" Remy smiled at the waitress, the little laugh lines around his eyes crinkling in amusement. Jinx rolled her own eyes when his dimples came into play. Whew, when he turned those whiskey brown eyes on a woman, focused his million-dollar smile and all that Cajun charm onto said females, apparently they melted into a puddle of melted butter—just like she had at the fishing shack. The rogue was definitely irresistible. Apparently, their waitress was no exception to the charming ways of the southern gentleman. Jinx decided to sit back and watch a master interrogator at work.

The waitress tittered. There wasn't a better word to describe it. A hand went to her hair and she patted it absently, before tugging on the pencil shoved into her messy topknot. Within seconds she whisked a chair from a nearby table and plopped herself down at the end of their booth. Her flirty smile was solely directed at Remy, Jennifer completely ignored at this point.

"Oh, we have a grand time. The whole parish gets together. Most of the actual festivities are held in the next parish since they're bigger than we are, but it's only a short drive, or about a fifteen minute walk. There's carnival rides for the kiddies. Cooking competitions and bake-offs for the grownups. Even Darryl," she pointed back toward the kitchen with her thumb before continuing, "he's got pies in the bakeoff."

She leaned forward toward Remy. "The big draw though is the noodling."

A frown creased Remy's brow, and Jinx chuckled at his puzzled look. His gaze shifted to hers, and she put the tips of her fingers in front of her lips to cover her smile, struggling to keep her laughter in check. It was blatantly obvious he had no clue what noodling was.

"Noodling? I thought we were talking fishing?"

The waitress nodded. "Sure am. Noodling is catfish hand-fishing. Basically, you stick your fingers in the catfish's mouth and pull it clear out of the water with just your bare hands. No rods or reals, not bait or anything like that. Ask anybody, they'll tell you we've got the best noodling competition in the entire parish." She leaned forward in her chair and whispered in a conspiratorial fashion, "Though to tell you the truth, if you ask me, we've got the best noodlers in the state right here in our own back yard." She nodded to him and Jinx, crossing her arms across her bosom. "Heck, ole Jack Perkins caught a 70 pounder at last year's contest."

"Huh, I guess I never heard it called that before." Remy appeared impressed, and Jinx couldn't blame him. Catching a 70 pound catfish using regular fishing equipment seemed like a pretty big deal. She couldn't imagine doing that with her bare hands. A shudder ran up her spine at the thought of sticking her fingers inside a fish's mouth. Have those wiggling whiskers touching her? Eww. *Yep, I'm a girly girl, fishing with my hands? No thank you very much, I'll just watch from the sidelines.*

"It's called by lots of names, but folks round here call it noodling. Everybody's probably down at the lake already. You can bet there will be some big ole catfish cookouts tonight for dinner."

A yell from the kitchen had her jump up from her chair. "That's your order, I'll be right back with your food."

Jinx couldn't hold back her laugh any longer. "The

look on your face," she sputtered and Remy grinned as his laugh joined hers.

"Well, I know what hand-fishing is, but I'd never heard it called anything else before. How'd you know what it was?"

"Television."

"Huh?"

"There was a TV show about this guy who taught people how to hand fish. It was hysterically funny, so I watched it a few times." At his raised brow and decided smirk, she defended, "Hey, I've got very eclectic taste, what can I say."

By then, their food arrived and the scent of the bacon and sausage set Jennifer's mouth to watering. Breakfast was her favorite meal and she dug right in, almost shoveling the first bite in at record speed. She moaned as the flavors of the blueberry pancakes exploded on her tongue.

"Oh my word, these are delicious." She moaned aloud, while cutting another forkful off the stack, and swirling it around in the syrup before filling her mouth again. Her eyes closed in bliss. Remy's laughter caused her to flip him off, and she kept chewing.

Their waitress strolled back over, coffee pot in hand. She quirked her brow, holding the pot aloft, and Remy nodded. Jennifer smiled her appreciation.

"We were supposed to meet up with some friends of ours here. Are you sure nobody else stopped in?" Remy asked quietly. "Since you mentioned the big noodling competition, I wondered if we were the only folks who didn't know about it."

The waitress cocked her head, giving Remy the once-over look only somebody digging for information can give. "Funny you should ask. Two men headed through here late yesterday evening. Big burly guys. Didn't seem like they were from around here 'cause they had strange accents. I couldn't place 'em, but Cookie said they sounded foreign to him." She leaned forward, and her voice dropped down to a whisper even though nobody else was within hearing distance. Except for the lone diner seated at the counter, but he was clear across the room. "He thought maybe they were Russians."

She straightened up after her big announcement and watched them intently, waiting for some sort of reaction, and Jinx knew they couldn't disappoint her. That would seem even more suspicious.

"Really? Russians? Wonder what they wanted in the middle of Louisiana?" She glanced over at Remy, noted him reaching for his wallet and kicked him underneath the booth, making contact with his shin. When his eyes met hers with a surprised glint, she shook her head, and mouthed "no", jerking her head toward his wallet which he shoved back into his pocket.

"You let Darryl know this is the best breakfast I've ever eaten, will you?" She put another bite of sausage in her mouth, but it tasted dull and bland now, her appetite gone.

"I agree, this is excellent. Plus, you can't beat this great coffee." Remy winked at their waitress, and she blushed like a schoolgirl.

"Honey, I've got an idea." Remy smiled at Jinx and she leaned back against the seat and folded her arms across her chest. She didn't like his tone; he was up to something. Keeping her mouth shut she looked at him, waiting for him to expound on his idea.

"Sweetheart, since we've got a little time to spare,

waiting for our friend, why don't we head on down and join in the festivities? I'm dying to see the noodling up close and personal, now that I've heard all about it. How about you?" The twinkle in Remy's eye dared her to say no.

Oh, she was going to get even with him. First a fishing shack in the back of beyond with no electricity. Well, okay, that had turned out pretty great, since they'd spent the entire night making love. But, watching people catch fish? Not exactly her idea of a dream date. Then again, with the Russians ahead of them now, at least according to their waitress, spending a little time letting them get farther up the road and putting miles between them didn't seem like such a bad idea.

"Honey, that sounds fabulous. Finish eating so we can get there right away."

Jinx turned to the waitress. "Do you have any muffins or bagels or anything portable we could take with us to munch on?"

"Don't you worry about food. There are tons of booths and things set up with everything you'd possibly want to eat, right there on the grounds. You definitely won't go hungry."

"Thanks." Remy reached across the table and squeezed her hand, just a little too tight. Tempted to give him another swift kick, but instead she smiled and fluttered her lashes at him.

"I'm ready whenever you are, honey." Her words sounded sweet, but Remy was a sharp cookie, and knew he was in trouble. *Fishing?* She'd show him fishing. "Pay the nice lady. The faster we get there, the sooner the fun begins."

Chapter Twenty-Two

They ended up down on the lake, teeming with people. The waitress had been right. It looked like everybody from miles around had shown up. Huge barbeque smokers were set up around the outer perimeter, the grassy areas filled with endless tables holding so much food they overflowed. Metal washtubs filled with ice held a variety of cans and bottles of cold sodas, juices and beer.

If they weren't on the run for their lives, Remy thought, this would actually be fun. He glanced at Jinx, watched her lean down to pet a black lab puppy on a leash held by a young boy, maybe ten or eleven years old. His glazed expression caused Remy to smile. Yep, he understood exactly how the kid felt. Jinx didn't have a clue how much appeal she had without even trying. Lush, generous curves, a killer smile, and a genuinely sweet personality. She drew people, especially men, like flies to honey. *Why wouldn't she?* They knew the real thing when they saw it, and she was one hundred percent the genuine article. Damn, why couldn't he have met her without all the drama of her brother being shot, fleeing from Dubshenko and the Russian mob and trying to figure out exactly why Dubshenko was so desperate to find Jinx in the first place. She still hadn't given any clue to what Dubshenko thought she had—or why it was so important.

He needed to check in with Max or Captain Hilliard, see if they'd made any progress on finding her brother, or why Dubshenko was so hell bent on getting his paws on Jinx.

Wouldn't it kill Dubshenko to know I've had my paws all over her already, and plan to again as soon as I get the chance?

"Jinx?"

She looked up at the sound of his voice, her hand still scratching behind the puppy's ears. He crooked his finger at her and she gave the dog a final pat, said good-bye to the kid and glided over to join him. Even dressed casually in wrinkled clothes, and sneakers, the woman looked mouthwateringly gorgeous. Like stop-you-in-your tracks stunning. She didn't flaunt her assets, though she had some great ones with plenty to spare. She was simply Jinx.

"Will you be okay here for a few minutes? I'm going to call Captain Hilliard, see if there's any news."

She bit her lower lip, and Remy wanted to pull it free from her teeth and lave it with his tongue before sucking it into his mouth. Such a simple thing, yet he wanted her with a fierceness he couldn't explain. This impossible woman aroused feelings he'd never experienced before, and unfortunately didn't have time to explore fully now. He wanted this entire mess finished first. Over and done. Then he'd get to know her, explore whether they had something to build a future on.

Chapter Twenty-Three

Daniel Delaney lived for the spotlight, which left him with two basic choices, acting or politics. Then again, weren't they both two sides of the same coin? He spotted his wife across the room, impeccably groomed in an ice-blue sheath dress, diamonds glittering in her ears. Blonde hair in an up-do that had cost a fortune, makeup perfect. She was a striking counterbalance for him, with his dark-hair and brown eyes. She was talking with the senator from Florida, the one who'd been on the fence about giving support to his candidacy. Leave it to his darling Amy, she'd have him eating out of her hands in no time. Fortunately, his lovely wife was nearly as ambitious as he was, and had set her sights on the Governor's mansion. She played her part to perfection.

Another charity event, this one a five hundred dollar a plate event, had he and his opponent shaking hands and making small talk with their constituency. Thank goodness it was an afternoon thing, and he didn't have to spend his entire evening dealing with people he couldn't stomach.

Not three feet away from his wife, Jonathan Caine

Kathy Ivan

smiled at the chairman of this charity extravaganza, schmoozing and butt kissing, things he excelled at.

Daniel looked at it as an integral part of life in politics. If you wanted to get ahead, you needed to shake a few hands, kiss a few babies and know where all the skeletons were buried.

Fortunately, he was very good at what he did, and had dirt on every influential person attending this party. Knew when to play his cards close to the vest, and when to bet it all. He smiled at the thought.

Might be time to head to Vegas soon. He did love a good poker game.

"Daniel." Jonathan Caine stood beside him, hand outstretched. His white smile reminded Daniel of a barracuda, teeth all sharp and pointy and ready to tear you to pieces without provocation.

"Jon." Knew the barb struck home with Caine's moue of distaste. The fool hated to be called by the diminutive name. *Which was exactly why he did it.*

"Less than a week until the special election, and we're still neck-and-neck in the poles."

Daniel hated the smirk on the other man's face, like he knew something he didn't. Caine was an upstart, thinking to rise through the ranks of Louisiana's hierarchy without paying his dues first. Unlike Daniel himself—he'd been carefully groomed for his position all his life. Nobody was taking away his big chance.

"May the best man win." Daniel held out his hand, knowing everyone's eyes were on them. "If you'll excuse me, I need to join my wife." Another little barb, sure to dig at Caine. The man wasn't married, never had been, and that was a sticking point with a lot of voters.

"Give her my best." With that, Caine walked away,

208

leaving Delaney feeling victorious. In this little skirmish he'd been the clear winner, just like on Tuesday, he planned to be the victor no matter what it took.

Chapter Twenty-Four

Guilt gnawed at her, but Jinx didn't have a choice. Remy'd told her absolutely no phone calls, no internet. No contact with anybody until they'd heard from his brother, Max, or from Captain Hilliard. Yet sitting around and waiting wasn't in her makeup. Here at the festival everyone milled around, small groups and families moving from table to table. Make-shift stalls were decorated to entice, selling food and handcrafted touristy items.

People weren't paying close attention to anybody, even strangers, which made it easy for Jinx to let old habits rise to the surface, long forgotten skills she'd hoped forgotten, but some things never change. The cell phone in her hand was a perfect example. Within seconds it had gone from her mark's pocket to hers, without him any the wiser. Guilt raised it head, but she beat it down into submission. Heck, she only needed to make a single phone call, then she'd make sure it got returned to its rightful owner.

Dialing her home number, she prayed Carlo picked up, knowing it a longshot at best. Damn, she wished she know where he disappeared, how badly he was hurt. His voice, weak and thready on Dubshenko's call replayed through her head for the hundredth time. At least she knew he was alive—or had been during that fateful call.

After four rings, the call switched to her voice mail system. Thankfully, it was part of her cable/phone package, so she didn't need to keep an antiquated answering machine. *Three messages.* Mentally crossing her fingers, she entered the pass code and listened. First message was Sally Ann from work, wondering why she hadn't shown up. Oh well, maybe she'd still have a job when this was all over, maybe not. The next call was from her mother. Uh oh. Mama yammered on and on— why hadn't she come to visit? Why did Carlo never call? When was she going to find a man and settle down and give her grandbabies? Nothing new there, either. Her mother called every couple of weeks, expecting Jinx to drop everything and come home. It was a longstanding argument, but mama hadn't won yet. Jinx valued her independence, and refused to be pulled back into the grifter lifestyle.

Third message. *Bingo!* Carlo's voice.

"Jinx, picnic. You've gotta remember. Picnic."

The beep ended. No more messages.

A jolt of adrenaline raced through Jinx's blood at her brother's words. To anybody else those few words wouldn't mean a hill of beans. She knew better though. When they were younger she and Carlo searched for a hidey-hole for their treasures. Things had a habit of disappearing whenever the family decided to pick up and move on to their next big score. Or else it ended up gracing the front window of the local pawn show.

It took a couple of months of searching, trial and

error but they found the perfect place. A park where their grandfather took them on picnics during the summer—just her and Carlo. They loved spending time with the old man, whereas their brothers and sisters couldn't stand playing outside. They'd rather stay glued to the idiot box.

Close to the water, the park became their special place. Calm, serene, families brought their kids to play on the swings and slides. Sculpted alligators, fish and other aquatic beings carved from huge chunks of rock graced the perimeter of the green space. A wooden fort constructed of wood beams and rock pillars, half fallen in on itself sat to the side. It had long ago been torn down and hauled off by the city or the county, somebody in authority, but last time she checked the park was still there. It had been a magical wonderland full of possibilities for two kids used to being dragged from pillar to post, dreaming of stability and a better future.

With that one word, Carlo's message became crystal clear. He'd told Jinx in their own private code he'd hidden something in their special hiding spot. Could it be what Dubshenko was pursuing her for?

She hadn't thought about that place in years, but with one word Carlo had brought back happy memories and a potential clue. Somehow he'd put something there, and she knew exactly what she had to do.

There was only one problem. She had to convince Remy to return to New Orleans.

Dubshenko believed Carlo gave her something so important he'd sent his squad of goons to chase her halfway across the state to retrieve something she did not have in her possession. For all she knew, their hiding place wasn't even there any more, had been bulldozed and covered with a parking lot. But at least it was more info than she had up until now, a clue pointing her in a different direction. She'd been running, hunted by a madman. At least with Carlo's call, she now had an end goal in sight.

Her eyes frantically search the crowd, both for Remy and the guy from whom she'd *borrowed* the phone. A group of men clustered around a makeshift stage, their Zydeco music filling the air. The noise from the swelling crowd of men, women and children combined into a cacophony of sounds. Voices raised in laughter and good-natured shouts, all having fun times at the festival. She sighed. Fun—other than the night she and Remy made love, well, there hadn't been a whole lot of fun the last couple of days.

Jinx spotted Remy about twenty feet away, watched as he slid the Smartcard from the cellphone he held. He tossed the phone into the nearby trash can. The Smartcard flew end-over-end into the murky water, sinking beneath its muddy surface. This deep in the bayou, nobody was ever going to find that card.

She jogged toward him, waving to get his attention. The smile he sent her way shot a pang of longing through her. She wished they really were a couple in love, out spending time among the citizenry of the countryside instead of a cop protecting her from the epitome of evil, on the run for her life. If only...

"Hey, babe. I talked to Max." He reached forward and tucked a wayward curl behind her ear. She fought back the urge to lean into his touch, turn and place a kiss against his palm. "Carlo hasn't been spotted yet. I'm sorry."

She was practically jumping up and down with

restrained excitement. Finally, she had something to contribute. "Remy, I know you said no phone calls, but…"

His eyes narrowed and his smile disappeared. "You didn't!"

"It's okay, I borrowed a phone and called my house. I thought maybe Carlo went back there to hide out from Dubshenko, since it would be the last place he'd look for him. Only the call went straight to voice mail."

"Wait, you borrowed a phone?"

"Um, sorta. I'm gonna give it back." No reason to tell him how she obtained the phone, was there? "There was a message from Carlo on my voicemail."

"What?" Remy grabbed her upper arms, firm enough to hold her in place, but not hard enough to hurt. "What did he say? Did he tell you where he's at?"

"No. He sounded stronger—but that's not important. It's what he said that's important."

Remy sighed, the little crease between his eyes deepened with his frown. "Okay, what did he say?"

"Picnic." She couldn't help laughing at the confused look scrawled across Remy's face. The word held a world of meaning for her—for him it didn't mean a thing.

"Great, I'll bite. What's picnic?" His barely contained growl sent a ripple across her, and tingles marched up her spine. Dang, she loved his voice, that sexier-than-sin Cajun accent got to her.

"Not what. Where. It's a place Carlo and I used as kids to hide things, important stuff we didn't want disappearing, which happened a lot in our family." She was practically bouncing on her toes, anxious to get back on the road, head for New Orleans and home. Things were coming to a head, she could feel it deep in her bones. The answer to everything, Dubshenko, the bombing, nearly dying. Whatever Carlo had stashed in their secret hiding place was the key.

"Where is it?"

"New Orleans. We've gotta go back, Remy."

Remy cursed, spun on his heels and stalked several steps away. Jinx watched him muttering to himself. She knew he was arguing against going back, putting him smack dab in the middle of Dubshenko's territory. Might as well paint a giant bulls eye in the middle of her chest. But she also knew there wasn't any other answer. Carlo's message pointed them toward a way to stop Dubshenko and nothing was going to stop her from taking the bastard down. He'd tried to murder her brother, and he'd made her life a literal living hell for the last few days.

Well, except for meeting Remy. That part wasn't so bad. In fact, once the son of a bitch had been arrested, she'd make a point of personally thanking him for the unorthodox introduction. Her feelings for the cop had started out shaky to say the least, but with every hour she spent with him, getting to know him, the more she liked what she discovered.

It wouldn't take much for her to fall in love with Remy. Her eyes widened at the unexpected thought. Who was she kidding? She was already head over heels in love with the big galoot.

Remy stomped toward her, and she held her ground. If she gave an inch, he'd find a way to stash her and head back to New Orleans himself. He kept threatening to call his friends in East Texas—she wouldn't put it past him to make the call and have them escort her out of Louisiana and onto their ranch before she could say boo.

"Don't even think it, Remy. You'd never find the

exact spot. I'm going with you." Jinx crossed her arms beneath her breasts, and she noted his eyes zeroed in immediately on their display. *Hmm, might not be a bad idea to keep him a bit off balance, at least until we hit the road.*

"Hon, Dubshenko's got eyes all up and down the state looking for us. Looking for a man and a woman together. His men will spot us before we can get within fifty miles of New Orleans. It's better if I go alone."

"Hell, no. Other than Carlo, I'm the only one who knows where we need to go—and Carlo isn't here, is he? You need me. Besides, I owe it to Dubshenko to make sure he pays for what he did to my brother. You weren't there. You didn't see him with a gun pointed at your brother's head. I thought he'd killed him."

She reached up and cupped Remy's cheeks in her palms, staring deep into his eyes. "I have to do this, Remy. *Me.* I've run away from everything my entire life. I ran from the life I had with my family and their less-than-honorable pursuits. I've made myself run from living, burying myself in a job that I hate, simply because it was the polar opposite of the way I was raised. Now I'm running from somebody else's machinations, wanting to destroy everything I thought was important. Only none of it matters unless I stop running and face the reality that I'm a coward. "

"Jinx…"

"No, you won't change my mind, Remy. You can't stop me, either. I have to finally stop running and stand. You can go with me, be my strength, or step aside and let me go. Either way, I'm going to New Orleans, finding whatever it is that Carlo hid and to make Vladimir Dubshenko rue the day he messed with the Marucci's."

Remy stood stock still when she'd finished speaking, the vein in his temple pulsing, but that was the only indication he'd heard every word she'd spoken.

Did I ruin everything? Have I lost him before I even had a chance at happiness?

"You still got that phone?" He held out his hand, and she placed her purloined cell phone in his palm. With efficient movements, he dialed and put the phone to his ear.

"Max, change of plans."

After outlining the new direction the case had spun, and setting up a rendezvous back in New Orleans, Remy dug into his jeans pocket and pulled out a scrap of paper.

"One more call, sweetheart, and we return the phone to its rightful owner, and hightail it back home."

With a crooked grin, Remy dialed, putting the phone on speaker with a wink. Jinx wondered who he'd called. Not the three cowboys from Texas, no way they'd get here in time.

She started laughing when she heard the voice on the other end of the call.

"Princess Grace, it's Remy. We need a favor."

Chapter Twenty-Five

It had taken Ness a couple hours to meet up with them, by which time it was almost midday. The bayou noodling festival was in full swing, and the competition kept everybody in stitches. Remy'd never seen anything like it. If they'd had another couple of hours to spare, and didn't have hired killers stalking them, he'd love to give it a shot. He'd done enough old school fishing in his lifetime to know catfish could be ornery critters when using a fishing rod and bait on a hook—catching one of those suckers with his bare hands—that sounded like some kind of fun. Oh, well, next time.

Thankfully, Ness hadn't asked any questions except for their location, and drove straight through to meet them. He and Jinx backtracked to the diner where they'd breakfasted earlier. Remy was fairly certain her big rig would have been too recognizable to the local citizens if Dubshenko's mob squad came back with more questions. Better to meet up away from the crowd.

Once they'd hit the road headed for New Orleans, Remy silently watched Jinx. She chewed on her bottom lip, a habit he'd picked up on watching her. She did it whenever she was deep in thought, like now. The sunlight glinted off her red hair, and though it was pretty, he wished it was back to the long blonde strands she'd had when they first met. As a disguise it was adequate, but pretty damn soon it wouldn't be enough. She had a memorable face, those beautiful blue eyes surrounded by long dark lashes were a dead giveaway. Besides, not much could disguise him—a ball cap and sunglasses only went so far. A couple days of scruff from not shaving gave him a bit of an edgier vibe, but he was recognizable without a lot of difficulty.

"Dubshenko's probably going to have everybody on his payroll scouring the streets for us by now. How are we going to sneak back into the city?" Jinx's question was valid. He wished he had an answer.

"I'm working on it, hon. It's almost four o'clock now, so it'll still be fairly light out by the time we hit the city."

"Um, can I make a suggestion?" Ness broke into their conversation, keeping her eyes on the asphalt before her. "I got a buddy who could put you up for the night, no questions asked."

"Really?" Jinx's voice held hope tinged with a bit of skepticism. Remy echoed her sentiments. He'd learned the hard way, nobody did anything for free.

"That's a nice offer, Ness, but what's the catch?" Remy shifted in the seat facing toward the driver's side so he could watch Ness's face. Trust didn't come easy, especially when you were running for your life. His latest call to Max, right before contacting Ness for a lift, he'd found out the bounty on his head was now at fifty grand. A hundred grand for Jinx. Damned if he'd tell her that, though.

"It's not a catch exactly. Thing is, he's a reporter."

"Nope, sorry, but…"

"Hear me out, Remy." Ness interrupted him, glancing toward him with a frown before turning her focus back to the road. "I've known Hank for a long time. He's one of the good ones, I swear. Do you remember the misappropriation of funds scandal in the mayor's office a few years back?"

"I do." Jinx replied faintly from the back.

"Hank's the one who broke the story. You can trust him—he'll probably ask for an exclusive on whatever you find, but he won't report anything on the air until he's got your okay."

Remy stiffened when an awful thought occurred. He had to ask, though he hoped he was wrong. "Ness, did you tell him about us?"

Ness's body jerked nearly imperceptibly in her seat, and she took a deep breath before answering him. Staring him straight in the eyes, she replied, "Hell, no. I promised y'all I wouldn't tell a single soul about you and I haven't. Maybe the crowds you run with can't keep their mouths shut, but when I give my word, I keep it." She huffed and then slapped the steering wheel with her balled-up fist. "I really want to help you. Don't know either of you well, but you were honest when I caught you lying in the beginning. I think you're telling me the truth when you say this Russian dude is chasing you. Besides, I ran into a couple of goons a couple hours before you called. Tall, dark suits, close cropped military-style haircuts. Definitely mercenaries working for Dubshenko. Showed me pictures of you." She paused and glanced at Jinx's dyed hair, her lips turned upward in a smirk.

"They definitely weren't local guys, if you catch my

drift."

Remy's gut twisted at her words. Were they the same two that passed through asking about them at the diner? Or are a couple of different trackers hunting for Dubshenko's prey?

He thought about Ness's proposal. A safe place to hole up for the night, plus an outlet to the media if things went south fast. Contemplating the lengths Dubshenko had already gone to, chasing them halfway across the state for something they didn't even have? Nothing was going to stop him short of full exposure. If that meant going to the press he'd lose his job, his pension. Hell, he'd probably end up in a cell next to Dubshenko. But it would be worth it, if it meant keeping Jinx safe.

"Thanks, Ness. I think we'll take you up on your offer. Let your friend know we're heading his way. We can make further plans once we're out of sight."

Jinx sighed behind him, and without looking back, he reached between the seats and grasped her hand, squeezing gently. Whatever it took he'd keep her safe from Dubshenko. There was an ache deep inside when he thought about a future without Jinx in it. He'd only known her such a short time, but she'd managed to wedge herself firmly inside his heart without him realizing it. He was a man who loved easily. Friends, family, they were all important to him, but what he was discovering about his feelings for this curvy blonde with the big blue eyes wove deeper, gripped him tighter than anything he'd experienced before.

When had it happened? They'd been chased, shot at, running for their lives. Yet through it all, she'd become as necessary to him as breathing. He could only hope she felt the same about him. When this was over and

Dubshenko paid for his atrocities, maybe he'd be able to convince Jinx to give them a chance.

Still, he needed to start moving players into position. This chess game was kicking into high gear. Time to call Max and Captain Hilliard. At all costs they needed to protect the queen. Jinx held the key to ending the Russian's stranglehold on New Orleans. Other than her brother, she alone knew the hiding place where he'd stashed something so important Dubshenko was ready to kill to get his hands on it.

Remy laced his fingers through Jinx's and she scooted forward, resting her head against his shoulder. He'd take this solace, this few minutes of peace, because come morning all hell would break loose in his city.

The hypnotic thump, thump, thump of the wheels along the asphalt lulled him to sleep, dreaming about one more night with the woman of his dreams.

Chapter Twenty-Six

They'd spent hours going over what they had so far with Hank, Ness's friend. He was a reporter for a local affiliate, but had connections to the top brass, enough pull that if things broke wide open he could get it on the national broadcasts instantaneously. Good to know, since heaven only knew what Carlo had hidden in their secret place.

Jinx brushed out her hair, grimacing at the texture of it. The hair color hadn't been kind, drying it out and losing all the glossy shine. Looking in the mirror was like looking at a stranger. A natural honey blonde, seeing the red was strikingly different. It looked okay, but she preferred her own color. Plus, it felt strange not to have any makeup. She'd been going without for days. No moisturizer, no foundation, not even mascara.

Ugh! I probably look like a gargoyle. To say nothing about how my skin feels.

"You ready?" Remy's voice came from the other side of the bathroom door. Was she ready? She glanced down at the yoga pants she'd donned, the same pair she'd worn the first night they'd hit the streets. The night everything in her life imploded. For the thousandth time she wondered where Carlo was, how badly was he hurt? A shiver ran down her spine when she pictured the bullet striking him in the center of his chest, his body falling backward, hitting the floor.

Running from Dubshenko. Running from the bombing. Always running, never stopping. No—it ended now. Whatever they found, whatever Carlo had hidden, it had to be something big enough to take down the biggest fish in the Russian mob.

She pulled open the door where Remy stood on the other side. "I'm ready." Giving in to impulse she stepped into him, hugging herself close against him. She needed to feel his warmth, the safety she felt close to him. Her arms twined around him, and she rested her head against his shoulder, wrapped in the security of his embrace. He smiled when his arms came around her, pulling her closer. One brief moment out of time where there was no one else in the world except for them.

"We've gotta go."

"Did you get hold of Max?" Reluctantly she stepped back, already missing the warmth of his touch. It was harder than she'd imagined, stepping away from this man who'd come to mean everything to her in the last few days.

"He's ready to meet us. They're going to be at the park, waiting. Close enough to help, but they won't interfere unless…"

"Nothing bad's going to happen, Remy. We're going to go, pick up whatever Carlo hid and get back to a safe place to check it out. Easy as pie."

Remy laughed. "Honey, ain't nothing easy about pie. If you've ever made one, it's a whole lotta work."

Jinx rolled her eyes, but the corners of her lips tilted upward.

"Let's roll, folks. Daylight's wasting." Ness's voice boomed from the living room. Jinx watched Remy, saw his whole demeanor shift. No longer the joking, fun-loving man she'd spent hours and hours with, laughing even in the midst of danger. In his place stood a predator, lethal and deadly. Everything about him screamed danger.

"Remy?"

"Let's go." His hand cupping her elbow, they walked out to the car. Hank begrudgingly loaned them his, amidst protests he didn't want to be left out of all the action. He didn't get his way, though, since Remy wasn't about to have any more civilians in the line of fire. They still had one more battle line to cross, though, because they hadn't told Ness she wasn't coming with them.

She stood beside the shiny black sedan, keys in hand. The welcoming smile on her face faded at her first glimpse of Remy. He held out his hands without saying a word. Ness glanced over at Jinx. She looked at the ground not wanting to meet her new friend's gaze. She wasn't any happier about telling her she wasn't coming as Ness was at finding out, but she agreed with Remy. Nobody else needed to place themselves in Dubshenko's sights. Too many people who cross him ended up in the swamp with their throats cut.

Ness tossed the keys to Remy, gave Jinx a hug and stomped back into Hank's apartment. They climbed into the car, and headed toward the park. Just outside the city proper, Jinx had fond memories of her grandfather bringing all the kids to play while the adults handled *business*. Now she was older, knew what that business really was, and why they always left the city right afterward. Still, this was a special place from her youth.

It took about fifteen minutes to get from Hank's apartment to the outskirts of town. Hurricane Katrina had devastated the area. Nothing looked like her memories. Gone were the lush grassy areas where kids played soccer. Uprooted trees lay on their sides, covered with lichen and moss. Rusted out swing sets and slides, abandoned. No children's cries of joy rose from the playground area anymore. Instead, a visual reminder of devastation and hopelessness pervaded.

"This the place, hon?" Remy pulled the car to the side of the road, leaving the engine idling. Jinx watched his keen eyes scanning, searching for hidden dangers. He, more than most, would understand the loss of places like this from the fabric of New Orleans during its hay day, the changes a catastrophic event wrought even on the children.

"I had no idea…it's so desolate. When we came, everything was bright. Filled with kids. Now…" Her voice trailed off, fighting back tears. Another memory from her youth, destroyed by the realities of adulthood.

"Where is this secret hiding place? We've got to move quickly." Remy opened the door and got out, coming around to her side of the car, opening her door. Her eyes immediately strayed to the gun tucked into the waistband of his pants. That, more than anything else, seemed to enforce the gravity of what they were doing. People wound up dead when they crossed Dubshenko. For all she knew, Carlo was dead. Now she'd put Remy in the crosshairs, too. This had to end, and it had to end today.

"It's over there." With a wave, she pointed toward a

stone bridge crossing over a stream that meandered along the side of the deserted park. Ornate in design with small pillars, the concrete and brick structure arched across the water. Trees flanked either side, covered in Spanish moss which writhing and undulating in the breeze. Algae floated in a green, slimy film across the top of the stream. What had once been a feature of beauty and tranquility now stood as a stone reminder of better days. A bygone era of children racing across it, cries of laugher and joy now silenced.

"The bridge? That's where Carlo hid something? Please tell me I don't have to crawl underneath that thing. Who knows what's in the water under there." Remy gave an exaggerated shudder.

"It was our special place. We'd leave secret messages there for each other. Or a special treat. Then we'd leave for a while. When we came back, sometimes months later, our things were still there, so nobody had discovered our hidey-hole."

"Wonder if it's still there, though?" Remy asked as they strolled through the devastated landscape toward the bridge. She knew it'd be best if they looked like two lovers out for a cozy morning stroll, so she didn't say a word when he wrapped his left arm around her shoulder. He kept his right hand free, she noted, so he'd be able to get his weapon if he needed it. *Please don't need it.*

"I think it's still there if Carlo hid something."

"That's true."

They'd reached the foot of the bridge. Jinx looked at the stone edifice, struck again by the effects wrought by Mother Nature. The stone façade had worn in place. The carefully crafted design work with its etched swirls and flowery patterns, cobblestone bricks, broken pillars. They were abraded, falling away with erosion and the wear and tear caused by years of weather and neglect.

Stop wasting time, she told herself. Find whatever Carlo hid, it's important. She moved to the left-hand pillar near the opening of the bridge. Dropping to her knees, she began digging around the stone base. Grass and mud gave way beneath her hands as she dug, searching for the grooved opening in the rock.

"Ah, there's something here."

Wiggling her fingers into the hole, she felt plastic wrapped around something hard. It wasn't very big, and she easily pulled it free and held it up to Remy.

"A cell phone?" He snatched it from her, shoving it in his pocket, before pulling her to her feet.

"What's wrong?"

"We're being watched. We've gotta get out of here."

"Do you think it's Dubshenko?"

"Don't know, don't care. Let's go." Grabbing her hand, he hauled her toward the car, and she stumbled trying to keep up, her knees hitting the dirt and grass. Her hand slipped free and he spun, frozen in his tracks when he spotted the three men behind her, guns pointed at her head.

Jinx stayed on her knees, her heart racing. How were they going to get out of this? Dubshenko's men had found them! They'd been so careful, hadn't told anyone, yet here they were, guns drawn.

"Took you long enough." Remy relaxed, although the scowl on his face didn't make her feel better.

Wait, he knew these guys?

He reached forward, helping her to her feet. Mud and clumps of dirt clung to the knees of her black yoga pants, but her hands were shaking too much to reach down and brush it off. Remy pulled her close against his side, giving her a reassuring squeeze.

"Jennifer Marucci, meet my brother, Max." The tall dark-haired, gray-eyed man on the right smiled and winked. His brother? That meant these were the good guys. She slumped against Remy, relief flooding her.

"The other two are Stan Jennings and Mark Wilson, two guys I trust from the N.O.P.D."

"They've been watching us the whole time?"

"Well, we skirted the park first, since we didn't know exactly where your hiding place was, other than the name of the park." Max chuckled. "Next time a few more details would be nice. It's a damn big place."

"Shut it, bro."

Jinx elbowed Remy in the ribs, and he let out an exaggerated oomph. It looked like he had the kind of relationship with his brother that she had with Carlo. Nice. Whether you agree with everything they do or not, family is family. You gotta love 'em.

"We need to get off the streets. You got a safe place?" Max turned his attention to Remy. "Might be best to give me whatever you've got. I'll get it to Hilliard so they can start…"

The sound of a gunshot split the air, and Jennings body hit the dirt. Jinx spun toward Remy and he jerked his head toward the car, parked on the street. The single shot came from behind Max and the two cops, so the shooter had been facing them. Meaning the shot fired should have taken out either Remy or her. Her gut told her the bullet had her name on it.

Max and Wilson knelt over the fallen officer, guns pointed toward where the shot had emanated, ready to provide cover while Remy and Jinx sprinted for their car.

Damn it, Carlo, what is on this phone Dubshenko wants enough to kill you or me to get his hands on it?

"Run." The words had barely left Remy's mouth when he grabbed her and half-led, half dragged her to the car and shoved her inside. He slammed the keys into the ignition, gunned the engine, and the tires spun, squealing as they tore down the street.

"What about your brother? We can't just leave them there. Dubshenko will kill them."

"Max can take care of himself. I don't think that bullet was meant for him."

"No, it was meant for me." Jinx wrapped her arms around herself, fighting the chill spreading through her. All the running and hiding and they'd managed to stay one step ahead of the hunters. Back in New Orleans less than ten hours and they'd already been found and shot at. Damn it, Dubshenko was never going to give up.

"We need to find out what's so important on that phone Dubshenko's willing to kill to get his hands on it. Remy tapped his fingers against the steering wheel, deep in thought.

Things were spiraling rapidly out of control. Look at the players. Dubshenko was a given. He's the one who started this whole fiasco. Then there's Carlo. Definitely more than meets the eye with that part of the story. What kind of dirt did the truck driver have on the notorious Russian?

Then there was Jinx, who'd become the central figure in their game of cat and mouse. He wanted to trust her, knew most of what she told him was the truth, but was she holding out on him? A niggle of doubt crept in.

Captain Hilliard knew there was a leak in the N.O.P.D. Probably more than one. Dubshenko had deep pockets, and for most cops money was tight. They'd been working on plugging the leak for months, but it seemed like as soon as one bad cop got taken out of the equation, somebody else bubbled up to the top to take his or her place. Unfortunately, money talked in a city known for its excesses, and Dubshenko had more than enough money to continually have eyes and ears at the station.

"You're thinking way too hard over there. Spill it, flat foot." Remy smiled at her teasing nickname. They'd discovered a love of old classic movies, and she'd taken to calling him by the old-fashioned name for cops. He liked to consider it a term of endearment. At least he hoped it was.

"Running through a list of the key players trying to see a pattern, something to connect the dots."

"Okay, I get it. Definitely Dubshenko. He started this by trying to kill Carlo." Jinx chewed on her lower lip, and if they weren't running for their lives Remy would have pulled the car to the side of the road and kissed the living daylights out of her. She was just so damned cute.

"Actually, it looks like Carlo actually is the first player. He's the one who's got something— incriminating—on Dubshenko. Something big enough to kill for."

Jinx shifted to look at him. "You're right. I didn't know the company Carlo was contracting with, driving long-haul shipments for belonged to one of Dubshenko's holding companies. Could it have something to do with his shipments?"

Remy nodded. "Might be, but somehow this seems bigger. A lost shipment or missing merchandise, yeah,

Dubshenko might exact payment from your brother, probably in the form of a beating, maybe dismemberment."

"Uh, gee, thanks for that visual."

Remy grinned. She was adorable. "No, whatever Carlo has or found or transported, I think that's only the tip of the iceberg. Think, hon, Carlo said he lost the package. Did he give any clues, say anything about what the package was?"

Jinx closed her eyes, and Remy waited. Knew better than to interrupt her train of thought. Sometimes a witness will remember something days or weeks afterward, so he'd give her time to replay everything. He hoped some small detail might pull them in a different direction.

"Oh, crap! The package. Remy, he did slip one time and call the package *she*. Like it was a person!" Jennifer scrubbed her hands over her face, before looking back at him.

"Dubshenko was obsessed with the package, but then he said there were two things Carlo had of his. That's why he thinks Carlo gave me something." She picked up the plastic wrapped phone from the console between the seats. "This has to be the second thing he's after. But the first is a woman."

"Human trafficking? There've been rumors, but nothing concrete ever surfaced. If he's moving people, there's little to no chatter about it."

Remy hit the gas and the car shot forward through an intersection heading toward the city. "I need to make some calls, figure out where we're gonna hole up for the rest of the day. Dubshenko's not going to give up, especially since he knows we're back in New Orleans.

Let's find a phone and get this info to Hilliard."

Jinx picked up Carlo's cell phone. "We have a phone."

"That's not a phone, honey, that's evidence."

He reached over and squeezed her hand, and she clung to him, entwining her fingers with his. Not a problem, he could drive one-handed, and he welcomed the brief physical connection.

Things were about to implode, he felt it, that deep cop's instinct. There was a hell of a lot more going on right beneath the surface, but the waters were too muddied to see all the players. Wouldn't be that way for much longer, though. A plan unfolded in his head, piece by piece. A plan with Dubshenko at its core.

It was about time to turn the tables on the Russian mob, and he knew just how to do it.

Chapter Twenty-Seven

Carpenter had been right, the girl was terrified. Isabella Sokolov trembled so hard she could barely stand. Fifteen years old, one look and you knew she was going to be a beauty when she had a few more years to mature into her looks. White blonde hair fell in a straight curtain to her waist. She had piercing green eyes, when they weren't filled with tears they displayed an intelligence and wisdom beyond her years.

"Isabella, I promise I'm here to help get you back home to your father." Carlo waited while Samuel Carpenter translated. His gut told him to trust the man, though they'd just met. Knowing his reputation as former DEA helped, even the fact that he'd left after a bungled bust. The man had more money that Midas, for crap's sake, he didn't have to be a dirty agent and steal more. He'd never be able to spend the immense wealth he'd already accrued.

"She said you worked with the bad man." Carpenter quirked his brow. "Think she means Dubshenko?"

"No. I think she means Ivor Gregorski. He's the one who gave her to me in Houston."

Carpenter frowned at the mention of Gregorski's name. "He's a little fish in Dubshenko's pool, but he's vicious. Hope he didn't touch her." Carlo hoped Ivor hadn't touched her either. Heaven help him if he had, because from the look in Carpenter's eyes, he'd end the man's existence.

"Does she know, or has she ever heard of, Vladimir Dubshenko?"

Carlo didn't have to wait for an answer. Isabella spit on the ground at the mention of his name.

"Pig."

Carlo and Carpenter exchanged looks. Maybe...

"I think we need to take her back to the bedroom and have some fun." Carpenter said, eyeing Isabella suggestively. Carlo knew exactly what Carpenter was doing, testing the girl's story with scare tactics.

She ran forward, throwing herself into Carlo's arms. "Don't let him hurt me." Perfect English, barely a hint of an accent.

Why the little brat. She could speak English this whole time!

"I thought she might be pulling the wool over Foster's eyes. With the kind of education Sokolov can afford, she probably speaks several languages fluently, don't you, Isabella?"

"Of course I can. I thought it best not to let anybody know I could understand them. Information flows when people think you cannot understand them." She shook her head. "Stupid Americans."

Carlo decided to let the insult slide, though the corner of Carpenter's lip quirked up. "I really am here to help you. What do you know about Vladimir Dubshenko? The more you can tell me, the faster we can have him sent to prison and get you back to your father."

"My father will gut Dubshenko where he stands. He'll never make it to any American prison." Isabella promised.

"While I'd like nothing more than to leave Dubshenko to your father's tender mercies, there is more at stake here than just you, princess."

"What do you mean?" Isabella sat down on the edge of the sofa, perched for flight at their slightest movement. Carlo knew she didn't trust him, and why should she? Kidnapped and smuggled into another country, manhandled and drugged, those were only some of the things she'd endured. He really had no clue what else she'd been through, and she wasn't exactly forthcoming with info.

"Dubshenko has done a lot of very bad things, but there's somebody even more evil who's his boss. I have to find out who that is before we can send Dubshenko to meet his maker. He's also threatened my sister. For that alone, I'm going to make him bleed." Carlo's words held a promise filled with conviction. Carpenter's indrawn breath confirmed maybe The Ghost didn't know everything going on, though he knew enough.

Isabella studied him and Carlo left himself open, vulnerable to this fifteen-year-old woman-child, praying she'd read the truth in him. After what seemed like an eternity, she slowly nodded.

"My father talks about Dubshenko. Says he wants more and more. More money. More power. If he was an American citizen, he'd want to be President." She chuckled. "Can you imagine him as your leader?"

That thought alone had shivers of unease crawling up Carlo's spine, and he spared a glance toward Carpenter, who rolled his eyes. Yep, that would be really bad.

"He tells my father he wants a bigger cut of the profits. He's taking all the risks, he should have more rewards. My father tells him *nyet*, he can replace him like that." She snapped her fingers.

"Dubshenko met with my father several months ago, along with other business associates, at our home. My sister and I were kept out of sight, but…"

"But you couldn't help sneaking out to see what was going on, am I right?" Carpenter interjected with a pat to her hand.

"Like you, they treat me like a baby. Isabella, you can't come down to dinner, it's business. Isabella, you must stay away from the ballroom, your father cannot be disturbed." She plucked at a string on her jeans-clad thigh. "I didn't mean to cause trouble, but on my way back from the stables I snuck onto the patio, the one that backs onto the room they were meeting in, and peeked in the window. Vladimir Dubshenko was there, along with several others. He was the only one who saw me, though. There was this look on his face, like he'd been handed a prize. He winked at me and I ran—like a coward."

"Isabella—"

"I know my father does bad things. You don't have to tell me this, but you have to understand—he's my father and he loves me. I love him."

"We will get you back to your father, I promise." Carlo made the vow, knowing he'd do everything in his power to ensure she'd be reunited with her father. Growing up the way he had, he understood better than most that blood was thicker than water. His family wasn't perfect, but he loved them anyway.

"Where's Foster?" Carpenter's voice broke into Carlo's thoughts. He looked around. Good ole Foster was nowhere in sight.

"You don't think…" Carlo began but Carpenter cut him off.

"We're outta here, now." Carpenter pulled Isabella off the sofa and started for the front door. "Foster's been acting odd ever since he called me to talk to Isabella. He's been there every time we've talked, hasn't he, Isabella?"

She nodded, her hand within Carpenter's. They raced toward the front door.

"Him not being here, wanting to know what's happening, something's definitely off. We'll split and check with him later. Right now, we need Isabella safe or we'll have one hell of an international incident parked right at the steps of the White House."

Carlo pulled open the front door and froze. Foster stood on the small wooden deck's middle step, a shotgun pointed dead center at his chest. Damn, I'm sick and tired of having guns pointed at me, he thought. Behind him, nobody moved.

"Carlo, buddy, I'm sorry but the money is too good to pass up. Once Carpenter uncovered who our guest is, I couldn't resist. I'll cut you in on the reward. Man, we could be living the high life down in South America."

"Why, Foster? You're one of the good guys."

"Yeah, well, where has being one of the good guys gotten me? Stuck in this rat hole in South Texas, watching drug dealers and murderers rake in the dough hand over fist. My wife split, took the kids with her. I'm paying so much alimony and child support, I'm lucky to have enough to buy macaroni and cheese once a week."

238

"So it's all about the money?" Carpenter's disdain was apparent.

"Hell, yeah, it's about the money. You'd never understand, Mr. Moneybags. You've got more money than the gross national deficit of some small countries. So don't look down your nose at me when I'm barely scraping by."

Carlo took a step forward and Foster raised the shotgun up a notch higher. "Don't do it, man. We're friends. I don't want to hurt you. Gregorski's got guys on their way to pick her up. She'll be delivered to Dubshenko, and everything can go back to the way it was, except we'll be rolling in moolah."

Carlo shook his head. He, better than anybody else here, knew Dubshenko wouldn't let them live. When Ivor Gregorski got here, all three men would be dead, and Isabella thrown into the hands of a monster who'd either use her as a bargaining chip to control her father or rape her then sell her on the black market as a sex slave. Either way, her life would be ruined.

"Back inside. We'll wait until Gregorski's men get here. Carlo, get Carpenter's gun and put it on the table." Foster motioned with the shotgun, stepping forward and crowding everyone back into the entry. Carlo glanced toward Carpenter, nodded and the man pulled a Glock from behind him, gripping it by the muzzle to hand it to Carlo.

With a move worthy of those big blockbuster, Hollywood special effects Carlo spun and fired in one smooth movement, hitting Foster between the eyes. The shotgun discharged with a reflexive twitch of the dead man's finger on the trigger, the shot going wide as his body fell backward onto the front steps.

An eerie calm settled over the small entryway as the reality of what happened settled over Carlo. Another betrayal, another friendship lost due to the lure of filthy lucre. Everybody's brains seemed to be screwed up lately, with the love of money ruling out their common sense.

In the distance, the sound of an engine broke through the quiet. It had to be Gregorski's men. No reason for anybody else to be headed for Foster's place.

"Get her out of here." Carlo spun at Carpenter's voice, reflexively snatching the keys he'd tossed out of midair. Isabella's head darted back and forth between the two men, fear written across her young face.

"We all need to leave." Carlo replied.

"Sports car only holds two." Carpenter shot back, before grabbing up the shotgun lying beside Foster's prone body, and laid it on the floor.

"Never get past them, not on that crappy driveway. If they're smart, they'll block the end and we'd be sitting ducks." Carlo slammed the front door shut, flipped the deadbolt before shoving the hall table against it. Wouldn't hold for long, one good shove and they'd be through.

"Excuse me." Isabella's voice stopped him cold. He turned to her, waiting.

"We should take his truck." When Carlo stared at her, she shrugged. "Mr. Foster, he has a pickup truck behind the house. The keys are on a hook by the back door." When Carlo continued staring, she rolled her eyes. "What, did you think I sat around eating cookies all day? I looked for a way to escape. Then when he came," she jerked her head toward Carpenter, "I decided to take a chance, see if you would really return me to my father. But I'm not stupid, so I made sure I had a backup plan." Turning, she sprinted down the hallway toward the kitchen. Carlo heard Carpenter chuckle before both men raced after her. With a pickup truck, they might have a fighting chance to get away from Gregorski and his goons.

Isabella waited by the back door, tossing the keys up and down. Carlo snatched them on one of the up tosses, before handing Carpenter's Glock back to him. Bending, he reached into his boot and pulled out his Smith and Wesson.

"Don't I get a gun?" Isabella pouted.

"No!" Both men answered at once.

"Spoilsports." Seems like her English had improved dramatically, Carlo thought.

The screech of brakes from the front galvanized him into action. Peering through the glass panels on the back door, he didn't spot any movement. He tossed the keys to Carpenter, silently acknowledging the man's better driving skills. With a flick of his wrist, he flung open the door, gun pointed toward the wide open back yard. No trees or bushes close enough to provide decent cover, it also meant nobody was hiding, waiting in ambush.

There was a dusty black Ford, parked about twenty feet beyond the door. It seemed like miles of open space, but their options were slim.

"Ready?"

"I've got your back." Carpenter spoke from behind him, and Isabella patted his shoulder in a clumsy motion. He had a hard time remembering she was just a kid. A kid he needed to protect and get home to her family. She'd handled herself better than most adults would've in the same situation, thinking on her feet and staying one step ahead, pretending she couldn't speak English. That alone had been pretty darn smart.

"On three." He silently raised one finger, then two. On the third, he burst through the open back door and raced toward the pickup, Isabella directly on his heels. Carpenter dashed past, climbing into the driver's seat and shoving the keys into the ignition. Carlo opened the passenger door and shoved Isabella through before scrambling in beside her.

Carpenter threw the truck into gear, peeling out from behind the house, dirt spewing from beneath the tires in a spray of dust and grass. Foot to the floor, they rounded the side of the house, heading for the drive. Shouts in Russian filled the air, and the sound of gunshots. The distinctive ping as bullets hit metal. Carpenter wove in and out across the pitted driveway, never driving in a straight line. Leaning out the window, Carlo aimed at the tires of the black SUV parked in front of the house, but his shot went wide.

Ivor Gregorski's blond head was clearly visible above the roof of the SUV, where he stood, his gaze meeting Carlo's through the back window of the pickup. With a cool nod, Gregorski stood there immobile, while his men scrambled around him, firing wildly. Yet Gregorski himself never moved, only that single nodded, a brief inclination of his head once.

They were too far away now, but Carlo could have sworn the look that crossed Gregorski's face as they pulled onto the street and away from the Russians piling into the SUV was one of respect.

As they roared down the blacktop away from Gregorski and the Russians, Carlo's mind spun a million miles an hour. Instead of getting into the SUV and giving chase, Gregorski stood, delaying his men from leaving. What the hell was going on? It almost seemed like he'd wanted them to get away.

Once again he wondered what the bloody hell was going on?

Chapter Twenty-Eight

Dubshenko wiped the bead of sweat from his forehead. This infernal heat. He hated living in the Deep South, especially in the summertime. Instead he longed for the colder climates of his Russian homeland. Staring at the woman currently kneeling at his feet, he remembered there were some perks of living in America.

Her long blonde hair and blue eyes reminded him of his sweet Jennifer. This woman was a pale imitation, a facsimile of the real thing, but she'd been available and Jennifer—well, soon enough she'd be his. It was a shame he wouldn't get to keep her for long. He'd promised Carlo his sister would pay the price of betrayal, had explained in exquisite detail all the things he planned to do to the sweet innocent beauty.

She'd sparked his interest from the beginning. Her voluptuous curves and sparkling personality intrigued him. First things first, though. Carlo had to be found and the damning video destroyed. If that footage came to light everything he'd worked so hard for in the last ten years went up in smoke. Plus, Sokolov would put a bullet in his brain, if his American partner didn't beat him to it.

The damned American. What had Sokolov been thinking, getting in bed with the foreign devil? Hadn't he kept everything running smoothing in the southern region? Now he had to answer to some politician with delusions of grandeur.

It wouldn't be long now, though. He'd show both Sokolov and that upstart American politician who craved power exactly who held the real power in America.

He reached forward and patted the head of the girl still on her knees before him, head bowed. She hadn't murmured a word since being brought into his bedroom, only an occasional sniffle. Fear—it was a beautiful thing.

A sharp knock on the door interrupted. He called out to enter, not bothering to stand or dress. Bubba had seen him naked before, and nobody else would dare disturb him.

"Mr. Dubshenko. Carlo was spotted in South Texas." Bubba's deep rumble echoed. His hulking frame intimidated many, but Dubshenko knew where his loyalties lie. It's amazing the power some judicious old-fashioned blackmail could wield.

"Where?" Dubshenko stood, pulling on the robe, ignoring the woman at his feet as though she were invisible.

"Ivor Gregorski received a tip from an informant. Carlo killed the informant and escaped with your package."

"He has her?"

"He never lost her. She's been staying with the informant, the one who called Gregorski. By the time he and his men arrived, Carlo and the girl along with an unidentified male got away."

Dubshenko frowned, pacing the floor beside his massive four poster bed. "Why didn't Gregorski recover the package?"

"Apparently there was an exchange of gunfire, and in the chaos they got away. They chased after them, but lost them in the town."

Dubshenko cursed in Russian, and Bubba stood silent, a statue in the doorway, unobtrusive but present.

"I want him found. Now!" Dubshenko slapped his hand against one of the bedposts. "Double the reward. He's to be captured and brought in immediately. Keep him and the girl alive. She's still our best bargaining chip with Sokolov. We're running out of time. He will be in the States tomorrow."

Bubba cleared his throat. "Sir, there is more."

Dubshenko froze. "What?"

"The Marucci woman was spotted here in New Orleans."

Here? Oh, this was priceless. Capturing Carlo was top priority, but having the sister too, would be the final nail in his former employee's coffin. If he got his hands on Jennifer, Carlo would do anything he wanted, including turning over the cell phone. *That damned video was ruining his life.*

"She and Detective Lamoreaux went to a city park. Three other men were there, one of them his brother. When our men tried to shoot her..."

"Shoot her? Were my orders not clear? She is not to be harmed. Kill Lamoreaux, but the girl is *mine!*" Dubshenko took a deep breath, visibly calming himself, fisting then unclenching his hands.

Was it possible, both Marucci siblings within his

grasp? If he dealt with Carlo and his troublesome sister and retrieved pretty little Isabella, blackmailing Sokolov would be a piece of cake, as these Americans say.

But the icing on this particular cake would be never dealing with the American upstart again. The politician who would be king would die in a blaze of glory at his hands, and the whole world would know that ultimate power belonged to Vladimir Dubshenko.

"The shooter has been dealt with appropriately, sir. I have men tailing Lamoreaux as we speak. We'll soon know exactly where they are and we'll get her back."

"Excellent work, my friend." A sniffle from the floor drew Dubshenko's attention and he grimaced. He was finished with her. A poor imitation of the real prize, she'd been adequate at best, but still she deserved a reward.

"Take her home and make sure she's well compensated. I won't need her services again." With a wave of his hand, Dubshenko turned his back, knowing his orders would be carried out. Bubba always did exactly what he was told, never more and never less. Dubshenko liked that. A man with no ambition was a man easily led.

"Now, I think I'll have a little fun."

Picking up his phone, he started dialing.

Chapter Twenty-Nine

"I don't suppose it's safe to go by my house and pick up some things?" Jinx's half-hearted question had Remy wince. Crap. When they'd first taken off, he'd been too concerned with getting her out of New Orleans and keeping her safe. Once they were on the road, hiding from Dubshenko's goons, he'd forgotten to tell her about her house.

"About that. Jinx, I'm sorry."

"What?" She'd been slumped down in the seat of the car, but straightened at his words. "My house?"

"The night we left, it burned to the ground." At her sigh, he faced her.

"Was anybody hurt? My neighbors?" Wasn't that just like her, concerned about others before herself. One more thing he loved about her. And he freely admitted it, he loved her. Wasn't sure how he'd live without her once she was safe and he didn't have a reason to be in her life.

"All your neighbors are fine. We know Dubshenko did it, we just haven't been able to prove it yet."

"There's nothing left, is there?"

"I'm sorry, babe." What else could he say?

Comforting words wouldn't bring back her home, or the cherished memories it contained. It broke his heart to see her so desolate, so hopeless.

"It's not your fault. Damn Dubshenko. He's taken everything away from me. For what? We don't even know what's on the cell phone Carlo hid."

"Maybe I should call Captain Hilliard, and get the ball rolling on that." Remy reached into his car's console and picked up the cell phone they'd retrieved at the park, still wrapped in plastic.

"Should we check it out ourselves, Remy? I'm sorry, but I don't know who to trust at this point." She stared up at him, gently touching his cheek. "Besides you. I trust you with my life."

Remy's heart swelled at her words, hope burgeoning inside. Maybe they'd have a shot once the smoke cleared and life returned to normal. Or as normal as it could for a cop and a former grifter.

"Thank you for your trust, babe. I promise you'll never regret it." He hated what he was about to do, but lives depended on finding Carlo's information and getting it into the right hands. Unwrapping the plastic from the cell phone, he powered it on. Barely five percent power, but it turned on. He scrolled through it, leaning toward Jinx so she could see what he saw.

Nothing in the contacts that was unusual. No incriminating e-mails. Calendar had nothing. Pictures, photos, nothing.

"What's that?" Jinx pointed to an icon in the upper corner of the screen. Remy squinted at it.

"Looks like a video icon."

"Well play it, let's see if there's anything there. Although it better not be Carlo and one of his girlfriends.

Uck!"

Remy laughed before tapping the icon. The video played and Dubshenko's voice filled the sedan. The quality wasn't the best, but there was enough there to be admissible in a court of law. Dates, times, meetings, distribution runs.

A second figure, a dark-haired man, came into the frame, but was only visible from behind. Taller than Dubshenko, he was clearly giving the orders and Dubshenko just as clearly wasn't happy about it. Remy hit pause and stared out the windshield. Who was the other man?

"Is it enough, Remy, to put Dubshenko behind bars?"

"It's a damn good start." He tapped the button to continue playing, but the phone's screen went black and abruptly cut off.

"We need to get this charged and see the entire thing."

"Okay, I've got to ask." Jinx toyed with a piece of her red hair, and once again Remy wished it was back to its natural color. "Did you recognize the man with Dubshenko?"

"He's familiar. It's like I've seen him, but I can't place the voice. Unfortunately, we didn't get to see his face—yet. We'll get the phone charged and watch the rest of the video. If we're lucky, Carlo got a shot of his face and we'll know who Dubshenko's boss is, who's really running the New Orleans syndicate."

Remy turned on the ignition and pulled the car out of the parking garage they'd been hiding in, and drove out onto the street. "First thing, we need to get hold of Captain Hilliard. Let him know that somebody else is behind Dubshenko's reign of terror."

Jinx's expression didn't change, she just twirled that piece of hair around her fingertip, her eyes had a far-away look in them. "There is something so familiar about that other man. Where do I know him from? I swear I've seen him before."

Remy squeezed her hand, before raising it to his lips and placing a soft kiss on her palm. "We'll figure it out together, sweetheart. In the meantime, here, hold onto this." He picked up the phone and tossed it to her and she caught it.

"You went to a lot of trouble to get that, so keep it safe until we get it charged and see the rest of that tape."

"Carlo did well, didn't he?"

"Yeah, he got some pretty damning stuff there. He did well."

"Knowing my brother, this isn't the only evidence he's piled up against Dubshenko. He will have more."

Remy drove toward the outskirts of the city, thankful Dubshenko's men hadn't caught them yet. He wished he could call Max to find out about the downed cop, and make sure that Max himself was okay. Leaving him behind with gunfire around them left a cold ache in his gut. Max was his big brother and he loved him dearly, couldn't stomach the thought Dubshenko might take his revenge against Remy out on his brother. Though why not, Dubshenko was a sociopath without feelings or remorse.

"He's okay, Remy."

"What?"

"Your brother. I'm sure he's okay. They stopped shooting before we got to the car, and he was fine." She paused a second. "Do you want to call him, make sure he's okay?"

251

More than anything in the world, he thought. "No, it's okay. I need to call Cap though. We need to get this phone into a chain of custody, or it will be useless against Dubshenko."

"Remy?"

"What, babe?"

"Do you think Carlo's still alive?" Jinx's voice broke at the end of her question, and he wanted nothing more than to pull over and snatch her into his arms, give her the comfort she needed. Instead, he kept driving, eyes peeled in the rearview for a tail.

"Yes, I think he's still alive. I've thought about it and Dubshenko's men are spread too thin. They've been looking for us, sure, but honestly I'd expected to see a whole lot more men than we've encountered so far. He's got to have a good chunk of his force out looking for Carlo, too. It only makes sense."

Jinx took a shuddering breath and nodded, hugging her knees up to her chest. "He has to be alive, Remy. He has to."

Remy pulled into a convenience store parking lot, having spotted a payphone attached to the wall. Fingers crossed it worked. "Wait here, I'm going to call Cap."

"How about I get us some coffee? I think it's going to be a long night."

"Good idea." He pulled a twenty out of his pocket and handed it to Jinx. She climbed out of the car and headed inside and he walked to the phone. Bingo! Dial tone. Within seconds, Captain Hilliard was on the line.

"Remy, where the hell are you?"

"We're in New Orleans."

"I know that, idiot. I talked to your brother. Where the hell do you get off pulling two of my guys into this mess without getting my okay first?"

Remy sighed." Cap, you'd have given permission. I trust them both. How is Jennings? He caught a bullet right before we ran."

"He'll be fine. Through-and-through. Lost a lot of blood, but not life-threatening. Max said you found something."

Remy looked around. Jinx hadn't come out yet, but it had only been a couple of minutes. She was probably okay. "Carlo left Jinx a clue about where he'd hidden something."

"Jinx. Who the hell is Jinx?" Hilliard barked.

"Sorry, Jennifer Marucci. Jinx is the nickname her brother calls her. Anyway, we found a cell phone with a video on it."

"I know you watched it. What's on there?"

"Dubshenko. Lots of names, dates, shipping routes. Enough to send his ass to prison for the rest of his sorry life." Remy couldn't hide the satisfaction in his voice. He'd wanted to put the low-life drug lord away for a very long time. Looked like he might finally get his wish.

"Oh, man, that is the best news I've had all damn day." Captain Hilliard sounded almost as happy as Remy felt. He probably wanted Dubshenko's worthless hide beneath the prison.

"Something else, Cap. There's another guy in the video. It's obvious he's giving the orders, and Dubshenko's not happy about being told what to do. I didn't recognize him and the phone's charge went dead, so we haven't seen the whole thing yet. What do you want to do?

Silence filled the phone line, only the sound of papers shuffling heard. Remy waited, trying desperately to be patient, his eyes now glued to the store's doorway. *Where was Jinx?* She should have been out by now, she'd just gone for coffee.

Finally, the door opened and Jinx emerged, holding the door open with her hip, both hands containing a coffee cup. She grinned at him, walking past him toward the car. His gaze zeroed in on her ass, encased in stretchy black fabric. Somehow, he promised himself, before this night was through he planned to have that fine thing in his hands.

"Remy, you still there?" Hilliard questioned.

"I'm here, Cap." Focus, man, let's get this over with.

"Dubshenko's got his men crawling the streets big time tonight. You got a safe place to hole up until morning? I'm gonna call in a buddy with the FBI, he's a specialist at data retrieval. Think you can keep the phone safe until morning?"

"Might be best, Cap. You ever figure out who Dubshenko's got on the payroll?" Remy hated dirty cops, they were the lowest of the low. Stinking rat bastards, every one of them.

"We caught one, but I'm convinced we've got one more. That's why I don't want you coming in tonight. One more piece of evidence against him, and he's toast, and we should have that before morning."

"Okay, I've got a place in mind for overnight. I'll be in touch."

"Remy, be careful. We can't afford to lose you."

Remy's chest filled with warmth at his captain's words. The bigger-than-life man was a good friend and a father-figure, second only to his actual father in men he respected, so his words meant the world.

"See you tomorrow, Cap."

He climbed behind the wheel and Jinx handed him his coffee with a tentative smile. Took a swallow. For midday coffee it wasn't too bad.

"Thanks."

"Any decision on what we do with the video?"

"Captain is calling in a friend with the FBI who's a specialist on data retrieval, should be able to get anything and everything off the phone. We just have to hold onto it until tomorrow."

"Good idea, about calling in the FBI. But that still leaves the reset of today and tonight to get through."

"Right, plus Cap said Dubshenko's got all his guys out searching, so we're going to hole up and stay put until morning. I know a place that should be safe."

He slid his cup into the holder between the seats, next to hers. Without thinking about it, he leaned forward brushing his lips against hers. Her tentative response was all the encouragement he needed. His hand slid behind her neck, tangling in the red curls, pulling her closer into the kiss. Sliding his tongue along her bottom lip in a caress, she willingly opened to him. Velvety soft, her lips parted, gaining him access to the sweetness within. Her tongue tangled with his as the kiss deepened, a sensual battle, not for dominance, but for pleasure alone. His teeth caught her bottom lip between his as he broke free, giving her a quick nip before releasing her. She was breathless, but so was he.

"Let's go." Her shaky voice was all the confirmation he needed. Giving thanks with every ounce of his being that she wanted him helped, since he was nearly exploding with pent up desire for her.

They drove until they reached the French Quarter, parking in the general parking by the brewery. It was a bit of a walk, but with a little fancy footwork and dodging down side streets, they finally made it to his friend Theresa's shop. It was closed, since Max wasn't letting his woman out of his site until everything with Dubshenko was settled. Remy knew Theresa wouldn't have a problem with him using her apartment above the shop. Heck, he'd slept there dozens of times over the years. She was his best friend, and they had an unbreakable bond forged through pain that nothing could ever break.

One problem, though he had a key to her place, his keys were sitting on his dresser at home. As much as he hated it, he started looking around for a rock. Time for a little smash and enter.

"Wait." Jinx pulled a piece of wire from one of the planters on the tiny patio. She unbent it and then did something to the end of it. "Keep your eyes out for the coppers." She laughed, patted his chest with one hand and knelt down in front of the lock.

He watched her, mesmerized at the agility and deftness of her touch. With a flick of her wrist, the back door swung open.

"I didn't see anything, but thanks, sweetheart. I really didn't want to have to replace her window."

Once inside, they kept the lights off and moved straight to the staircase leading upstairs. Above her New Age shop, Theresa still maintained the apartment, even though she lived with Max. They were engaged and Remy couldn't be happier that his brother found the love of his life with his best friend. It had been a rocky road, but in the end they'd made it, and he was convinced they'd make it through the long haul.

The ringing of the phone startled him, and he stared

at it. Jinx grasped his hand. On the fourth ring the answering machine beside it picked up. Leave it to Theresa to have an old-fashioned answering machine, rather than voice mail. But then again, that was Theresa.

"Remy, if you're there, you should be okay for the night. There's plenty of food in the fridge downstairs. I have a feeling everything's coming to a head tomorrow, so be prepared and be ready. Love you."

The call ended and Remy relaxed. If Theresa said everything would be okay, then it would be. Gifted with psychic abilities from a trauma in her teenage years, when her gift spoke it was rarely wrong. She'd even been instrumental in finding a missing teenager, the case that she'd worked on with Max, finally getting through his bullheadedness and winning his love.

"You hungry? I can go down and get us something."

Jinx shook her head. "Oh, wait." Reaching into her pocket, she laughingly pulled out a cell phone charger. "I picked this up at the store when I got the coffee. It's a universal one, so it should work on Carlo's phone."

"Picked it up?" He quirked his brow.

She slapped his arm. "Paid for it, not stole it. You don't have any change, by the way."

He handed her the phone and she plugged it into the outlet. "I'd really like a shower, if your friend wouldn't mind. I'm still feeling dirty after falling down in the park. Ugh."

"Theresa's probably got something here you can wear. If not, I'll run downstairs to her shop. It's all New Age stuff, but she has a few touristy things, including shirts and stuff."

She smiled and just like that he wanted her. "Want some company for that shower, sweetheart?" *Say yes.*

"Yes." Without hesitation, no wavering.

Remy reached for her and she went willingly into his arms. He placed his fingers under her chin, lifted her face and touched his lips to hers in a light kiss. Her lips were velvety soft beneath his. With a controlled effort, he kept the kiss gentle, soft and full of promise. A bare brushing of lips, filled with sweetness. Pulling back, he stared deep into her eyes. His thumb rubbed a circle against her cheek, his lips only an inch from hers.

"Remy?"

His finger landed against the mouth he'd just kissed, stopping her words. Heat roared through him at the thought of his hands touching more than her mouth. Touching everywhere. Closing the short distance between them, he covered her mouth with his, unable to resist the pull of the siren standing before him. His mouth covered hers, diving into her moist depths. No longer the tender, gentle kiss of moments before. Instead, he ravished her lips demanding a response, and she opened for him like a flower blossoming. He brought their bodies together, wishing they were already in the shower together, skin on skin. Naked, so her softness played against him, without the layers of clothing separating them. He needed to feel the hard peaks of her nipples against his chest, to rub against the soft curve of her belly. He broke off the kiss and pulled back, gazing into her eyes. "Jinx…"

Her arms slid around his waist, keeping their lower bodies pressed firmly against one another. "No promises. I want this, too." Remy knew this might be the only time he could show her what she meant to him.

He peeled her top off over her head, and it fell to the floor. *Merde*, but he'd forgotten the sexy mini-corset she'd worn before, showcasing the curves and valleys, the hidden lushness of her body, but he wanted her out of it, out of all her clothing. The night they made love in the fishing cabin, it had been nearly dark. He'd memorized her by feel, but today he could look at every glorious inch of her.

One arm slid beneath her knees and lifted her in his embrace. With ease, he carried her into the bathroom, settling her gently on her feet, then turned and started the water. He adjusted the temperature until it was hot enough, but not too hot. He didn't want to burn her delicate skin.

With infinite care, he undid the first hook on her mini-corset. He worked his way down, and his long fingers brushed against the pale perfection peeking through with each fastener undone. The fullness of her breasts teased him with glimpses of her pink nipples. When the final hook released, he peeled back the lacy fabric to expose his prize, leaving her bare from the waist up. Jinx gave a shuddered breath before doing a little shimmy-type movement, and the garment fell from her shoulders onto the counter behind her.

Impatient now, he yanked his shirt over his head, only to feel another set of hands fumbling with the button of his jeans. He froze, afraid to move, anxious to feel her hands on him anywhere. Everywhere.

He looked down at her bared breasts, a soft, sexy sound coming from deep in his throat. With a light caress, he hooked his thumbs in the waist of her pants, dragging down both pants and panties together, before dropping to his knees. He tugged them down until they were around her ankles. Jinx placed a hand on his shoulder for balance, as she stepped out of them. Remy looked up and met her shining blue eyes smoldering with passion and something—more.

"You should never wear clothes."

Jinx smiled, running her fingertips through his hair, her nails scratching lightly along his scalp. He placed a kiss against her stomach, smiled when she took a shuddering breath. The lovely little pooch of her belly, its softness, fascinated him. So utterly feminine.

She stepped back out of his reach. "I think you're overdressed."

"I need to kiss you." Remy's raspy voice sounded abnormally loud, echoing over the water pounding in the shower. Jinx wrapped her arms around his neck and licked her lips in silent invitation.

"Yes, please."

Remy's lips met hers in a scorching kiss, the gentleness from earlier gone. The kiss deepened and she met his passion with her own. He spun her until her back pressed against the wall, shifting until more of his weight pinned her in place. He loved how hot her skin felt pressed so tightly to his. Shifting his hips, he bumped his thigh against her, demanding entrance.

Jinx spread her legs wider, enough to accommodate him. He broke the kiss and lifted his head enough to stare into her eyes. His hands splayed on her ribcage as he bent his knees, lifting her higher against the wall. Jinx slid her arms around his shoulders, shifted until her legs wrapped around his waist, locking her ankles behind him.

Lowering his head, he found the place at the nape of her neck where it joined the shoulder, trailing kisses along the sensitive flesh. Jinx shuddered in his arms, her breath catching in her throat. One thumb rubbed against the underside of her breast, before circling the areola. She moaned, and it was the most beautiful sound in the world to Remy.

"So beautiful. My precious Jinx."

"Remy, don't stop."

He helped lower her legs back to the floor, desperate to remove the final article of clothing separating them. His hands reached for his zipper when her hands stopped him.

"No, let me."

Jinx slid gracefully to her knees before him. His breath caught in his throat when her fingertips touched the taut skin of his stomach. She slowly eased the zipper lower and lower. He tensed when her hands shoved down the jeans, and his hard length sprang free.

Jinx chuckled. "Commando, huh?"

"Clean underwear hasn't exactly been a top priority, sweetheart." The gravely depths of Remy's voice belied the joking words. He couldn't remember ever wanting anyone as much as he wanted Jinx right now. There was no missing the thick, hard shaft standing free and proud. In a bold move, Jinx's hand encircled his heated flesh and Remy prayed he wouldn't expire right on the spot. Oh, so slowly, she traced him from root to tip and back.

The bathroom filled with steam, sweat dripping into Remy's eyes, and he finally remembered where they were. *Right, shower.*

"Come here, Jinx."

"Busy right now, babe." Jinx leaned forward and swirled her tongue around the crown. His knees threatened to buckle as pleasure roared through him.

"Jinx, wait."

"No more waiting." The tip of her tongue circled the

mushroom head, dipping into the little hollow beneath the tip. Remy nearly swallowed his tongue. The only sounds emitted from his mouth were strangled groans. When she wrapped her hand around the base of his shaft and slid the first few inches into the hot moist depths of her mouth, he nearly exploded on the spot.

She gave a hum of appreciation, and Remy threw his head back lost in sensations. His hands clawed behind him, seeking purchase, something to grab hold of and brace against. Jinx was relentless, nipping and licking and sucking until he closed his eyes, fighting not to lose himself to the ecstasy her touch rocketed through him.

No, he needed to make sure she was taken care of first. From this day, this moment forward, she always came first. Not just sexually, although he'd make sure she never went unsatisfied, but he pledged to give her the happiness she richly deserved.

"You've gotta stop, baby, or I'm going to explode."

"Good, since that's my plan, flat-foot." Remy attempted to smile at the nickname, but knew it probably looked more like a grimace. With gentle care, he pushed Jinx back, pulling free of her oh-so-talented mouth. It hurt, but it was a good hurt. Next time, he promised himself he'd let her finish, but right now he wanted nothing more than to be buried deep within her heat, in the most intimate bond possible.

He walked behind her, stepping into the shower, his body curled around hers, and let the hot water slide against his skin. Her delighted sounds at the luxury of not just running water but hot water sent a spiraling warmth curling like a well-fed kitten in Remy's chest. He grabbed the bottle of liquid soap sitting on the little cutout niche beside the folded washcloth. Delightfully wicked thoughts raced through his mind while he squirted the liquid soap onto the cloth.

Gently, he ran it over her shoulders and down one arm, soaping her skin all the way to her fingertips. He gave the same dedicated care and attention to the other side.

Jinx's head lolled back as he ran the cloth across her clavicles and down the center of her chest. Lifting one breast with his free hand, he plied the washcloth around the outside and the undersurface, paying special attention to the nipple area. The shower was steamy, the glass fogged from the heat, but Remy paid no attention to anything but the goddess in human form standing before him.

He gave the same loving attention to the opposite breast, again stroking and coaxing the nipple to a distended peek. Lowering his head, he laved his tongue across the tight nubbin of her right breast, and smiled at her sharply inhaled breath. *So good.*

The cloth eased along her stomach, loving the inward curve of her waist, flaring out to generous hips. Hips he had been aching to dig his fingers into, so he did. Pounding into her while he grasped her close—plunging deep as he rocked within her. Oh yes, that was at the top of his to-do list, right after he finished giving her a shower she'd never forget.

Dropping to his knees in the cramped small space, he continued his soapy journey, down over her thighs, stopped to drop a kiss on the dimple of one knee. He lovingly paid special attention to her feet, knowing they were probably sore from all the hiking she'd endured over the last couple of days. She'd never complained— well, hardly ever.

Jinx squirmed in his hold when he worked his way back upward, caressing her calves and thighs, edging ever so slowly toward the one area he'd saved for last.

"Remy, please." Oh, he loved that pleading tone in her voice, loved knowing she was close to the brink and he'd been the one to bring her there.

"Shh, I'm busy now." A planted kiss against her hip bone, and her hands were clawing at the shower walls. Another kiss against the top of her pelvic bone, a bare brush of lips, and her body pressed forward seeking more.

She mewled his name and the corner of his mouth quirked up. *Almost there.* He dampened the washcloth under the shower spray, and finally beginning rubbing slow circles at the juncture of her thighs.

"Ahhh!"

"Go ahead, sweetheart. I want to hear you scream," Remy whispered, the cloth now forgotten, dropped to the floor as his fingers trailed through her bare folds. He felt the wetness between her thighs, and felt ten feet tall knowing it wasn't from the water, but tangible evidence of her desire.

"Now, please, please."

Remy's groin tightened with every cry she uttered, with each clenching of her muscles. She was close, and he eased one finger deep inside, slid back out, and plunged in again. He wanted to give her this—needed to bring her pleasure.

When he pulled his finger out, he added a second one on the next inward thrust. Jinx's breathing sawed in and out, guttural cries falling from her lips pleading for release. He felt her muscles contracting, squeezing. *Almost, so close.*

Plunging two fingers deep inside, Remy twisted his thumb, rubbing against the bundle of nerves at her clit, round and round in small circles, and Jinx screamed out, her vaginal walls clamping down on his fingers. He continued stroking deeper and deeper, giving a little twist when he withdrew them, only to send them deep again. He pressed his face against her stomach, holding her steady as her body rocked with the orgasm he'd given her, gentling her with kisses and caresses as she wound her way down from the heights of pleasure.

Grabbing up the forgotten washcloth, he made quick work of cleaning her and did a quick personal wash down, before shutting off the water. He wrapped a towel around his hips, and grabbed another, lovingly drying every inch of her body, just like his fantasy at the motel the first night they'd spent together. Her gaze was drowsy, but filled with emotion. His heart swelled, but Remy didn't want to read more into what he saw there, not without the words. He knew his own feelings, knew he'd found the one woman he wanted to spend eternity with, but realized they'd only know each other such a short time. *Would that matter to her?*

Biting back the words felt like a punch to the gut, but he'd wait. When Dubshenko had been dealt with, he'd court her. Bring her roses and chocolates, take her to dinner. Let her meet *maman*.

He led her to the bed, covered in a deep purple velvet bedspread. He turned down the bedding, and helped her slide beneath the sheets. He stood looking down at her, this woman who'd come to mean more to him than his next breath.

"Aren't you coming to bed?"

"I'll be right there."

"Okay." She snugged down deeper, and he pulled the bedspread up lovingly tucking its warmth around her. Then he stood looking down at her, knew the moment she fell asleep.

He felt a twinge of guilt at what he was about to do, but squashed it down. Deception and lies had been a part of this investigation from the beginning, right down to her name. Once he made the next call, plans would be put into action which couldn't be stopped. He just prayed she'd forgive him.

Walking to the living room, he pulled out the final burner phone. If he did this, he could lose her. If he didn't, she could die.

He didn't have a choice. With a ragged sigh, he began dialing.

Chapter Thirty

Another fabulous press opportunity wasted while he twiddled his thumbs. His unworthy political opponent was late. Again. These debates had been scheduled months in advance. Didn't he have a blasted social secretary to remind him about the important stuff? He'd shown up on time. Then again, being elected Lieutenant Governor of Louisiana was a major coup in his political journey.

He had big plans and he didn't plan on wasting any more time in this backward state than he had to. He belonged on the national platform, not dealing with crawdads and curfews.

It wouldn't be much longer, though. This special election was in the bag, bought and paid for by others who wanted him in this potentially key position. That was the lovely thing about political favors. It was a buy-now, pay-later scenario. Like a chess game, it was all skill and timing.

The pieces were positioned on the board, and he'd played them with precision and finesse. Another two moves and he'd be sitting in the Governor's mansion. He wasn't worried about the necks he stepped on along the way. The ends justified the means, and the ends in this case came with an oval office and unlimited global power.

The flash of cameras to his right heralded the arrival of his rival.

What an ass! Did he really think there was a bat's chance in hell he'd be elected? He might put on the airs and polish of gentility, but this backwater bayou nobody wasn't a match for him.

Digging up dirt was a time-honored tool of the trade, and when you couldn't find anything—which unfortunately he hadn't—well, then you bend the truth just enough to make a palatable lie. People were sheep, easily led and wanting to believe the salacious rather than truth. The juicier the gossip the more the tabloids, and thus the gullible, ate it up. They were ravenous for more.

It was time to play dirty.

Pulling out his personal mini-tablet, he pulled up his e-mail account that was carefully hidden beneath layers upon layers of falsified trails. Only the finest hackers in the world would be able to break into its encrypted contents, and only if they knew where to look.

With the press of one button—send—the demise of a candidacy began.

Humming *Hail to the Chief*, he strode forward to take his place behind the podium. Time to give the people what they wanted.

# # # # #

"Is everything in place?"

"For the hundredth time, stop worrying. The meeting is all set."

"Wasn't Branson suspicious when you called instead

of me? Carlo paced the spacious hotel room floor. Carpenter had rented out an entire suite in downtown New Orleans. Stated the best place to hide was in plain sight. They'd never look for them in the exclusive five-star hotel. Hell, he was probably right, but Carlo's gut was coiled tighter than the trigger on a brand new pistol.

"The man comes with food." Isabella stepped back from the door. She'd constantly peered through the peep hole ever since they'd called in the room service order.

"Both of you in the other room." Carpenter barked. "I'll get it."

The closing of the door had all three converging on the wheeled cart. They hadn't stopped the entire drive from South Texas to New Orleans, other than for gas.

"Give me that!" Isabella snatched the cheeseburger platter right out of Carlo's hand. She'd taken to treating him like a big brother, most of the wariness and fear now absent.

"Hey, that was mine." He groused, but it was half-hearted at best. The girl could stand to put on a few pounds, she was pretty much skin and bones. Spying the rib eye steak and loaded baked potato on another plate he raised a brow at Carpenter, who waved his hand at it. Carlo snatched up the plate and silverware before he changed his mind, striding toward the coffee table. He eyed Isabella drag a french fry through a puddle of ketchup and felt a momentary twinge. Burger and fries—his kind of comfort food. But then again, a tender, juicy steak with all the fixin's wasn't a bad second choice.

Carpenter plopped down sodas next to each of their plates, and Carlo mumbled his thanks, his mouth full. Isabella never stopped shoveling food in. If she didn't slow down, Carlo thought, she might choke.

"I had a friend contact Branson before I called, and explain our dilemma, so he wasn't surprised at my contact. By the way, they uncovered the rat in his department. Branson's clean."

Well, that took one worry off Carlo's list. Branson had never out and out given him a reason to doubt him, but then again, he'd never exactly been the most forthcoming with info or intelligence, either, when it would have helped. Still, he was glad he wasn't on Dubshenko's payroll, though he doubted he'd ever become best buddies with the guy.

"Where's the meeting?"

Carpenter took a sip of his coffee before answering. "The DEA is coordinating with the FBI and the local authorities to retrieve the information you've got. Pretty smart hiding most of it around the city."

"Well, Dubshenko didn't suspect me until this last SNAFU." He glanced over toward Isabella, oblivious to everything except the burger she was shoveling into her mouth. "I never really had enough concrete evidence until I stumbled upon him meeting with…" He broke off abruptly, his eyes shifting to Isabella.

Carpenter nodded, understanding the unspoken words. They wouldn't say much in front of Isabella. They trusted her, but she was still a kid and might unknowingly say something to her father once she was returned. Better safe than sorry.

"I'm worried about Jinx though. I left her a coded message only she'd understand on her voice mail. If she's even got it. N.O.P.D. has a cop watching her."

"Got a name?"

"Yeah, Remy Lamoreaux. I haven't had time to check him out, but what little I know about him, he's a pretty good cop."

Carpenter pulled out his phone and began typing. Within seconds, he sent the text and smiled. "Give me five minutes and we'll know everything there is to know about Remy Lamoreaux."

"Your guy's that good?" Carlo was impressed. Whenever he needed info, the DEA pencil pushers took forever.

"She's the best." There was an undercurrent of something in Carpenter's voice, but Carlo didn't have time to try and puzzle it out. They needed to get Isabella back to her father, and Vladimir Dubshenko and his partner behind bars.

They ate in companionable silence for several minutes when there was a beep on Carpenter's phone. He answered, listened for several minutes, then hung up.

"Lamoreaux's clean. Good cop, trusted by fellow officers and a favorite of the division's captain. Whole family seems to be squeaky. Brother's a former cop, now a P.I. Future sister-in-law runs one of those woo-woo shops in the French Quarter. She's a supposed psychic, and apparently a pretty good one. Worked with the cops on several cases. Has a good track record. Father is retired military. Mother worked as a nurse until she quit to travel with their father."

"That's good. So Jinx should be safe for now."

A knock on the door interrupted them. Carpenter pulled out his Glock and Carlo retrieved his Smith and Wesson. He motioned for Isabella to stay behind him, as Carlo opened the door just enough to talk to the person outside.

After a few words were exchanged, the door swung open and Branson walked inside. Carlo huffed, but eased down on his weapon. Carpenter said Branson had checked out.

"Marucci, where the hell have you been?" Branson marched straight up to him, and surprised the hell out of him when he pulled him forward, slapping him on the back. *What. The. Hell?*

"I believe the FBI and N.O.P.D updated you on the information Mr. Marucci uncovered with regard to Dubshenko?" Carpenter shoved the Glock back into his waistband, and picked up his salad. Carlo almost snorted at the look of surprise on Branson's lined face. His brows shot up beneath the wire-rimmed glasses, and not for the first time Carlo thought he looked like a bookworm instead of a man capable of running the entire southeastern division of the DEA.

"Besides, I called you and set up this little meeting, didn't I?" Carpenter shoved a forkful of salad into his mouth, and Branson was speechless. Carlo raised a hand across his mouth to hide the smile threatening to break free.

"That's another thing. Who the hell are you? I got a call to deal with you directly, but nobody gave me any information. They wouldn't even tell me your name." Branson stood with his hands on hips, trying to be intimidating and failing miserably. He might be great behind a desk, but in the field he was a total washout.

"Didn't I introduce myself? Names Carpenter." Another bite of salad slid between his lips.

"Carpenter?" It took a full minute before Carlo saw the light bulb, ah-ha moment flash across Branson's face. "Samuel Carpenter?"

"Yep."

"How'd you get involved in this? You're not DEA

anymore." Branson's chest jutted out like a banty rooster, and Carpenter rolled his eyes. Carlo didn't blame him. Branson always seemed to think of himself as being above everyone, which endeared him to no one.

"Not important. What is important is this— Dubshenko is going down, and it's happening soon, maybe in the next twenty-four hours. You can either be in or out."

Branson glared at Carpenter before turning to Carlo. Before he opened his mouth, he spotted Isabella, arms wrapped around her middle standing right behind Carlo.

"Who's she?"

"She's part of the key to bringing down Vladimir Dubshenko. The final straw that breaks the camel's back. Meet Isabella Sokolov." Branson's eyes rounded behind his wire rims, so big the whites shone all the way around.

"Sokolov? As in—"

"Oh, yeah." Carlo chimed in. "That Sokolov."

He could practically see the gears turning in his brain. Branson might be a wimpy little bugger, but he had a brilliant mind. He'd connect the dots without any explanation.

Branson puffed out his chest. "Let's all sit. Finish your meals. We've got some planning to do."

"We know. That's why we called you."

Chapter Thirty-One

Jinx snuggled closer to the warm body spooned around her back. The strong arm across her middle tightened, and breath stirred the hair beside her ear. *Remy.*

They'd spent the entire day making love, only stopping long enough to grab some food from Theresa's stocked kitchen. When she'd remarked on all the fresh produce, Remy laughed and said Theresa probably knew they'd show up there, and didn't want them to starve.

"Morning, sweetheart." His raspy greeting was accompanied by his lips nuzzling against her nape, and she tilted her head giving him greater access. The arm draped across her shifted, and his hand cupped her breast. This was perfect. She'd give anything to wake up like this every morning for the rest of her life.

"Hi." Wow, was that throaty growl her voice?

"Yes, good morning." Jinx yelped, and Remy's arm across her tightened. The voice had come from the end of the bed, though she didn't need to look to recognize it. Dubshenko's massive bodyguard lounged against the wall with his arm across his enormous chest, a SIG Sauer resting easily in his right hand. The perpetual scowl from his scarring had her stomach pitching and heaving, and she slammed her lips closed against the instinct to heave.

"Mr. Dubshenko would like to see you—both." Her skin crawled as his gaze raked her from the top of her head to her toes, pausing to linger on her exposed breasts. Remy yanked the sheet up, thankfully covering her, and glowered at the giant.

"We're not going anywhere."

"Detective, I believe you and the lovely Ms. Marucci will accompany us," he motioned with the gun to the three other men positioned in the doorway, "or your brother and his lovely fiancee will take your place. Trust me, you don't want their fate in the hands of Mr. Dubshenko. He's not a happy man when he doesn't get what he wants."

Remy flopped over onto his back rubbing a hand across his face, and Jinx felt bereft when his arms were no longer embracing her. There was no way to get out of this room, not with four armed men and only one door, which they were currently blocking.

Come on, Jinx, think. What would Pop-Pop do?

Her eyes darted around the cramped bedroom, searching for answers. Hands gripped the sheet tight when she spotted the cell phone. They'd remembered to plug it in yesterday in between their bouts of lovemaking, but something didn't look right.

She swung around to Remy, and he shrugged and kept his mouth shut. *The louse!* Didn't he trust her at all? That wasn't Carlo's phone in the charger. Somehow, during the night he'd switched it for the burner phone he'd carried all day yesterday. Damn him!

Obviously Dubshenko's comrade-in-arms, A.K.A. Mr. Scarface, had followed her gaze because he walked over to the phone, unplugged it from the charger and placed it into the inside pocket of his jacket. He laughed, and the darkness in the sound caused the little hairs along her arms to stand on end.

"Thank you, Ms. Marucci. Mr. Dubshenko will be very happy to have this. Of course, he'd be happier if he had Carlo as well, but this will suffice. For now."

Jinx's heartbeat tripped over in her chest, beating faster at his words. Dubshenko didn't have Carlo! If he was still searching for him, that meant he wasn't dead. She felt the imperceptible stiffening of Remy's body beside hers, and she tugged the sheet tighter and higher.

"Get dressed, now. Mr. Dubshenko is waiting." The muscular giant nudged a pile of clothing with his foot, a look of distaste crossing his face. *What, he didn't like people making love on possibly their last night alive? Well, too stinking bad.*

"Wait in the hall while she dresses," Remy barked, his face hard, his tone intractable.

"You don't give the orders here, Detective Lamoreaux."

"How will Vladimir feel if he knows you've seen her naked? I'm pretty sure he plans to keep her all to himself, and from what I've heard he doesn't share." Remy flipped back his portion of the cover, and stood tall and nude, unashamed before the gun-wielding mobsters. "She hasn't done anything to earn your disrespect. Wait outside the door and let her dress. We're coming with you—it's not like we have any choice."

Remy bent and picked up the clothing off the floor, tossing Jinx the wrinkled shirt and pants she'd worn the previous day. Crap. She'd planned on raiding Theresa's closet and finding something fresh to wear, but beggars can't be choosers, at least not while a pistol is pointed at you.

"Um, can I use the bathroom?"

The three men had left the room, leaving only Dubshenko's bodyguard still remaining, though she knew the others could be back inside in a heartbeat. There was no way out except to comply with his demands.

Remy had dragged on his jeans while she hadn't been looking, and now yanked on his shirt, ignoring the fact it was inside out. He sat on the edge of the bed and slid his feet into his runners, and just like that he was ready to leave. How like a man, she thought.

"I'm sorry, but I've got to pee."

"Go, but make it fast. Take too long and…" The gun pointed at Remy's head centered between his eyes. Yeah, she got the message. Yanking the sheet from the bed, she wrapped it around her nakedness. She fisted the clothes in her hand and with the dignity of queen, strode across the floor to the bathroom. The same bathroom where she and Remy shared intimate moments. Had it been only yesterday?

She raced through taking care of her personal business, and tugged on her clothes. It didn't matter how she looked, she had a pretty good idea how things would end. Bayou bait.

In less than ten minutes she'd gone from secure and safe within Remy's arms, to huddled in the back seat of an SUV headed toward a meeting with the man who, when all was said and done, would end her life.

Yep, today totally sucked.

# # # # #

Dubshenko didn't even try to hide his smile as the naked dark-haired girl presented the tray with his breakfast. This day kept getting better and better. After a night of mindless sex with the stunning creole beauty, he'd gotten word lights were seen in the shop above Theresa Lamoreuax's French Quarter shop.

He'd had the place watched, knowing instinctively the good detective would figure it was a safe hiding place. After all, his future sister-in-law's place had already been searched when he and Jennifer first disappeared. Other than bugging the phones, which they had done, why keep an eye on a place where nobody lived anymore?

No one could ever accuse Dubshenko of being stupid. He was a master manipulator, and looked at life like a chess match. Always stay at least three moves ahead of your competition. Remy Lamoureaux had become his adversary long before he'd interfered in the life of Jennifer Marucci. But he'd loved the cat and mouse nature of their encounters. Enjoyed making the good detective look the fool at every turn.

He'd made a mistake, though. Underestimated the good detective's white knight impulse to protect the damsel in distress. Taking a sip of his chicory coffee, he sighed. This was one of the many things he loved about being in a position of power. All the finer things in life were available at a snap of his fingers, or for the right price. For him, the price was always right. People knew that or people disappeared, and somebody else took their place who realized the foolishness of crossing him. No one did it more than once.

He'd sent Bubba to retrieve Remy and the lovely Jennifer. While he'd admired the chase they'd given him, they should have known they couldn't win. He was powerful, and when his candidate won the upcoming election, his power base would increase exponentially.

The metal doors of the warehouse slid open with hardly a sound, and two black SUV's pulled into the empty bay. Excellent, his quarry was within his grasp. He remained seated. Make them come to him. Soon all the players on the chessboard would be in place, and the game finally concluded. He so looked forward to tipping the final piece, proclaiming "checkmate" and claiming his prize.

Remy alighted from the vehicle first, and reached inside to help Jennifer out. Ah, ever the gentleman, Dubshenko thought. He truly is the white knight. Too bad he will not win the fair maiden. Bubba and his elite crew stood beside the couple, weapons drawn. After all, you can never be too careful around the police, even when they are unarmed.

Without hesitation, Remy marched forward, Jennifer's hand wrapped around his arm. Dubshenko noted the tremble in her fingers as they gripped the other man, and a moue of distaste crossed his mouth before he let all emotions drain away. It wouldn't do to tip his hand too soon.

He could play the gentleman, show Jennifer the good detective wasn't the only one with perfect manners. "Remy, Jennifer, good to see you." He waved a hand at the other seats at the table beside him. "Won't you join me for some coffee? It's an excellent chicory blend. There's also croissants and rich butter."

"No, thanks." Remy's tone was blunt. "Let's get this over with."

"Hey, speak for yourself. I'm hungry." Jennifer

moved around the table, sitting in the chair across from where Dubshenko sat. "I'd love some coffee."

"Of course, my dear." Dubshenko snapped his fingers, and the naked girl nobody had noticed cowering in the corner ran over and began filling the coffee cups.

"What the…" Jennifer broke off and sat silent, which was good. Dubshenko smiled at her. She was a quick learner. That might help her in the short term. How he wished he could keep her. He frowned though, when he finally noticed her hair."

"What have you done to yourself?"

"What?"

"Your lovely hair. This," he gestured toward the unruly hair piled atop her head, "is an abomination." Something would have to be done. Her buyer had been very specific, long blonde hair. This reddish atrocity would negate the sale.

"It was the best I could do under the circumstances. You try coming up with a disguise while running for your life. Let's see how you look." She flung herself back in the chair, coffee cup raised to her lips.

"Still insubordinate, I see. We'll fix that." Dubshenko loved seeing the slight stiffening of her body as his words sank in. Ah, yes, now she was getting the full picture.

Bubba walked forward and placed the cell phone onto the table beside Dubshenko's coffee cup. "They had this."

"Excellent." He left it on the table without touching it. Watched Remy closely. The man was always so calm, so cool. Let's see him sweat—know that his life was about to end.

"It's been a good game, Remy. Unfortunately, you

lose. I have won. I told you in the beginning you could not best me."

Remy reached for the cup of coffee the girl had filled, and took a sip. "Dubshenko, you haven't won anything. Maybe I won't be the one to take you down, but someone will. Captain Hilliard, Carlo. Could even be Max. But your days running New Orleans are over."

"Without this," he touched the phone with one fingertip, "the authorities have nothing."

Remy shook his head and took another sip of his coffee, not saying a word. *Damn it, why wasn't he breaking?* Dubshenko had waited months to have him like this, at his mercy. The cop wasn't playing the game by the rules.

"Admit it, detective, without Carlo's so-called evidence, which I'm assured wouldn't stand up in a court of law since it was obtained illegally, what do you have? Nothing."

A beep sounded from the front of the warehouse, and Dubshenko's face lit with another smile. Ah, yes, the rest of the party was here. Time to get the show on the road.

"My dear, Jennifer, I hope you'll excuse me. I have a bit of business to attend to, and then we'll finish this conversation." Taking her hand, he lifted it brushing a kiss across the back. Yes, indeed, they'd finish what they'd started, and then she'd be leaving the country, never to return. She'd probably not enjoy her future accommodations, but, then again, business was business, and she'd bring him a small fortune.

The doors slid open and a black Lexus drove inside, its tinted windows obscuring the occupant. Right on time. He did love punctuality. He left Bubba standing guard over his two visitors, and walked toward the newcomer.

The tall, dark-haired man alighted from the driver's side and stretched to his full height. Dubshenko heard Jennifer's gasp of surprise when she recognized their visitor. It didn't matter though. Neither she nor Remy would be telling anyone about Mr. Caine's visit. They wouldn't be around long enough to spill the beans.

"Why the hell did you want to meet in this godforsaken spot, Dubshenko? I've got a press conference in under an hour. The election is in the bag, but appearances still need to be kept up for the paparazzi. People need their 6 p.m. sound bite to feel like they're part of the campaign."

Jonathan Caine looked spotless. The dark, charcoal-gray suit and burgundy, striped tie was the perfect picture of the next Lieutenant Governor.

"Mr. Lieutenant Governor, in a few more days you'll practically be running the state. We'll have very little time to meet then. Besides, I wanted you here to greet the people who've ensured your election." Dubshenko gestured toward Remy and Jennifer, in their rumpled clothing. Remy sat unshaven, and Jennifer's hair looked like a giant ball of fluff on top her head. Together they presented a picture of debauchery, an example of life lived in excess.

"These two? How did they ensure my election?"

"Come, let me show you." Dubshenko led Caine to the small bistro-like table where his prey sat, still sipping coffee and snacking on fine French pastries.

"Mr. Jonathan Caine, this is Detective Remy Lamoreaux of the New Orleans Police Department."

"He's a cop? What the hell is a cop doing mixed up in this, Dubshenko?" Caine narrowed his eyes, staring at

Remy. "Is he on your payroll?"

Dubshenko let out a full-throated laugh at his words. "Remy, on my payroll? Oh, that is rich. No, no, Caine. He's so clean he squeaks. Nobody could bribe this one. But he was instrumental in returning something important. You need to see this."

Dubshenko picked up the cell phone, activated the video app and hit play. Silence filled the air before the small screen filled with Remy's face.

"Hello, Dubshenko. I guess you finally caught us if you're looking at this video. Much as I hate to burst your bubble, old friend, I'm sure if you're watching this you've realized this isn't Carlo's phone." Remy's huge grin on the screen had Dubshenko gaze locking with his in reality. Remy just shrugged and took another sip of coffee. The video continued playing.

"I knew you'd catch up to us at Theresa's place. That's part of the reason I chose it. You're not stupid, I knew you'd have the area staked out. Still, I had enough time to put a few plans into action. The phone you've been searching for, desperate enough to try and kill an innocent woman for, well right now it's in the hands of the FBI."

"No!" Dubshenko's howl of denial echoed through the warehouse. Remy gestured toward him with his cup.

"Keep listening, jackass." Jennifer reached up and swatted Remy on the back of his head.

"Stop antagonizing him."

"I used this burner phone, had Max make a few other calls for me. Wanna know a secret, Vlad? Carlo Marucci, your employee, the one who recorded you and Jonathan Caine conspiring to assassinate the governor following the election—he works for the Drug

Enforcement Administration."

Dubshenko heard Jennifer's indrawn gasp of surprise. So even the traitor's sister hadn't known about his extracurricular activities. *Bastard.*

The video droned on. "You're done for, you son of a bitch! The FBI and DEA now have all the evidence they need to throw you in prison for the rest of your natural life."

Dubshenko drew his arm back, ready to throw the phone across the space. Remy tsk'd from his seat at the table. "You don't want to do that yet. There's more."

Gritting his teeth, Dubshenko hit the play button again. "If Mr. Caine is there, and I'm sure you called him to gloat in your victory, let him know he's under arrest, too."

"What!" Jonathan Caine screeched loud enough to pierce Dubshenko's eardrum. *Why had he surrounded himself with such stupid people?*

"Remy, I don't think you are in any position to arrest anyone. After all, you are unarmed, and at my mercy."

Remy smiled. "I never said I was arresting you."

The doors to the warehouse exploded open, and dozens of people in black uniforms raced through, guns in hand.

"This is the FBI, everybody freeze."

"Drug Enforcement Administration. Hands in the air!"

"New Orleans Police Department, put down your weapons and nobody gets hurt."

Pandemonium ensued as people were rounded up without a single shot being fired. Dubshenko watched his hired men, the men he'd paid to protect him, surrender without any struggle or fuss. They laid their weapons on the ground, knelt down and put their hands in the air. Even that snake, Bubba, put his SIG Sauer on the table in front of Remy, and twined his fingers behind his neck, surrendering to the feds.

Within minutes everyone was surrounded, handcuffed and led from the building. Finally, only Dubshenko, Caine, Remy and Jennifer were left. Fury roiled deep in his gut—how could he have been betrayed by those he trusted? Didn't they know who he was? He was the king, the chess master. No one defeated him.

"This isn't over. I'll beat this, you know it, and I'll come after you. It's not over, I tell you!" Dubshenko needed to make sure Remy and Jennifer knew they weren't safe—they'd never be safe as long as he still breathed.

"Oh, it's over, jackass." A voice called from the doorway.

Carlo Marucci walked through the door, and Jennifer launched herself into her brother's arms. Dubshenko struggled against the cuffs, his hands secured behind his back.

"Traitor! I'll kill you!"

"Dubshenko, I'm the least of your worries right now. Remember the package you had me pick up in Houston?" All the blood drained from Dubshenko's face. "Ah, good. I see you do remember. That package has been returned to its rightful home."

Carlo walked up to stand face-to-face with Dubshenko. He leaned forward to whisper, "If I were you, I wouldn't worry about Remy or Jinx or even me. Daddy's coming and he's pissed. You better watch your back."

"No!" Dubshenko repeated over and over, as he was

led away in handcuffs, with Jonathan Caine trailing behind. Looked like the election was over—and he'd lost.

Chapter Thirty-Two

It was over. It had been three long, tortuous days of interrogations, paperwork, dealing with the FBI, more paperwork, consulting with the DEA, and still more paperwork. Remy sat behind his desk at the police station, feet propped up on its worn, battered surface. They'd finished processing Vladimir Dubshenko, Jonathan Caine, and debriefed every single alphabet agency regarding the whole sordid nightmare.

Who'd have thought this one case would burgeon into massive corruption that reached the Governor's mansion, and if unchecked all the way to the White House. Not to mention the kidnapping a minor, who just happened to be the daughter of one of the biggest crime czars in Russia, transporting her internationally and having it land smack dab in the middle of the Dubshenko investigation. Remy rubbed his hand over his face. Damn, he was tired, surviving on pure adrenaline alone—well, that and coffee.

Jinx and Carlo finally left the station earlier that morning, after their own endless rounds of interviews. He wanted to see her desperately, hold her, but knew she needed time. Time to process everything. Time to make decisions about their relationship, if they had anything to build on. It wasn't every day you find out your brother worked undercover for the DEA, have to run for your life, get kidnapped by the Russian mob and find out the man you're sleeping with kept you in the dark about his plans. Even if those plans kept her safe.

"Lamoreaux." Remy jumped to his feet at the sound of his name. Damn, he was still jumpy. Probably would be for a long while.

"Cap."

"My office, now." Hilliard turned and strode down the aisle, now cleaned of all the debris from the explosion. Repairs were well under way, but at least cases could be still be handled, the day to day operation of the station kept right on chugging along. After all, crime didn't stop because the walls got blown down.

Hilliard stood outside his office door waiting for Remy to catch up. *What's going on?*

"There are some people inside who want to talk to you. Your choice whether I come in or not."

Remy gauged the captain's words trying to read him, but he was inscrutable. "I'd rather you be there, sir."

Hilliard snorted. "Don't start that sir nonsense. Listen to what they've got to say. Then we'll talk."

Remy was even more confused. Hell, it didn't matter, he was so tired nothing made any sense. Might as well get it over with. He pushed open the captain's office door to find several suit-clad men inside. One he recognized instantly. He immediately straightened to attention.

"Sir."

Governor Bradley stepped forward, offering his hand.

"Detective Lamoreaux, it's a pleasure to meet you." He indicated the other men in the room. "Agent Branson, DEA. Special Agent Richards, FBI."

"I thought I'd answered everyone's questions. Was there something else you needed?"

Agent Branson stepped forward. "Detective Lamoreaux, Carlo Marucci explained how you risked your life not only keeping his sister safe, but retrieving crucial information and keeping it secure and out of Dubshenko's hands. That evidence along with other vital information obtained by Mr. Marucci will put Dubshenko behind bars for a very long time, with any luck the rest of his life."

"I was just doing my job, sir."

"Which you did very well. The DEA is very impressed. You'll be receiving an official commendation." Branson stood straighter, smoothing his tie before adjusting his wire-rimmed glasses. "If you ever decide you'd like a change, contact me." He handed Remy a business card that he took automatically. "I looked into some of your past cases, when Carlo first mentioned your name. Your ability to blend in is an asset which would serve you well in the Drug Enforcement Administration."

"Before Agent Branson steals everybody's thunder, the FBI also thanks you, detective. Believe it or not, we've been trying to get a foothold into Dubshenko's operation for years, but he's always been one step ahead."

"That's how he plays it." Remy replied. "He's a master manipulator. Got the better of me more than once."

"Regardless, you've done your country a valuable service, and you have our thanks." Agent Richards looked over at Branson. "Off the record, Lamoreaux, you ever want to change jobs, call me first."

Everyone in the room chuckled, except Hilliard. Remy noticed he stood with his back leaning against the wall, his arms crossed. The mutinous expression on his African-American face looked hewn out of stone. *Uh oh, Cap was not a happy camper.*

"I want to add my personal thanks," Governor Bradley added, once again stepping forward. "Chances are good Jonathan Caine would have won the special election for Lieutenant Governor in a few days. It looks like you saved my life."

"Indirectly, sir, if at all." Remy replied.

"Nonsense. Jonathan Caine's lead in the poles was growing. He would have won, and my life would have been the prize." He shook his head. "Hearing him plot my assassination on that recording—let's just say I've had my eyes opened. Truthfully, there are times I wish I'd never gone into politics. I want to help the people of Louisiana. I have no interest in personal gain and no aspirations of sitting in Washington."

"So what happens now?" Remy felt he had earned the right to ask.

"Isabella Sokolov and her father have already returned to Russia. Fortunately, Sokolov was so grateful to Carlo Marucci for keeping his daughter safe and out of Dubshenko's clutches, he agreed no further retaliation was warranted. Dubshenko's legal sharks are circling, trying to cut a deal—which will never happen. He's going to stand trial unless he pleads, but either way he's never walking out of prison a free man." Governor Bradley shook his head sadly.

"As for Jonathan Caine, he's denying any ties to

Dubshenko. Swears to anybody listening he was working behind the scenes to bring down corruption and the Russian mob. Nobody's buying it. At the end of that video, he's clearly seen ordering Dubshenko to orchestrate the hit on me after the election results were finalized. Sokolov confirmed Caine was doing business with the Russian mafia. He was calling the shots, not Dubshenko. He'll be a guest of the penitentiary for a good long while.

"Wish I could say that was the end of things, but somebody else will slide in and take over Dubshenko's territory, and we'll start all over again." Hilliard's words had everybody shaking their heads, even though they knew it was the truth.

"We won't take up any more of your time, Captain. Or yours, detective. Thank you both for the fine job you're doing to protect our wonderful city and its citizens."

They left. Just like that, everything was over and done. Hilliard motioned him to the wooden mission-style chair in front of his desk, and Remy sank down into it scrubbing his hands through his hair, which hadn't seen a comb in a couple days. Then again, he'd just talked to the Governor of Louisiana, and he hadn't brushed his teeth since he'd been at the station. Wow, great impression to make on one of the most powerful men in the state. Ah, hell, screw it. He just wanted to go home and get some sleep.

"You're taking a couple weeks off."

"No, couple days and I'll be fine." Remy protested.

"You're not listening. That wasn't a suggestion. A couple of weeks. I don't want to see your mangy backside here for at least two weeks."

"Fine, I'm not gonna argue about it. I could use the down time." Remy rolled his shoulders, more than ready to go home and get some sleep.

Hilliard shuffled some of the papers on his desk. Nothing alarming in that, but it had Remy scooting further down in his chair. Cap was a neat freak, didn't have papers scattered over his desk top. Except when he was frazzled or pissed. Which one?

"You planning to take 'em up on their offers?"

Huh? Did Cap seriously think…?

"I don't know. Honestly hadn't expected it." Remy sat back, arms across his chest, and waited. He couldn't believe Hilliard thought he'd even consider leaving the New Orleans Police Department. This was where he belonged—he wasn't going anywhere unless they kicked him out.

"Don't. I mean, I can't tell you what to do, but you need to stay here. You belong at N.O.P.D. and you damn well know it." He scowled at Remy, and Remy had to bite the inside of his cheek to keep from laughing.

I'll be damned, he really thinks I'm considering leaving.

Should he prolong the moment—nah, much as he enjoyed seeing the captain wriggling on the hook, he respected the man too much to torment him any longer.

"Cap, I'm not going anywhere. I'm honored they'd consider me, but N.O.P.D. is my home."

"Damn straight." Hilliard's gruff response touched Remy because he knew it was sincere. Cap wanted him to stick around.

"One more question before I kick your ass out of here."

Remy started to rise from the chair. "Gee, only

one?"

"What are you going to do about Ms. Marucci?"

The question hit him right between the eyes. Or maybe like an arrow to the heart. Too bad he didn't have an answer.

"Honestly, Cap, I have no bloody idea. I figure I'll get about twenty-four hours of sleep, then I'll call her and..."

"Wrong answer, bub."

Remy squirmed in his seat now. Conversations about work, sports, anything else with the captain were fair game. But discussing his love life, there was a conversation he'd never felt he'd be sharing with the big guy.

"Okay, what should I do?"

"I watched you, and I watched her at the warehouse takedown. Even before that, the night she first came into the station. There was something between you even then, an undeniable spark."

Remy remembered the instant attraction he'd felt for Jinx the moment he'd seen her walk through the doors. Disheveled, dirty, and clearly in shock, there'd been more than chemistry blooming between them. He didn't believe in love at first sight. That was for fools and sissies. Real life didn't work that way. Yet spending the last few days with her, getting to know her under less-than-ideal conditions, there wasn't a doubt in his mind she was *the one*.

His *maman* swore when he'd found the right woman he'd know, and in his gut Remy knew Jennifer Marucci, with her big heart and generous spirit, was the woman he'd waited his whole life to find.

"Don't wait, son. I know you're tired, but if you let

this one get away you're gonna regret it for the rest of your life." Hilliard stood and walked around his desk, stretching out his hand toward Remy. He took it and Cap pulled him from the chair and hugged him. Hugged him! One of those manly hugs, more of a slap, slap, slap on the back and release, but that ball of tightness in Remy's chest unfurled, and he pulled in a huge breath. He hadn't even realized how much Cap's approval meant. Though it should have, the man was like a surrogate father to him. His own parents traveled so much now that they were both retired, and aside from Max, Cap was the rock solid haven he'd come to depend upon.

"Go get your woman, and don't take no for an answer." With a little push, he steered Remy toward the door. "And don't show your sorry hide around here for at least two weeks."

Remy turned and started down the corridor toward the front of the station.

"Remy." Cap's voice floated behind him. "Call and let me know how it goes."

"Will do."

Remy stopped at the front steps to the precinct and looked around. Yep, this was where he belonged. This city, these people—this was home.

Taking the steps at a brisk clip, he stopped short realizing he didn't know where Jinx was staying. Since Dubshenko burned her house to the ground, she'd have to be temporarily living someplace else. But where?

He grinned. Good thing he had an in with the best private investigator in New Orleans. Yanking his phone out of his pocket, he called his brother and within minutes had an address.

Time to find his woman and bring her home.

Chapter Thirty-Three

Jinx hated everything about the hotel suite she and Carlo shared. After a frustrating couple of hours dealing with the insurance company, who wanted to give her a hard time about her property claims, her head felt like it was going to split open. So far the aspirin hadn't dulled the pain, and she wanted to crawl into her queen sized bed with its overstuffed comforter pulled up to her neck, close her eyes and block out the rest of the world.

Only she couldn't. Her queen sized bed was gone. Her overstuffed comforter burned to ashes. The haven she'd created for herself destroyed in a fit of pique by a man bent on her domination. But she'd survived, and he was going to spend the rest of his natural life behind bars. The District Attorney, the FBI, the DEA and everybody associated with this case assured her of that.

"I've got a couple of loose ends to tie up. You going to be okay here, sis?"

"For the last time, Carlo, I'm fine. I'm going to take a couple more aspirin and pull the covers over my head and pretend none of this ever happened."

Carlo walked over and wrapped his arms around her

shoulders, pulling her close. It felt good to be held in her big brother's embrace, but she couldn't help wishing it was another set of arms that held her. *Stop thinking about him. He did his job, it's over. He's moving on and you should to.*

Easier said than done.

"Branson said he'll have his assistant deal with the insurance company if they keep giving you a hard time. I'm sure they don't want to have the government crawling up their butts." Carlo stepped back and stared at her, and she glanced away. Sometimes her brother saw too much.

Plus, she was still pissed he hadn't told her he worked for the Drug Enforcement Administration. All this time she'd thought he'd fallen back into the shadier side of the law, when he'd actually been trying to take down one of its major players. He still hadn't told her how he'd gone from being in prison to working for the good guys, but he would. She'd drag the story out of him, just not today.

"Go. I'm fine."

"You've got my number if you need anything. Anything, Jinx. I can be back here in ten minutes tops."

She pushed him toward the door. "Go already. The faster you leave, the sooner you'll get back."

The door closed behind him with a gentle snick, and she headed toward the bathroom in search of more aspirin. She'd just picked up the bottle when there was a knock. Seriously, he was back already? Unless he'd forgotten his keys, she was going to bop him over the head. She was a grown woman, she didn't need a babysitter.

When she flung open the door, instead of Carlo standing there it was Remy. Her eyes devoured him, from his long dark hair to his whiskey brown eyes. Dark circles, a couple of days of dark growth shadowed his chin, and he looked ready to drop. Yet here he stood on her doorstep.

"Remy?"

"Jinx. We need to talk."

Uh oh, that sounded serious. She waved him into the room. Were there more questions? Surely they'd covered everything. She'd answered questions until her voice was hoarse, and they'd finally let her go that morning.

"What's wrong?"

Remy jerked at her words, a half-smile curving his lips. Those lips that had kissed hers, brushed along her skin in silken caresses—whoa, don't go there, girlfriend. Business, strictly business now.

"Nothing's wrong. I had to see you. Make sure you're okay."

Yep, she was right. It was strictly business between them now. She loved him, and all she was to him was a means to an end, a case solved. Okay, she'd assure him she was fine and let him go on his way while she nursed a broken heart.

"I'm fine. Dealing with the insurance fallout from the house, but otherwise everything's great." *Lie number one.*

"Really?"

"Of course. Carlo's boss totally said he'd put the squeeze on them if they don't cooperate, so you don't need to worry."

"I wasn't worried about the house, although I'm glad it'll be covered. I wanted to check on you."

"Me? Couldn't be better." *Lie number two. Is my nose starting to grow?*

"I've missed you." Remy's gravely growl sent a frisson of desire coursing through her. She loved his voice, and when it went all rough and sexy, she wanted to melt into a puddle at his feet.

"Can we sit? I'd like to explain…"

"What's there to explain? You switched out the phones. I got it, and it was a really good plan. I'm guessing you knew they'd find us at your friend's place, so you set us up to be found, right?"

Remy nodded, and Jinx gave herself a mental high five for having guessed right. She'd had a lot of time to think about everything since the takedown in the warehouse. Initially hurt that he'd kept her in the dark, the more she thought about the chain of events she not only got it, she'd probably have done the same thing in his place.

"Jinx, forget the case. Forget Dubshenko. Forget everything else except you and me."

Hope blossomed inside Jinx. Only a tiny spark, but for the first time since they'd been apart she let herself wish. Could he care about her as more than a means to an end? What she felt for him consumed her, the love she felt was like nothing she'd ever felt before.

"Us?"

"Jinx, I know we haven't known each other long." He reached out and caught both of her hands in his, his thumb rubbing across the back of her hands. His touch sent a thrill coursing through her, that little zing she felt whenever he was near.

"A few days, but it seems like a lifetime, doesn't it." She stared at his face, looking for clues. Where was he going with this?

"But those few days were packed with more living

than most people do in a year. I just...the thing is..."

"Remy, whatever it is, just say it."

Remy stared at her, and she read the indecision in his gaze. Please, don't back out now, she thought. Say something. Anything. Give me a freakin' clue here. She bit her lip, still uncertain where he'd take this conversation.

"Ah, the hell with it." Remy let go of her hands to cup her face. His touch was gentle, but the fire in his eyes blazed with an intensity hot enough to burn her alive. He swept his lips over hers, gently at first, but the kiss grew increasingly more demanding. Jinx parted her lips, wanting to get a taste of him, see if her memories of their time together were more than an illusion or a dream she'd built of her own desires.

His unique blend of assertiveness and repressed power surged forward and the kiss became more, building from sweetness to carnal in the space of a heartbeat. He took his time, forcing her to acknowledge the growing heat between them. Jinx was thrilled her feelings, her needs, weren't all one-sided. Remy wanted her, and the slow burn began to build.

She curled closer against him, eager for his touch. Her fingertips brushed against his unshaven cheeks, felt the scratchy stubble beneath her hands. That masculine edge only added to his appeal. But she wanted more. Deeper, hotter. Her tongue danced with his, but Remy insisted on controlling this melding of mouths and teeth and tongues.

A sweet heat built between them and Remy's hand slid along her collarbone, sweeping lower and cupping the heavy weight of her breast. Through the layers of clothes, he exerted just the right amount of pressure to have her nipple standing at rigid attention within seconds. He kept kissing her mouth, tasting every inch of her he could reach. Desire coursed through her, her body alight with wanting the man in her arms.

Finally, breaking the kiss he leaned his forehead against hers, his breath ragged. "Damn, I needed that."

Jinx laughed, the sound bubbling up freely with her happiness. She'd take this moment, secure it away to pull it out when the unhappiness threatened to consume her. The memories of this special man, this shared moment.

"I know you'll think I'm insane, but I've got to say it. Jinx, I love you."

Remy's words froze the breath in her chest. *He loved her?* Wait. *He loved her!* She blinked back tears while the reality of his words sank in. This wonderful man who'd kept her safe, put himself in danger to protect her, the one who'd made her laugh, made her hope—the man who'd made her *feel*—loved her.

"Oh, Remy, I love you, too!"

His answering smile was all the confirmation she needed. This was right. They were right. Sure, they'd known each other for what, a week? But in that week they'd lived a lifetime. She had never been more sure of anything in her entire life. This was her soul mate, the man she wanted to spend eternity with.

"Move in with me." Remy voiced the question as a statement, and Jinx grinned. More than anything she'd love to live with him. Wake in his arms every morning, go to sleep after making love, knowing he belonged to her.

"I know it's too soon for marriage and the white picket fence and everything else, but just so you know, I plan on proposing the second I'm convinced you'll say yes. But come live with me and be my love. We can make it work." Remy started laughing after he'd finished that sentence. Wait a minute, what was so funny?

"You'll have to meet *maman* first though. Since it's her house, it might be a good idea for you to know her before I move you in lock, stock, and barrel." He reached forward and rubbed the strands of a curl between his fingers before tucking the lock of her still red hair behind her ear.

"I don't mind the red, but I'm looking forward to getting my blonde beauty back. There was something about you, when I saw you standing in the glaring overhead lights of the station—even then you pulled at me like no one ever had before."

Jinx wrapped her arms around Remy's neck. "There was definitely an attraction there, right from the start. And I'd love to meet your *maman*. What if she doesn't like me?" Worry laced her words.

"Jinx, I love my grandmother dearly. She's a huge part of my life. But *you are my life*. I'll move out in a heartbeat if that's what it takes to keep you by my side. I actually have an apartment I keep in the French Quarter, when I need some privacy. I moved in to take care of her, since she's getting up there in years."

He placed a quick kiss on the tip of her nose. "Trust me, though, she's gonna love you. You're more alike than you know."

"Well, as long as you know you get my family, too. The whole Marucci clan is going to descend on us like a swarm of locusts the second they hear I've met the man of my dreams."

"The man of your dreams, hmm. I like that."

He stood, holding out his hand, and she rose off the

sofa. In a wildly romantic gesture he slid his hand beneath her knees, cradling her in his arms. She gasped and protested, knowing she was a big woman and didn't want him straining to hold her.

"Stop it. Which way to your room?" She pointed and he strode easily forward, and gently laid her across the white duvet.

Wow, look at that. He's not even short of breath. He really is the man of my dreams.

With infinite care he removed each item of clothing, tossing them all onto a chair. His grin widened at the matching bra and panties she'd worn beneath her demure skirt and blouse.

"I love the wicked lingerie you always wear. It's like unwrapping a sexy package decorated just for me." He made short work of ridding her of them, and she stretched out fully, letting him look his fill. One fingertip brushed across the roundness of her belly, and she sucked in a breath. His frown grew, and she exhaled. While she knew her body and loved all her curves, most guys wanted the skinny chicks. Then again, Remy wasn't most guys and he seemed to exult in her lushness.

"Mine." He placed his palm against her belly, and she smiled.

"Yours."

His hand traveled down to cup her mound, naked now that he'd removed everything. "Mine."

She quirked her brow, but nodded. "Yours."

With a final touch, he laid his hand between her breasts, directly over her heart.

"Mine?"

Tears blurred her sight of him, but she didn't hesitate. "Yours, Remy. Forever."

Remy stared down at the beautiful woman spread before him like a sumptuous buffet. The warmth flooding through him had nothing to do with the temperature and everything to do with the love coursing through his heart.

"Forever." He yanked off his shirt, uncaring where it landed and shucked his jeans, toeing off his runners, anxious to be with Jinx. He leaned forward, sucking one breast into his mouth, savoring the ample more-than-a-mouthful womanliness of her. He ran his tongue around the nipple, and it peaked into a rigid nubbin. Keeping her occupied with the sucking and licking, his hand slid along her torso, down to her mound. He threaded his fingers between her naked folds, feeling the slick wet flesh beneath his fingertips.

She wanted him and this was further evidence she was ready for him. Her gaze lifted to the crystal chandelier above the bed and she started to sit up. With a gentle nudge, he pushed her back against the bedding.

"Where are you going?"

"To turn down the lights."

"Why? I want to see you. I love looking at you."

He sprawled beside her, watching the play of emotions across her face, knew the moment she acquiesced to his request. Good, because he'd planned on getting his way. Looking at her was a joy he didn't plan on giving up for a very long time.

"You have such perfect breasts," he murmured. He bent down and licked the nipple again, "Sweet. You taste like honey." He ran his tongue over the valley between her breasts and continued to the swell of the other. His teeth closed over the stiff peak and gently tugged. She murmured something unintelligible, pressing his head closer against her.

He didn't hurry. Instead he inched down, oh so slowly until she was squirming, impatient for him to continue his trek lower. With an unexpected move she shoved him onto his back, crawling up to straddle him. Remy laughed, joy coursing through him. Ah, his unexpected vixen had grown claws and wasn't afraid to take charge. He liked it—a lot.

She pressed her body against his, and he delighted in the feel of skin against skin. Her softer body felt perfect against his hardness. Running his hands over her back he cupped the swell of her bottom in his firm grip. Caressed and squeezed until she moaned aloud.

"Remy, oh…" She broke off as he rocked his hip, brushing his hard length against her moist heat. "Do that again," she demanded.

At his full-throated laugh, she lightly punched his arm, a pout on her lips.

This was what had been missing for so long. This connection to another person, their wants, their needs more important than his own. He speared both hands into her hair, dragging her down for a passion induced kiss.

"In case you've forgotten, I love you." She placed a kiss against his left pec. "Adore you." She trailed her tongue across his chest, and Remy raised up propping himself on his elbows, watching her every movement. "Worship you." Her legs straddling his groin squeezed tight, and it was Remy's turn to let out a groan.

"Love you too, sweetheart. More than words can say."

Without missing a beat, Remy rolled, positioning Jinx beneath him. All playfulness evaporated as need spilled through him. He loved sharing the laughter and humor that came so easily with this woman, but time for play was over. Making love to Jinx, knowing she felt the same, elevated this moment to a different plane. He wasn't going to get all sappy and call it spiritual or something corny like that, but it felt different.

He trailed a hand along her hip, before sliding between her thighs, spreading them wider with his body. An ache coiled inside him, the need to spill inside her, claim her as his, was somehow foreign, yet felt right.

His fingers slid through her desire-slick folds, finding her wet and ready. Positioning himself at her opening, he eased forward. He felt her welcoming heat encircling and embracing him as he slid within her welcoming folds, felt her stretching to accommodate him.

He stared down at her, hair spread out about her across the snowy white bedding, her skin the perfect pink, flushed with desire. Her eyes began to flutter closed as he slid forward, and he stopped to lean down and press a kiss to each lid.

"Eyes on me, sweetheart. I want to watch you while I make love to you." Her eyes opened, a yearning so deep he nearly wept. He felt inadequate, unworthy of the love of this special woman, but he'd do everything he could from this day forward to make sure she knew how special, how precious a gift she was, and one he'd never take for granted.

"Remy, make love to me." Her whispered words were all it took for Remy to surge forward until he was buried deep within her. Nothing ever felt so right, made him feel so alive.

"Love you, my Jinx." He pulled out only to slam forward, again and again, riding the waves of passion, her body undulating beneath his. Her breaths quickened, the soft pink flush painting her skin with a warm glow.

"Love you, Remy." Her words sent a shockwave of desire searing through his body. He arched into her, surrendering, letting her take everything he had to give. Felt her opening herself for him, accepting him with each thrust deeper. Her body cradled his as he took her over and over, possessing him in a way no one ever had, touching the deepest part of his heart and soul.

"Take me," she whispered. He shuddered, braced above her and plunged into her welcoming body. Felt her contract around him, her back arching off the bed when her orgasm hit, a cascade of brilliant stars exploding behind his eyelids as he floated on wave after wave of ecstasy.

His world fractured into a million tiny pieces, fragments of sensation and pleasure burst around him. Felt the warmth as he filled her, and peace as he fell into her embrace. She held him tightly refusing to let go, not wanting their time together to end.

He brushed a soft kiss against her lips, brushing her sweat-streaked hair back from her face. Rolling to his back, he pulled her spent body alongside his, keeping her wrapped securely within his embrace.

"You are moving in with me. I want this every single day. We'll make it work, I promise." Remy pulled in a deep breath, inhaling the scent that was uniquely Jinx.

Her soft lips kissed the pulse at the base of his throat before pulling away. "That's all that matters, Remy. If we love each other, we'll find a way to make it work." She smiled, her eyes shining brightly with a blaze of love so strong it humbled him.

"I'm willing to take a chance, because I'm not sure I

can live without you. I don't want to even try. Love is worth the risk." When she put it that way, who was he to argue.

He covered them both with the sheet, tucking her up beneath his arm. Resting his head atop hers he played with one of the curls, fingering its softness.

"You've always considered your nickname unlucky. Never again. You're *my jinx*, and meeting you was the luckiest day of my life."

Remy meant every word. His luck changed the day she walked into his world and blew everything to smithereens. If she was a jinx, he'd take being jinxed for the rest of his days.

THE END

Newsletter Sign Up

Thank you so much for reading my book. If you want to find out about my other books, new releases, contests, free reads, and other things that are going on, sign up for my newsletter at http://eepurl.com/baqdRX

I take your privacy seriously. I will not sell your email or contact you for any other reason than to send you publication updates when a new release is available.

REVIEW
I hope you liked reading Relentless Pursuit, part of the New Orleans Connection series. I'd love for you to post a review so that other readers can find these books and enjoy them as well. Thank you.

"Kathy Ivan's books give you everything you're looking for and so much more". –Geri Foster, USA Today and NYT Bestselling Author of the Falcon Securities Series

"This is the first I have read from Kathy Ivan and it won't be the last. Desperate Choices had it all…" Night Owl Reviews

"I highly recommend Desperate Choices. Readers can't go wrong here!" Melissa, Joyfully Reviewed

"I oved how the author wove a very intricate storyline with plenty of intriguing details that led to the final reveal…" Night Owl Reviews on Second Chances

Desperate Choices

Winner 2012 International Digital Award—Suspense

Best of Romance 2011 –Joyfully Reviewed

Acknowledgements

My boundless thanks go out to so many people who helped while I struggled writing this book. As always, to the Plotting Princesses for their invaluable help when I'd find myself stuck in a scene. Being able to talk the story helps me make it through each day.

To Dalla Area Romance Authors, one of the finest groups I've ever had the privilege of meeting. Without this kind, gracious and informative group, my writing journey would never have gotten off the ground.

To my beta readers, Tanya Newbern and Karla Eakin, who read through the book, finding all those little details that I missed, and lending me their support and encouragement all through my writing. Special thanks, my friends.

Finally, and as always, to my sister Mary Sullivan. Her unwavering and unflagging support is the bedrock I rest upon when the writing sometimes overwhelms me. Her steadfast confidence and belief in me means EVERYTHING!

Author Bio

Kathy Ivan

Kathy Ivan spent most of her life with her nose between the pages of a book. From best-selling authors to just-getting-started writers, as long as it was a good story, she devoured it and happily searched for the next romance novel. It didn't matter if the book was a paranormal romance, romantic suspense, or action and adventure thrillers, sweet & spicy or sexy novella. As long as there was an alpha hero and a feisty heroine who got their happily ever after, she'd gladly spend her time with a psychic in New Orleans, or a mysterious stranger manipulating the fates of lovers. You might find her deep in the woods with her werewolf lover, or being wined and dined by the sexy vampire who loves her, or talking to ghosts.

Kathy turned her obsession with reading into the next logical step, writing. Her books transport you from a paranormal lodge in the Colorado Mountains in her Destiny's Desire Series, to the sultry splendor of the French Quarter in New Orleans in her award winning romantic suspense and mysteries. Kathy tells stories people can't get enough of; reuniting old loves, betrayal of trust, finding kidnapped children, psychics and even a ghost or two. But one thing they all have in common - love (and some pretty steamy sex scenes too).

A Florida native, Kathy has island hopped from one set of islands to another, having spent several years in Key West and Hawaii. Happily living in North Texas, she's always on the lookout for a cowboy of her very own. (And if he's a billionaire cowboy, well, she won't say no to that.)

You can find more on Kathy and her books at www.kathyivan.com or visit her facebook page at https://www.facebook.com/kathy.ivan.5 and follow her on twitter at @kathyivan.

Ultimate Betrayal (New Orleans Connection Series Book #3)

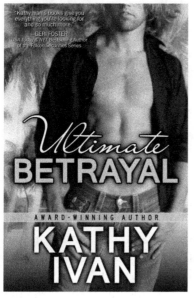

With his cover blown to hell after a media frenzy in New Orleans, all DEA agent Carlo Marucci wants is a week of rest and relaxation. Add in a Bed and Breakfast in Key West and a beautiful woman, and he thinks he's hit the perfect trifecta. Macie Branson has come to Key West to reconnect with her family after her sister's messy divorce. Cavorting with a tall, dark and sexy stranger isn't part of her plans. Until she meets Carlo.

The chemistry burns fast and furious between them, but when Macie's nephews vanish, evidence connects the boys' disappearance back to New Orleans and the newest party drug flooding its streets. It's a race against the clock as Carlo and Macie search for the missing boys. Will they find her nephews before time runs out?

Ultimate Betrayal Excerpt:

Sprawled on his back, Carlo Marucci felt the warm sunshine ooze into every pore of his skin. Dark glasses covered his eyes, which were closed at the moment, and the soft Texas drawl of George Strait playing through the earbuds obliterated the outside world. Oh, yeah this was exactly what he'd needed.

Rest and relaxation. Those had been his chief's orders when the case he'd been working exploded all over the front pages of every newspaper in the country. After all, its big news with the head of the New Orleans Russian mafia is taken down in a major sting operation, netting not only said big fish, but also a candidate running in the special election for Lieutenant Governor of the state of Louisiana. Ah, yes, corruption at its finest.

Of course, no one in the media mentioned the kidnapped daughter of one of the biggest Russian syndicate leaders, who'd been smuggled into of the country and landed literally in Carlo's lap. Those details were kept on a strictly need-to-know basis and the vultures of the press definitely didn't need to know. The explosive situation was diffused before retribution

rained down from the heavens. Anatole Sokolov was satisfied everyone connected to his beloved daughters abduction had been dealt with by the United States government and currently resided in the Louisiana State Penitentiary, having made plea bargains or awaiting trial. Keeping a lid on that potentially explosive international incident—yep, total media blackout.

A splash sounded from the pool at his feet, but he didn't bother opening his eyes. Probably the teenage boys he'd met the day before. Vacationing in the Florida Keys had been a stroke of genius on his sister's part. She'd suggested it, arranged every detail, right down to the bed and breakfast reservations, plane tickets. Carlo was halfway convinced she'd been instrumental in his boss's unyielding demand he take an extended leave, at least a week. His sister, Jinx, was a walking, talking miracle and he'd never forget how close he'd come to losing—and it would have all been his fault.

No yells from the boys followed the splash. No tidal waves of water soaked his chair from their horseplay like they had the previous day. Opening his eyes, he took in the sight of long golden limbs gliding seamlessly across the surface of the water, toward the far end of the pool. The deep ruby red of a one-piece bathing suit encased what appeared at first gland to be a voluptuous woman's curves.

He slid the sunglasses further down on his nose, peering over the top to get a better look. Oh, yeah, long dark hair flowed over her shoulders with each stroke. He watched her flip beneath the surface and kick off the far wall, pushing forward with a strength and speed he envied. He could swim well enough to get from point A to point B, but nothing like this. This woman's movements were poetry in motion.

When she reached the pool's edge where his chaise was, without even a curious glance his way, she turned again, headed for the opposite side. Not that it was a problem, he wouldn't mind watching her for hours. Folding his arms behind his head, he leaned back with a grin. Oh, yeah, this was his kind of vacation. Sunshine, an ice cold beer, and a nearly naked beautiful woman.

End of Excerpt
Coming Soon

Keeping Secrets (New Orleans Connection Series Book #4)

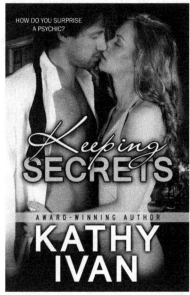

Keeping Secrets Excerpt:

Theresa unlocked the door to her New Age shop, and spun the closed sign to open. Tourists lined the streets of the French Quarter on this beautiful fall morning, milling through the various shops, and she was ready to begin a brand new day.

The wooden floors shone with an aged patina that gave a warm character to the space. The walls were painted a buttery yellow, a neutral and calming color which had the added benefit of highlighting her brightly colored stock.

Trinkets and Mardi Gras beads lay scattered across the display tables along with fancier crystals and charms.

One-of-a-kind handcrafted jewelry hung from miniature tree stands of weathered wood, white with age. The more expensive pieces were locked behind the glass-fronted cabinet. This shop was her livelihood and she loved bringing a little something extraordinary into people's otherwise ordinary day.

The bell above her front door tinkled, announcing customers and Theresa looked up with a welcoming smile. Alyssa Scott and Jinx Marucci stood inside the doorway, the sunlight behind them shining brightly and seemed to outline them like an invisible aura. With her friends showing up bright and early, it was definitely going to be another beautiful day.

She'd recently met both women and they were fast becoming good friends. Alyssa had been married to Max's cousin, Connor Scott, a New Orleans firefighter. They'd had a rocky relationship, separating and eventually divorcing. She'd moved to Florida to start over, but fate and a couple of elderly matchmakers threw them back together—straight into the dangerous path of revenge and betrayal which nearly cost them everything including their lives. Fortunately, they'd survived, although Alyssa was still reluctant to talk about everything she'd endured at the hands of a maniac. Theresa knew if it hadn't been for Connor's love, Alyssa wouldn't have survived. Now they were happily remarried.

Jinx was a different story entirely. She and Remy were in the early stages of their relationship, so in love and filled with the joys of learning new things about each other. Theresa couldn't be happier her best friend had found a woman so perfect for him. Beautiful and curvy, she'd finally managed to rid her hair of all the artificial red color and it was back to its original golden blonde. She'd been forced to alter her appearance when she'd been on the run from the Russian mob, and had died it a dark auburn, vastly different for her natural honey blonde curls.

Funny, how fate could bring people into your life who quickly became important, became closer than sisters, in such a short time.

"Good morning, Theresa." Alyssa smiled, picking up a green crystal from the countertop and turning it over. She watched the play of light, the prisms of color sparkling from its depths and reflecting on the scarves draped nearby.

"Hi." Jinx grinned at Theresa and gave a little wave.

"Want some coffee?"

"Yes." Both women responded in unison then laughed. Theresa was renowned for her coffee-making skills in the Lamoreaux family. They swore she had the *magic touch*. She'd tried teaching Max, but gave up after he burned two coffee makers beyond redemption.

"Come on back to the kitchen. We'll hear if anybody comes in." Theresa led them back to the little kitchenette area behind her shop. Before she'd moved in with Max, she'd lived in the one-bedroom apartment above her retail space. The living and sleeping areas were upstairs and the kitchen downstairs.

Within a minute she had everybody's cup ready, and slid the creamer and sugar on the countertop.

"You know, I never really got to look around much the night Remy and I stayed here." Jinx glanced around the space with its cozy warmth and inviting vibe. It wasn't modern or updated, no contemporary granite or stainless steel, but it felt welcoming.

"Well, you were kind of busy, hiding out. You were barely here overnight before you got hauled out by the Russians. Checking out my kitchen probably wasn't high on your list of priorities."

Jinx chuckled. "I was way more interested in getting Remy out of his pants. Chances were good we were going to die and I wanted one last night with him."

"But it worked out and you're together. I've never seen Remy so happy."

There was a companionable silence for a few minutes, before Theresa decided to wade right in.

"I know why you're here."

"You do?" Alyssa met her stare directly, not backing down or intimidated by Theresa. "Why are we here?"

"Max sent you. Darn it."

Alyssa looked at Jinx, who shrugged and rolled her eyes, before turning back to Theresa.

"Sorry, Madame Psychic, but we haven't talked to Max."

That couldn't be right. Max had been pushing all week, wanting to set a wedding date—and she couldn't. Not yet.

"Of course he sent you."

"Actually," Jinx interrupted, "I sent us. I mean it was my idea to come here, because—Remy and I are engaged!"

She held out her left hand, showing Theresa the diamond ring on her finger.

"Really! That is so awesome."

"Seriously—you kept that thing hidden from me the whole drive over here?" Alyssa playfully smacked Jinx's arm. "When did he pop the question?"

"Last night."

"Was it all romantic—Remy seems like he'd be the kind to get down on one knee and propose." Alyssa sighed dramatically and fluttered her eyelashes. Theresa looked at Jinx and they burst out laughing.

"Remy down on one knee, please, girlfriend, pigs will fly out of my butt before he'd do something so normal." Jinx chuckled at the look on her friend's face.

"How did he propose then?" Alyssa demanded.

Theresa felt a tickle at her psyche right before a picture of Remy popped into her mind's eye. She watched the events unfold, like a mini movie playing behind her eyelids, which flew open along with her mouth, forming a perfect O."

"He didn't!"

Jinx's cheeks turned bright pink at the realization that Theresa *saw* Remy's proposal.

"Oh, yeah, he did."

End of Excerpt
Coming Soon

Connor's Gamble

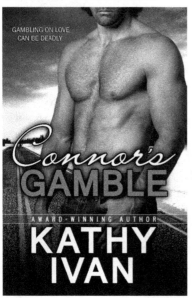

Connor's Gamble Excerpt:

A pool of matted dark red blood spread out in a macabre halo beneath the gray hair of Mrs. Abigail Spencer. For one brief moment, Connor gave thanks he hadn't eaten breakfast yet. It wouldn't do to spew chunks all over the poor old woman.

He whirled around at Alyssa's sharp intake of breath right behind him. Damn it, he'd told her to wait outside. Then again, why was he surprised she hadn't listened? The whole time they'd been married, she'd never listened to anything he'd said then, either.

"Connor? Is she . . .?"

"Dead?" Connor knelt beside the old lady, careful

not to touch anything. Reaching forward, he pressed his fingertips against the side of her neck, checking for any indication of life. He felt nothing. No pulse. No rise and fall of her chest. "Looks that way."

"Oh dear," she whispered. "There's so much blood."

"Yeah."

Standing, he took a couple of steps back, reached into his pocket for his cell phone and dialed nine-one-one.

"I need the police at the Wayward Wanderer Inn on I-10. There's been a death . . . That's right . . . No, there are two of us in the room . . . Yes, ma'am, we'll wait right outside the door for the officers to get here. Thank you."

Within minutes the familiar wail of sirens drew closer, accompanied by flashing lights. Killing the siren, one uniformed and one plainclothes officer alighted from the patrol car and walked toward him. Since all the rooms were located on the ground floor, spectators filled the parking lot and milled about in the now crowded hallways.

Connor spotted several folks from the tour group standing a few doors away, anxiety and concern clear in their expressions. Mrs. Spencer was one of their own. He knew Alyssa would deal with the aftermath of this tragedy, offering compassion and sympathy to each Whispering Pines resident. Who'd share a little sympathy with her, he wondered?

"Lyssa, why don't you talk with your group while I explain to the officers what's happened." The only thing that would keep her from dwelling on finding a dead body, especially someone she knew, was to keep her busy. He knew Alyssa well enough that giving her something to focus on, a task to perform, made the most sense. Pale, in obvious shock, she went into immediate helper mode. He wished he could hold her, comfort her through the trauma of what she'd witnessed, but he had to deal with the cops.

The people from Whispering Pines Senior Living Center needed to be handled gently.

Damn. First a bus crash and now one of them is dead. How much more can these old folks take?

The clearing of a throat brought things rushing back to the here and now.

"Officers, I'm Connor Scott. I called in the death."

Without a word, the uniformed police officer, a tall, rail-thin Hispanic man walked through the door into Abigail Spencer's room. The other stayed next to Connor. Pulling out a notebook and pen, he got right down to business. That's good, Connor thought.

"Mr. Scott, I'm Detective Taglier. How did you know the deceased?" The southern drawl followed by an 'I'm your good buddy' grin immediately grated on Connor's nerves. Hell, he didn't even know this guy and already the hairs on the back of his neck stood at attention and he wanted to growl a warning to back the hell off.

"Mrs. Spencer was a passenger on our tour bus. We had an accident yesterday afternoon. Slid on an icy patch on the interstate. Veered off the road."

"Yeah, I heard about it down at the station. Was she injured in the accident?"

"Nothing serious that I'm aware of." Connor stood with arms akimbo, looking at the policeman. Something didn't sit right about him even though he was just doing his job.

"She had a bump on her forehead, I think. It bled a bit but she was checked out at the emergency clinic by a physician and cleared. Everybody was, except for the driver." At the officer's raised brow, Connor continued. "Broken leg, fractured pelvis and a concussion."

"Ouch." Jotting down notes, the detective glanced through the open doorway behind Connor.

"The young lady with you, where does she fit into all this? Was she with you when you found Ms. Spencer?"

Connor bristled at his tone but answered. "Her name's Alyssa Scott. She's the Activities Director for the tour group. Works at the senior living center where they're from." The officer nodded again. He gave an exasperated sigh before continuing. "A few of the other passengers were worried when Abigail, Mrs. Spencer, didn't come to the restaurant for breakfast. They sent Alyssa to check on her. I came with her."

"Was the door locked when you arrived?" The officer's question was directed at Connor, but his eyes kept straying to Alyssa, and it pissed Connor off.

"No. I knocked several times. When there was no answer, I turned the knob and it opened."

"Uh, huh."

The second officer came out of the room, pulling the door closed behind him. After a quick whispered conversation with his partner he strode over to the patrol car, his wide steps quickly eating up the distance.

"So, Mr. Scott, you opened the door and . . ."

Connor turned back to the cop. "I told Alyssa to wait outside and I went in to check on Mrs. Spencer. Immediately upon entering the room I saw feet sticking out from beside the bed. When I got closer, that's how I found her."

"And Ms. Scott stayed outside the whole time?"

He would like to say yes but knew forensic evidence

would show she'd been in the room. "No, she came into the room and saw the body as well."

"Did you notice anything else, Mr. Scott?"

"Yeah, I noticed blood on the edge of the night stand by the body."

The officer jotted down a few more notes in his bent, crumpled notebook before continuing.

"Anything else? See anybody hanging around the parking lot?"

"No. I called nine-one-one and waited here for you."

"Okay. Thanks. I'll need to speak with Ms. Scott, take her statement. Same last name. Any relation to you?"

"Ex-wife."

"Huh. Amicable I take it."

Connor quirked a brow, refusing to rise to the subtle baiting question.

Connor knew most of the questions were standard procedure, he'd been around enough cops in his job with the fire department to know it, but he didn't want this guy talking to his wife.

Ex-wife, dammit.

End of Excerpt

FOR BOOKS BY KATHY IVAN VISIT:
www.kathyivan.com/books.html

READING ORDER FOR NEW ORLEANS CONNECTION SERIES
Desperate Choices
Connor's Gamble
Relentless Pursuit
Ultimate Betrayal
Keeping Secrets

OTHER BOOKS BY KATHY IVAN
Second Chances (Destiny's Desire Book #1)
Losing Cassie (Destiny's Desire Book #2)

Printed in the USA
CPSIA information can be obtained
at www.ICGtesting.com
LVHW061647110823
754980LV00003B/168